MOVIE CAT

MOVIE CAT

GARRISON ALLEN

WHEELER
CHIVERS

This Large Print edition is published by Wheeler Publishing, Waterville, Maine USA and by BBC Audiobooks Ltd, Bath, England.

Published in 2006 in the U.S. by arrangement with Kensington Books, an imprint of Kensington Publishing Corp.

Published in 2006 in the U.K. by arrangement with Kensington Publishing Corp.

U.S. Softcover   1-59722-210-0   (Softcover)
U.K. Hardcover 10: 1 4056 3793 5   (Chivers Large Print)
U.K. Hardcover 13: 978 1 405 63793 0
U.K. Softcover   10: 1 4056 3794 3   (Camden Large Print)
U.K. Softcover   13: 978 1 405 63794 7

The text of this Large Print edition is unabridged.
Other aspects of the book may vary from the original edition.

Set in 16 pt. Plantin by Christina S. Huff.

Printed in the United States on permanent paper.

British Library Cataloguing-in-Publication Data available

Library of Congress Cataloging-in-Publication Data

Allen, Garrison.
    Movie cat / by Garrison Allen.
        p. cm. — (A Big Mike mystery)
    ISBN 1-59722-210-0 (lg. print : sc : alk. paper)
    1. Big Mike (Fictitious character) — Fiction.   2. Warren,
Penelope (Fictitious character) — Fiction.   3. Booksellers and
bookselling — Fiction.   4. Women cat owners — Fiction.
5. Arizona — Fiction.   6. Cats — Fiction.   7. Large type books.
I. Title.
PS3551.L39227M68 2006
    813'.54—dc22   2005037450

For Diane,
Nicole and David,
Gina and Sam

FADE IN:
EXT. DESERT. DAY.
OPENING CREDITS roll over the bleak Arizona desert. A fierce, blinding sun rises over distant mountains.

A CLARENCE
DAVIS MASTERLY FILM
THE EARS OF THE ELEPHANT
SCREENPLAY BY
CLARENCE DAVIS MASTERLY
AND HARRY DUCHETTE
BASED ON AN ORIGINAL STORY BY
CLARENCE DAVIS MASTERLY
STARRING

Big Mike AKA Mycroft, Mikey. A twenty-five-pound Abyssinian alley cat from Abyssinia. He has seen the ears of the elephant and was not impressed.

Penelope Warren. She, too, has seen the ears of the elephant (flapping menacingly

7

in the rearview mirror of the Land Rover she happened to be driving at the time with the snows of Kilimanjaro in the background) and *was* impressed. That was not her primary reason, however, for moving to Empty Creek, Arizona, to open a mystery bookstore called Mycroft & Company.

Empty Creek, Arizona. The strangest little community one could ever hope to find. If *The Twilight Zone* ever makes a comeback, it will be set here.

Cassandra Warren AKA Storm Williams, Stormy. An actress of considerable talent who has starred in any number of B movies. Her role in *Elephant* is her breakthrough part. In real life, she is Cassie, Penelope's little sister and Big Mike's favorite auntie.

Clarence Davis Masterly AKA C.D. He is the greatest director to hit the American film industry in recent years, following in the tradition of Cecil B. De Mille, Orson Welles, and Steven Spielberg. Unfortunately, he has never heard of De Mille or Welles, considers Spielberg a third-rate talent, and thinks Jane Austen and Bill Shakespeare are script doctors living in

Encino. Most of the people who work with him think his initials stand for "creative differences."

Brynn Moore. Once the reigning sex symbol of Hollywood, she graduated to serious actress and has triumphantly starred in film and on Broadway. At the age of fifty-seven, she is still a Babe with a capital B.

Bobby Danes AKA the Masked Madman. A professional wrestler plucked from the ring by Brynn Moore. He is twenty-six years her junior, but needs his vitamin B_{12} and the occasional hormone shot to keep up with her.

Peter Benedict. Head Suit of Century Cinema. He green-lighted *The Ear of the Elephant.*

James Stapleton. Another Suit. Head lackey to Benedict, and producer of *Elephant.*

Amber Stark. A former Miss America third runner-up from Mississippi who used her scholarship money to major in communications. Century Cinema publi-

9

cist and the woman of Peter Benedict's attentions. Fortunately, her studio golf cart is faster than his.

Craig Halliday. The villain in *The Ears of the Elephant.*

Harry Duchette. Once an Academy Award–nominated screenwriter, Harry has been reduced to the lowly status of a schmuck with a metaphorical Underwood.

Brock Hackett. Second assistant director and Masterly's chief gofer.

Dominique Anders. Personal assistant to Mr. Masterly. It is a recent promotion (or demotion, depending upon the point of view) from Constant Companion.

Vixen DeVaughn. Constant Companion to Masterly. In addition to her many charms, Ms. DeVaughn has a real talent for screaming, her chosen career path in Hollywood.

Buffy Anne Mulholland. Masterly's Junior Constant Companion. She plans to marry C.D. and spend the rest of her life shopping on Rodeo Drive and hosting fund-raisers to save the rain forest.

Hilly Hollander. A dapper gossip columnist for *The Millennium,* one of the trashier tabloids of this, or any other, planet.

Base Camp Elephant. Headquarters of the location shoot where crew and non-union extras spend a lot of time hanging out next to the coffee urns while the stars await their calls in luxurious trailers.

Harris Anderson III AKA Andy. Stalwart editor of the *Empty Creek News-Journal* and Penelope's Constant Companion.

Nora Pryor. A single mother and author of the definitive guide to Empty Creek and its history.

Regina Pryor AKA Reggie. Nora's seventeen-year-old daughter. She has inherited her sexy mother's freckles, strawberry-blond hair, and sultry voice.

Anthony Lyme-Regis. A tweedy English gentleman who is much sought after as a director of successful television commercials. He keeps company with Nora when he does not have to be in Los Angeles.

Elaine Henders AKA Laney. A redheaded

11

romance novelist with a startling imagination for placing her always-ravishing heroines (and their bodices) in erotically charged predicaments in frontier Arizona.

Wally. An unemployed cowboy, Constant Companion, and always willing research assistant to Ms. Henders.

Alexander and Kelsey. Yorkshire terriers who live with Laney and Wally. Alex is Big Mike's best friend, while Kelsey is their pinheaded nemesis.

John Fowler AKA Dutch. A former L.A.P.D. detective who thought a quiet job as chief of the Empty Creek Police Department would be a nice way to ease into retirement. Boy, was he mistaken, but he did meet and woo Stormy, although he believes the Sisters Warren will drive him bonkers before he can get Stormy to the altar.

Larry Burke and Willie Stoner. The Tweedledee and Tweedledum of the E.C.P.D. Robbery-Homicide Bureau. In fact, they *are* the Robbery-Homicide Bureau.

Samantha Dale. A no-nonsense bank president by day and somewhat of a free spirit by night, who occasionally astounds herself by entering a wet T-shirt contest or posing nude for the Women of Empty Creek Sixteen-Month Calendar. Nor has she ever lost in strip poker while playing Big Jake Peterson, her favorite man.

Lora Lou Longstreet. Owner of the Tack Shack and Art Gallery. A past president of the chamber of commerce, Lora Lou is a willowy beauty who spends much of her non-working time posing in the nude for her youthful artist companion, David Macklin.

The Double B Western Saloon and Steakhouse. The watering hole of choice for the locals, where almost anything might happen — and has.

The Dynamite Lounge. The watering hole of choice for the film crew. They find the New Age music and Andrew Lloyd Webber tunes relaxing after a hard day on the set. The topless dancers don't hurt either.

Kathleen Allen. A vivacious college student who works part-time at Mycroft & Company. Penelope is her heroine.

Debbie Locke. Voted "Cocktail Waitress I'd Most Like to Spend the Twenty-first Century With," Debbie has a degree in psychology (Phi Beta Kappa) from the University of Pennsylvania but found her true profession at the Double B, where she breaks hearts on a nightly basis because she is enamored of Sam Connors, a member of Empty Creek's finest.

Timothy Scott. The poet laureate of Empty Creek, whose considerable body of work is devoted solely to commemorating in iambic pentameter the charms of the aforementioned Kathy Allen.

Lola LaPola. An intrepid television news reporter.

Myron Schwartzman. Stormy's agent. His nostalgia for the golden age of strippers inspired Stormy's stage name.

The Crew. A few assistant co-executive producers, second and third assistant directors, production assistants, a best boy, a gaffer, cameramen and camerawomen, wardrobe people, makeup artists, script girls, clappers, actresses and actors, paparazzi, various creatures of the animal persuasion, stunt men and stunt women, cops, demented senior citizens, Oscar Wilde, W. C. Fields, John Wayne, Pat Boone, Wolfgang Puck, Sean Connery, Marlon Brando, Gerry Spence, Peter Sellers and *The Goon Show*, Diana Rigg, and Elfrida Fallowfield.

DISSOLVE TO:

Casting Call

There was only one sane person left in the entire community of Empty Creek, Arizona, and he was a cat.

Penelope Warren usually blamed such mass aberration on some mysterious property contained in the municipal water supply or, at the very least, a full moon — even a spell cast by the spirit of the Indian maiden who gave Crying Woman Mountain its name. This was not to say that the citizens of Empty Creek were normal. Hardly. But their customary eccentricities indicated a healthy independence of mind and soul, unfettered by the herd instinct or the beat of *any* drummer. But the appearance of a single full-page advertisement in the *Empty Creek News-Journal* sent them into a collective twitter.

OPEN CALL
Extras Needed for a
C.D. Masterly Film
The Ears of the Elephant

Which was how otherwise rational — in the Empty Creek definition of the word — people suddenly lined up to be cast in the epic Western to be filmed on location, including, she was chagrined to admit, Penelope Warren, Ph.D. (English literature), former sergeant in the United States Marine Corps, former Peace Corps volunteer in Ethiopia, and now sole proprietress of Empty Creek's only mystery bookstore, Mycroft & Company.

Penelope looked around the reception room at her friends, all nervously awaiting an audience with the great C.D. Masterly, reigning wunderkind of Hollywood, who dispensed with his casting director when there were women to be interviewed and chosen for bit parts or walk-ons. The group had dwindled as one or another of the women had been cast — Kathy Allen, Penelope's assistant at the bookstore, was in the crowd scene at the lynching of Brynn Moore, the mother of Annie Two Guns, a leading role played by Storm Williams, Empty Creek's own resident movie star, and Penelope's little sister. Debbie Locke, renowned cocktail waitress, had been cast against type as a God-fearing member of the Women's Temperance Union. Ditto, Lora Lou Longstreet, prominent businesswoman, and the most un-likely candidate in town to play a straitlaced fundamentalist. Leigh Kent-Maxwell, of sexy-librarian fame, had been anointed Dance Hall Girl Number Two. Teresia Sandia, co-owner of the Desert Surf and Flower Shop (with *her* lover, Harvey McAllister, a displaced surfer from California), had, in the mysterious wunder-kind thought process, been cast in the role of a society belle from New York despite her Mexican heritage.

"I can't believe I'm doing this," Penelope announced for the third time to those re-maining in the waiting area.

"Oh, come on, Penelope, you've always wanted to be in movies."

"That's fine for you to say, sis, you've al-ways been an exhibitionist. I, however, am perfectly content with my own splendid persona."

"This is absolutely the last time I come to lend you moral support," Stormy said. "Exhibitionist, indeed."

"What about all those films you made, running around half naked, dispensing wicked Viziers by kicking them in the groin?"

"I was learning my trade. Besides, I didn't see the nudity clause in the fine print."

"Speaking of that, sis, I saw Masterly's last picture. How you can make naked women boring is beyond me."

"You don't have the proper sexual orientation to judge."

"I wasn't talking about me. Andy likes naked women, and he fell asleep, for God's sake."

A door opened and Nora Pryor, local historian and author of *A Guide to Empty Creek*, and her daughter, Regina, emerged from the office.

"Well?" Penelope demanded.

"Floozy Number Three," Nora announced.

"And I'm a floozy in training," Reggie cried gaily.

"You are not!" Nora said. "You're my daughter and I'm saving money to send you east to finishing school."

"I'd rather be a floozy."

"All in good time," Penelope said happily.

"Reggie," Nora warned. Mother and daughter took turns grounding each other for improper behavior. The record was six months — for Nora upon her nude appearance in the Women of Empty Creek Sixteen-Month Calendar.

"And you are the most unlikely floozy I

know," Penelope said. It was true. Walking past a Victoria's Secret shop caused Nora to blush furiously. "Who are Floozies One and Two?"

"I don't know."

"Samantha Dale," a six-foot Amazon in tight black jeans, black pumps with stiletto heels, and an *Ears of the Elephant* T-shirt about six sizes too small for her surgically enhanced chest said icily, looking at her clipboard. "Dominique Anders, personal assistant to Mr. Masterly," she had announced haughtily to each aspiring actress when they checked in for their appointment. "Mr. Masterly" was said in a tone of voice that implied God was traveling incognito among them.

"Wish me luck," Sam said, gently dislodging Big Mike, a twenty-five pound cat who moved only with reluctance. In Sam's real-life persona, she was president of the Empty Creek National Bank.

"Break a leg," Stormy said.

The door to the inner sanctum closed.

"I still can't believe I'm doing this."

"Four," rang out the chorus.

"Well, I can't," Penelope said sheepishly.

Big Mike, Penelope's friend and partner in life's little adventures since falling unceremoniously out of the bougainvillea in

Africa (narrowly missing the gin and tonic Penelope was enjoying at the time), looked around for another likely lap. Possessing a definite eye for the ladies, he decided to make a new friend and headed for Amazon Lady, rubbing against her leg with a friendly purr. Amazon Lady teetered away on her high heels. "Scat," she said.

Rebuffed, Big Mike leaped into Stormy's lap and settled down to stare malevolently at Amazon Lady. Scat, indeed.

Serve her right, Penelope thought, if Mikey put a curse on her, something along the order of shrinking her jeans and T-shirt until her tongue popped out. She was pondering even more dire torments for Ms. Anders when the outer door swung open and Elaine Henders swooshed in, dramatically tossing her thick mane of red hair.

"Sorry, I'm late. I had to finish the chapter I was working on."

"Name?" personal assistant to God demanded. She looked at the new arrival with the disdain reserved for writers, who were always consigned to the last circle of Hollywood hell.

"Elaine Henders. You can call me Laney."

"You can call me Ms. Anders. Take a seat."

Laney frowned and sat down next to Penelope. "Who got her underwear in a bunch?" she whispered.

"Mikey."

"Good for him."

Samantha came out of the casting office with a worried expression on her face. "Floozy Number One," she said. "What will my board of directors think?"

"They'll be proud of you," Penelope said. "As long as you keep making money for them."

"I certainly hope so. Well, I better go tell Jake. I know *he'll* be proud of me."

"Elaine Henders."

"What about me?" Penelope protested. "I was here first."

"Her name is ahead of yours." Ms. Anders turned to Laney. "Please go in. He doesn't like to be kept waiting."

"Nor do I, dearie, nor do I."

Laney closed the door behind her with an emphatic thump.

"Cue the malcontent," Stormy said.

"I wasn't going to say anything."

"You were thinking it."

"I was thinking that pink roses are very soothing."

"Ha!"

"Floozy Number Two," Laney huffed

when she returned. "What an insult. I've *never* been number two. In anything. Who's number one?"

"Samantha."

"She'd be much better as number two. I'm taking this to higher authority."

"C.D. is higher authority," Stormy said.

"My first role and already I'm having creative differences."

"That's what his initials stand for," Stormy laughed.

"Penelope Warren."

"Finally."

Penelope was disappointed. C.D. Masterly didn't look like God at all. He wore blue jeans and black cowboy boots. His shirt was Western, and he had a long black cigar stuck in his mouth. It looked like smoking had stunted his growth halfway between five feet and six feet.

"Name, sweetheart?"

"Penelope Warren, ammonia breath."

C.D. grinned. "Stormy's sister?"

"Yes."

"You're the madam," C.D. Masterly said, making a note on a sheet of paper before him. "The head floozy. You wanna take your clothes off now?"

"Certainly not!"

"Oh, well," he said with another grin. "It was worth a try."

"Did you ask the others?"

He shook his head. "You're special. Stormy said you were beautiful. Would you like to stay after the party?"

"Can you spell harassment?"

"Nope," C.D. said cheerfully.

"How about incorrigible?"

"My middle name."

"I'll see you at the party, but I'm bringing my boyfriend. He's Bad Guy Number One."

"You can always change your mind."

Penelope briefly considered doing her Charles Barkley imitation and tossing C.D. through the window. Instead, she chuckled. "You *are* incorrigible. Have a great day."

Penelope and Amazon Lady passed in the doorway. Stormy, Laney, and Big Mike all waited expectantly.

"I'm the madam," Penelope said, "the head floozy herself."

"Mom will be so proud," Stormy said.

"Mom will kill me, and maybe C.D. Masterly for good measure."

"She'll have to get in line," Stormy said. "Everyone wants to kill C.D."

Chapter One

By the standards of Beverly Hills, Bel Air, or Malibu, those lush enclaves for the rich purveyors of taste in American film, Paradise Regained was pretty low rent in the socioeconomic scale. In Empty Creek, Arizona, however, Paradise Regained was a fabulous villa high atop Crying Woman Mountain with expansive views from all points of the compass. At five thousand square feet with six bedrooms, five and one-half baths, den, family room (added to the architect's plans only for resale value), library, four-car garage, swimming pool, and hot tub, Paradise Regained listed at $2.1 million — walking-around chump change for the likes of C.D. Masterly — and rented for $25,000 per month only because Tater (he had a fondness for gourmet potatoes) O'Brien, the Realtor of record for the home, recognized gold in them there cameras and prima donnas trekking into town. But Tater later berated himself for not raising the ante to $30 or

$35 thou when Masterly sniffed and said, "It's not much, but I suppose it'll have to do."

Had Phineas C. Morgenstern, D.Litt., late professor of Old English, heard those words, he likely would have taken his hickory walking stick and thrashed the wunderkind of American film soundly. Having won $41 million in the Arizona state lottery, Morgenstern had immediately announced his retirement — before having to read all those tedious student papers on *Beowulf* — and set about building Paradise Regained, dreaming all the while of luring a particularly shapely coed, or two or three, to share his hot tub. Morgenstern's only regret before being run over by a speeding lorry driver while taking a summer holiday in his beloved London was having to delve into another period of English literature to name his retirement home. He just couldn't see coeds rushing to a place named Grendel, after the monster in England's epic poem. Still, had Morgenstern remembered to look right first, rather than left, he would have approved of the babes who now frolicked in the hot tub he had barely christened with a bottle of Dom Pérignon before his untimely demise.

Not so with Harry Duchette, who had been summoned for an audience with the wunderkind himself, the great C.D. Masterly, knowing he was in trouble when he arrived to find Brock Hackett, the second assistant director, gleefully using his script as kindling for the barbecue. He consoled himself by staring through the patio doors at Vixen DeVaughn and Buffy Anne Mulholland, the latest of Masterly's Constant Companions, gamboling playfully in the hot tub, displaying their glistening, perfect (unless the dimples on Vixen's derriere could be considered a flaw), and nude bodies without a hint of shyness for the members of the master's entourage. After all, how else could one attain the perfect tan?

Harry Duchette became a writer for two reasons — Miss Evelyn Ericson, during honors English his senior year in high school, praised his early creative efforts highly and, more important, Harry thought it would be a great way to meet girls while reading poetry by candlelight and drinking red wine.

Wrong.

The Vixen DeVaughns and Buffy Anne Mulhollands simply did not gravitate to writers. In all his years in the Business,

Harry had never found even a blonde dumb enough to sleep with the writer — God knows, he had tried hard enough.

And now the ubiquitous Dominique Anders spitefully blocked his view, which was not really a bad thing in Harry's opinion, considering she was fully clothed and hiding most of *her* tan. As an eleven on a scale of ten, the statuesque Dominique had once rollicked in Masterly's hot tub until she made the critical mistake of forgetting to lie about her age, admitting to being thirty (champagne made her tipsy) over a not-so-intimate dinner at Wolfgang Puck's Spago in Beverly Hills to celebrate what Masterly thought was her twenty-sixth birthday. Shortly thereafter, Dominique had been named personal assistant to Mr. Masterly, duly announced in all the trade papers, and Vixen DeVaughn moved to Senior Constant Companion (without benefit of a press release). "Mr. Masterly has some notes," Dominique said with all the warmth of a crocodile contemplating lunch.

"Is that a wrinkle I see on your face, Dommie?"

Dominique bared perfect teeth. "Don't call me Dommie," she spat out.

His stomach already beginning to hurt,

Harry walked through the open sliding glass doors onto the patio and the presence of the wunderkind.

"I have some more notes," Wunderkind said, glancing at his Rolex. He was wearing about a hundred grand's worth of clothing and accessories.

Harry checked his Timex, wondering if Masterly wanted to synchronize watches before going over the top, and sighed. Notes were just another of the innumerable ways Hollywood had for showing additional contempt for the writer. Schmucks with Underwoods, Jack Warner had once called the writers on his studio lot. Harry looked wistfully at the bar.

"Have a drink, Harry," Masterly said magnanimously. "This won't take long."

"Scotch and milk," Harry told the bartender. "A double."

The young man behind the bar poured the drink without snickering. He even managed to accomplish the task without spilling a drop, a remarkable achievement considering he never took his eyes off Vixen and Buffy Anne.

"Lose the snakes," Masterly said when Harry reluctantly took *his* eyes off the Constant Companions and focused on the impromptu story conference.

"C.D.," Harry replied with what he hoped was a reasonable tone of voice. "You can't film a Western in Arizona without a rattlesnake or two." The rattlesnake den had been yesterday's addition to the script. Harry knew Masterly suffered from herpetophobia, and exacted his small measure of revenge. Use my script to light your damned fire, will you?

Wunderkind shuddered and then snapped his fingers. "I hate snakes. Lose the snakes."

Ms. Anders scribbled in her notebook. No snakes.

"Yes, C.D."

"Remember, creativity is spontaneous."

Ms. Anders recorded that pronouncement.

"Yes, C.D.," Harry said, thinking spontaneity was crap. "What about gila monsters? Can I put in a gila monster?"

"No monsters either. But cactus is good. Use lots of cactus. Those big, skinny ones."

Skinny cactus, Ms. Anders inscribed.

"Saguaros," Harry said. "They're called saguaros."

"Whatever. I'll need the revisions first thing in the morning."

"No party?"

"No party, Harry. Remember, creativity is work."

Ms. Anders entered that in the chronicle verbatim.

Penelope Warren swung her Jeep into the circular drive of Paradise Regained and pulled up behind a white stretch limousine. Valets scurried to open limo doors, allowing egress for a publicist, a personal assistant, two secretaries, and a youthful, bronzed boy toy with bleached hair who was close to bursting the seams of his blue polo shirt.

"Who's that, I wonder?" Harris Anderson III asked eagerly.

"Visiting royalty, I should imagine," Penelope replied, "from the amount of subservience being displayed."

"No, look, it's Brynn Moore. My God, she still looks great."

Once the hottest sex kitten in Hollywood, Brynn Moore had aged gracefully (without benefit of plastic surgery), transforming herself all the while into a talented actress. She entered Paradise Regained like she was walking down the red carpet into the Academy Award presentations.

Penelope pulled her humble jeep into the space vacated by the limousine. Although her entourage was not so grand as that of the magnificent Brynn Moore, Penelope's had a certain cachet about it, consisting of Andy and Big Mike, still a little grumpy over having his afternoon nap cut short. Not bad for a couple of extras, albeit the head floozy and Bad Guy Number One.

Perhaps tantalized by the smell of barbecuing ribs or the more subtle aromas of a variety of canapes, Big Mike scampered ahead and disappeared through the grand entranceway.

"Mikey seems ready to party," Andy said, following in the big cat's wake, practicing his John Wayne walk — unsuccessfully, it might be added. He looked like he had a severe case of saddle sores, compounded by two arthritic knees and a blister on the sole of his right foot.

"I can't believe we're doing this," Penelope said. "And, by the bye, Mikey does a better John Wayne imitation than you."

"Does not, and it'll be fun. I can't wait to meet Brynn Moore."

"I'll bet she's saying the same thing about you this very moment. 'Who *is* that handsome chap with the funny walk? I must *have* him.' "

They entered the foyer to find Brynn Moore in the throes of a bad script day. "Six of my lines have been cut!" she screamed at C.D. Masterly. "Tell the writer to put them back or else!" She turned to Andy and offered her hand politely. "How nice to see you, darling. I'm Brynn Moore."

"I knew that," Andy stammered, clasping her hand.

After extricating her hand from Andy's, she turned again. "And you must be Penelope. Stormy's told me so much about you."

Andy looked at his hand in a daze. "I'll never wash it again."

Penelope smiled despite her previous resolve to hate everything about Hollywood — except her sister, of course. "It's a pleasure to meet you. I've admired your work, especially in *Hearts of Despair*. You should have won the Oscar for that."

"You're very kind to say so."

"Hi, Mom," Stormy said, joining the party with Dutch Fowler, her fiancé and the Empty Creek chief of police. In *Elephant*, Stormy was cast as Brynn Moore's gunslinging daughter. She kissed Brynn's cheek in the designated manner required in Hollywoodland.

"Don't call me that," Brynn said, returning the kiss affectionately. "People will think I have stretch marks. Hi, Dutch. Good to see you again."

"Nice to see you, Brynn." He wasn't very good at the kiss and damned near missed her cheek.

"Everyone go in and have a great time," Masterly said nervously.

"Six lines," Brynn warned, "and good lines, not that drivel you've been feeding poor Harry, or I'll have Bobby do a double grand slam whammy on you, or whatever it's called. Bobby's a wrestler, you know. The Masked Madman."

The young man with muscles rippled them, then glowered at Masterly.

"Yes, Brynn. Six lines."

Andy watched the Masked Madman and decided he wasn't in love with Brynn Moore after all.

Vixen and Buffy Anne, now formally attired in thong bikinis and high heels, circulated among the guests, inducing heart palpitations among the men of Empty Creek and a lively dose of cattiness in their women, particularly the floozies and temperance women who had gathered in a corner of the large living room close to a manned wet bar and a plentiful supply of wine bottles.

"You have to admit their plastic surgeons are very good," Nora Pryor said. "Perhaps I should ask for a referral."

"Nora!"

"Go for it, Mom," Reggie said.

"Reggie!" Penelope exclaimed a second time.

"Well," Nora said, "Tony might like it." She was looking across the room at her beloved Anthony Lyme-Regis, who stood talking with Craig Halliday, the male lead playing the diabolical enemy of Brynn Moore in the movie, but Tony's attention seemed focused on Vixen.

"I'm sure Tony likes you au naturel just fine."

"And, I've never won a wet T-shirt competition."

"Neither have I," Penelope said. "I'm sure it's vastly overrated."

"Oh, I don't know," Stormy said. She had triumphed over the legendary Debbie Locke in a memorable contest that some still argued was fixed.

"Vixen and Buffy Anne were laughing at the calendar," Andy interrupted indignantly. He was the nude male of the month for the Men of Empty Creek Sixteen-

Month Calendar, which had followed in the wake of the success of the women's calendar, raising almost as much money for a local children's charity.

"I hope it wasn't April," Penelope said sympathetically.

"They said I was too skinny."

"Don't worry, sweetie, I'll restore your ego later. They don't know what they're missing."

"They better not have been laughing at my honey," Stormy said. "I'll have Mikey scratch their eyes out."

Since Mikey was, at the moment, happily stretched out in Buffy Anne's lap, Penelope didn't think there was much chance of that. "Better have Dutch arrest them for public indecency instead."

"Good idea," Laney said. "Throw them in solitary."

"Dip them in honey and stake them out for an ant picnic," Debbie Locke said.

"No, they'd probably like that."

"Tie them up and tickle them with feathers."

"They'd probably like that too," Nora said.

"How would *you* know?" Penelope asked.

Nora blushed. It was something she'd rather not get into just then.

"Entice them to the Faire," Kathy Allen interrupted to Nora's gratitude, "and have good Queen Bess put them in the pillory so we can pitch rotten tomatoes at them." Kathy knew that experience all too well.

"Better yet."

"Scold's bridle and the ducking stool," Stormy recommended, recalling her ordeal during a peasant rebellion at the Empty Creek Elizabethan Springe Faire.

"Burn them at the stake," Alyce Smith suggested. She had once confronted that unpleasant prospect, a sorceress condemned by a murderer at the Faire. "No, forget it. They'd probably like that too." While standing around tied to a stake with fagots piled to her hips wasn't so great, Alyce remembered her rescue by the knight of her dreams with great fondness.

Andy decided never to incur the wrath of the women of Empty Creek.

As parties went, Masterly's soiree for the local residents cast as extras in *Elephant* was more than nice — food and drink was plentiful and excellent in every respect, white-jacketed waiters and waitresses were quick to attend to every need, and to

Penelope's surprise, she found everyone in the film company quite sociable, with the possible exception of Dominique Anders, also a definite candidate for the pillory. Penelope even warmed to the Junior Constant companion, who engaged her in a passionate conversation about saving the rain forest, a project Penelope thoroughly approved of, although she found it disconcerting to participate in serious dialogue with someone as skimpily clad as Buffy Anne.

But, as parties went by Empty Creek standards, it was pretty boring, failing to match even the *Monday Night Football* gatherings at the Double B for entertaining rowdiness — until Hilly Hollander crashed the party. That perked things up considerably.

Hilly Hollander, star gossip columnist for the trashiest of tabloids, *The Millennium*, seemed to have taken his fashion tips from both Truman Capote and Tom Wolfe. He appeared wearing a white linen suit (jacket worn in the European style loosely draped over his shoulders), white loafers (tasseled), a white silk shirt with ruffles, a red ascot plumped at his neck, and a long cigarette holder cocked jauntily between his teeth, but the pièce de résistance was the purple cape atop his linen suit.

Stunned by this apparition suddenly in their midst, the locals stared. Not so with C.D. Masterly — he was still trying to convince Penelope to take her clothes off — who turned when the silence fell over the party. "Who let that pimp in here?" he bellowed, instantly turning an angry red before charging the new arrival with a furious rush.

Nonplussed, Hollander casually removed his cape and goaded the charging Masterly like a bullfighter enticing the bull to his sword. Penelope gave him a nine on the graceful veronica he performed, but lowered the score when Masterly became entangled in the cape and crashed to the floor, bringing the columnist down on top of him.

Big Mike, sleeping with half a turkey dog between his front paws and startled by the commotion, provided the sound track for the melee, issuing a dire warning. "Meorgh!" he yowled. "Stay away from my turkey dog!

Before the astonished eyes of the assemblage, the two men sat on the floor, flailing wildly at each other. Masterly landed a good right cross on Hollander's nose, which started bleeding. Despite his wound, Hollander retaliated with a decent jab to Masterly's mouth.

"Shouldn't someone break it up?" Brock Hackett asked. "In about an hour, maybe two?"

"Let them fight," Brynn Moore said. "It's good for them."

"Oh, hell," Dutch said, "why am I always the only cop around?" He went to the table with the punch bowl, hefted it, and poured it over the combatants. The deluge was followed by more outraged howls.

"My suit," Hilly Hollander cried, "my nobe. You've broken my nobe."

"You chipped my tooth," Masterly shouted, scrambling to his feet. "I'll sue you again."

"Meorgh!" Big Mike's fur bristled in preparation for repelling food thieves.

"It's a good thing they outlawed dueling, or my seconds would call you out at dawn."

"I accept. Choose your weapons."

"Oh, shut up," Dutch said, "or I'll throw you both in the slam."

"He started it. And besides that, he's trespassing."

"I was invited."

"Not by me. Get out."

"He's my guest," Brynn Moore said.

That shut Masterly up. He had no desire to find out what a double grand slam whammy was.

"Now you boys shake hands and play nicely," Brynn said, "or I'll be very cross with you."

Vixen and Buffy Anne led Masterly away to tell him how brave he was and what animal magnetism he exhibited. After two minutes of that, Masterly elevated the schoolyard encounter into a stupendous victory over the forces of evil.

"And you, Hilly, you're not to write a word of it."

"Yes, Brynn."

"Now go tidy up."

"I'm curious," Penelope said. "If they're such enemies, why did you invite him?"

"You know what Oscar Wilde said," Brynn replied.

" 'There is only one thing in the world worse than being talked about,' " Penelope quoted, " 'and that is not being talked about.' "

"Exactly. C.D. has taken a pretty good script and screwed it up with all his notes and changes. I don't want to be in a picture that bombs, so a little good publicity in the beginning won't do any harm."

"Even in *The Millennium?*"

"Especially in *The Millennium.*"

"Meorgh!"

"It's all over, Mikey, you can relax now."

Easy for you to say. They weren't after *your* turkey dog.

And that was pretty much it for the party. The principals said their good-byes and the extras drifted toward the door, perhaps disappointed that no one had to go to the emergency room for treatment. It hadn't been much of a fight, considering the high standards by which such events were judged in Empty Creek, but, as Oscar Wilde might have said, "Even a dinky little fight is better than no fight at all."

"Well, that's over with, thank God," Masterly said, waving and watching the last of his guests drive away from Paradise Regained. He was flanked by Vixen and Buffy Anne. Dominique Anders stood behind them, pad and pencil ready to record any creative pronouncements passed down from Mount Sinai. Brock Hackett stood at her side.

"You two are in charge of the cleanup."

"Yes, Mr. Masterly," Dominique said.

Hackett sighed wearily, "I started the barbecue."

"You can put it out too," Masterly said. He put his arms around the respective waists of his Constant Companions. *"Now* let's party."

Dominique snapped her pencil in half.

Hackett made a rude gesture toward Masterly's back.

Making movies was such fun.

Driving home, Penelope recapped the afternoon and early evening succinctly. "Well, I for one fail to see the glamour."

"Great view from the house."

"Yes."

"Brynn Moore is nice."

"I agree."

"You're prettier than any of them."

"Oh, I am not. You're just saying that because they thought you were too skinny. Which reminds me, how's your ego?"

"Damaged beyond repair."

"We'll see about that — after we feed the critters," Penelope shared her twelve-acre ranchette with Big Mike, Chardonnay — a laid-back Arabian mare — a multitude of rabbits who gathered each evening for a handout of lettuce and carrots, a rattlesnake named Clyde, and the occasional coyote, usually new in town, who hadn't yet seen Big Mike's imitation of a fierce grizzly bear, where he reared on his hind legs and skittered sideways toward his victim, caterwauling all the while. One or two wauls was usually enough to send unwanted visitors heading south toward the Mexican border.

At the mention of food, Big Mike's ears perked. "Meow," he said hopefully.

"You've had enough," Penelope said.

She stopped the Jeep in the driveway and said, "Get ready to party, sweetie."

Seated at the vanity in the master bathroom of Paradise Regained much later — it was nearly midnight — Vixen DeVaughn enjoyed her fourth cigarette of the day, even though she had to sneak it because C.D. didn't allow cigarette smoking in his presence, despite those awful cigars *he* smoked. She limited herself to four because she aspired to be a Scream Queen — it worked for Jamie Lee Curtis — and she didn't wish to ruin her wind (Vixen had seen *Friday the 13th* twelve times before refusing to rent it again because she was superstitious). Thus, she smoked a king-sized, ultra light cigarette after breakfast, lunch, dinner, and sex.

She puffed away contentedly and contemplated her career. When location shooting for *Elephant* was completed, C.D. had promised to use his influence to get her a role in *Scream for Your Life 6*. Vixen intended to use the time on location in preparing for the part. She was on the payroll as assistant script person, which meant all she had to do was hang out, observe, fetch the occasional cup of coffee or diet soft drink for C.D., and massage his neck and shoulders when the tension of genius became unbearable.

Vixen snuffed out her cigarette and stood before the mirror. Her long blond hair was slightly tousled — the proper effect for a young woman in *Scream for Your Life 6* about to confront a deranged meat market butcher with a very big cleaver. She jiggled, watching her reflection critically. The jiggle was excellent, even perfect, she thought. That was also a major requirement for an actress in a fright film. Jiggling and screaming. Damn, I'm good. She blew herself a kiss and then went out to show off her jiggle and exact a few more career-enhancing promises from good old C.D. before nighty-night.

Unfortunately, C.D. was not there to appreciate her dramatic entrance, which was strange, indeed, considering she had left him handcuffed to the headboard.

Chapter Two

Officer Sam Connors was parked in the view area on the slopes of Crying Woman Mountain, minding his own business in the waning hours of his shift, when he heard the scream, and a woman, wearing nothing but a pair of thigh-high boots, flashed past his windshield, arms pumping, breasts bobbing, buttocks bouncing.

In the grand tradition of Sherlock Holmes, Connors immediately deduced that something was amiss, although in Empty Creek one could never be certain. "Something's wrong," he said, immediately glad he didn't have a partner to hear his witless remark. He started the black-and-white and pulled out behind her, hitting the red lights and a short, quick blast on the siren. The woman glanced over her shoulder, shrieked again, and picked up her pace.

Never having stopped a naked woman for speeding before, Connors wasn't sure of the procedure. "This is Cactus One. I'm in pursuit down the mountain and I need backup. Better send Peggy Norton."

"I'm on the way," Peggy cut in. "ETA two minutes. What's the make of the car and the license number?"

"She doesn't have one."

"She?"

"It's a naked woman."

A male voice broke onto the net. "Hot damn. Cactus Three ETA in four."

"Cactus One, have you been drinking?"

"No, dammit! I'm chasing a naked woman. She's hysterical."

"Something's wrong."

"No kidding. Did you think she was out for a midnight jog?"

"Well, make her stop."

"I'm trying, for God's sake."

Peggy Norton in Cactus Two swerved her black-and-white in front of the woman's path and stopped.

The woman didn't. She skipped, measuring her leap, and performed an excellent imitation of a high hurdler, jumping on the hood in full stride, leaving a couple of good dents before hitting the ground on the other side, howling maniacally and running downhill at a pretty fair clip.

Sam circled around Peggy's black-and-white and drew alongside. "Lady, will you chill? What the hell's wrong with you?"

She looked at him briefly with blank eyes. Had her features not been contorted with fear, she would have been very pretty, even beautiful, with her long blond hair streaming behind her. She screamed again and picked up her stride.

"Christ, I hope she's not practicing for a marathon."

Officer Phil McCutcheon in Cactus Three stopped and got out of his car. He stood in the middle of the road, legs akimbo, and held up his hand. "Stop!" he ordered. "Police officer!"

The woman thundered by, emitting a shrill wail that hurt McCutcheon's ears.

He took off in foot pursuit.

Big mistake. His playing days as a third-string linebacker at the U of A were long behind him. After a hundred yards, McCutcheon was puffing and wheezing. After two hundred yards, he was hunched over, hands on his knees, gulping frantically for breath.

Cactus One and Cactus Two cruised by. Connors now had the spotlight trained on the woman. The view was mesmerizing.

The chase might have continued through the warm Arizona night had not the usually diligent city road crew missed filling in a pothole. The unidentified woman had just kicked in her afterburners after another piercing wail — great lungs, Sam Connors thought — when her right foot dipped into the unintentional speed trap and the chunky heel on her right boot snapped off. Her stride broken, the woman fell, tumbled over once, and lay on the ground, sobbing uncontrollably.

Peggy Norton jumped from her car, grabbed a blanket from the trunk, and rushed to help, throwing the blanket over the nude body.

"Shouldn't we examine her for injuries or something?" Sam asked.

"Pervert," Peggy responded disdainfully without looking at him.

"Apple One, what the hell's going on?"

"She broke her heel."

"I'll dispatch the paramedics."

"The heel on her boot, dummy."

"Oh."

"Send the paramedics anyway," Connors said. "And a psychiatrist."

"Good God," Peggy said, holding up the broken heel. "How could she run in this? I couldn't."

Phil McCutcheon drove up and parked. The headlights lit up the scene.

"Kill the lights," Peggy said.

"Not till she's cuffed. I ain't chasing her no more." McCutcheon was still breathing heavily, and sweat beaded his plump but still handsome chocolate-brown face.

"Just kill the lights. All of them."

"Killed." The sound came from beneath the blanket between sobs. "Somebody killed him."

"Killed who?"

"C.D.," the woman cried.

The police officers exchanged glances. This was not going to be good for the tourist trade. Sam Connors called into the station. "Better wake up Dutch," he said. "I think we got a situation here."

The head floozy happily rehearsed her role, running through it for a third time, although Bad Guy Number One's chaps had long since wilted. After all, Penelope reasoned, striving for excellence, even in something as trivial as a walk-on role in a dumb movie, was a worthy goal. And, despite the fact that this particular scene called for nothing more than the head floozy to take Bad Guy Number One's hand and climb the steps of the saloon in the background of the scene while the principals made goo-goo eyes at each other across a poker table, Penelope was deter-mined to be the best stair-climbing floozy in the history of film. She had mastered flouncing, cocking her hip seductively, and started practicing her enticing look.

"Can't we just go up the stairs and be done with it?" Andy groaned.

"Absolutely not," Penelope said, leering at him. She decided to try for beguiling. "It's knowing what's waiting for you in my boudoir that provides motivation for the scene."

The telephone rang.

Penelope looked at the instrument on the nightstand. A post-midnight phone call was ominous. Andy sighed with relief, hoping that rehearsal was over.

Penelope answered, listened briefly, and replaced the receiver gently in its cradle, staring at it for a full minute. Finally, she said, "Get dressed, sweetie, we have to get back to the party."

"It's still going?"

"Yes, but it's turned into a wake."

"Whan that Aprille with his shoures sote/The droghte of March hath perced to the roote," Lola LaPola and Jacque Prideaux, her devoted husband, celebrated their first meeting. This fourth-anniversary rite was little different from the others, which meant a sensuous dinner of champagne and escargot in prelude, and then prolonged fooling around with many sweet kisses, and a great deal of gentle fondling while Lola was slowly divested of her garments.

The disrobing had reached a critical point when the telephone rang, interrupting Lola's happy cooing. "Let it ring, Jack darling," she whispered.

Engrossed in his task, Jack made no reply.

"Mmm, yes," Lola murmured at the third ring. "But what if it's World War Three?"

"It'll be over before you can get there," Jack replied.

"Probably, but we'd better answer anyway."

Jack stretched for the phone with one hand while continuing another task with his other. He held the receiver to Lola's ear.

"Mmm," she said. "I mean, hello." She frowned as she listened. "Thanks," she said, nodding to Jack that the conversation was over.

"World War Three?"

"Almost. I've got to go. Damn."

For the second time in less than twelve hours, Penelope drove up to the gates of Paradise Regained. There were no valets now to see to the black-and-whites, their lights flashing eerily, unmarked cars, coroner's van, and Dutch's personal pickup truck that crowded the drive, forcing Penelope to park the Jeep on the street.

Again, the double doors were open, but there were no entourages, no sounds of gaiety, no director to greet them effusively, if insincerely, no anything, in fact, except a bunch of cops, starting with Phil Mc-Cutcheon, who was guarding the entrance. He greeted Empty Creek's foremost amateur detective, her faithful assistant and reigning monarch of the feline world, and Scoop Anderson in a more accustomed role, his reporter's notebook at the ready. "Wacky," McCutcheon said, shaking his head.

Andy recorded the brief comment. It was a start.

"Where are they, Phil?" Penelope asked.

"Out back, by the pool. You ain't gonna believe it."

"Probably not, but I'll suspend my disbelief."

They found Dutch standing in the patio

doors, watching as several of his police officers searched the backyard with flashlights.

"What are they doing?"

"Looking for a rattlesnake."

"Dutch, with all the commotion here, any self-respecting snake, rattle or otherwise, has packed up his family and moved to Tucson."

"It's evidence," Dutch said.

"Oh."

Andy recorded the absent rattlesnake and then underlined wacky — twice.

"All clear, boss," Sam Connors shouted.

"I don't want it all clear," Dutch answered. "I want the damned snake."

"Well, it isn't here."

"You sure?" Larry Burke, one-half of the Robbery-Homicide Bureau, asked. Tweedledee was standing in a circle of light, looking around nervously, hand resting on the butt of his service weapon. If someone said, "Boo," he would probably leap into the pool, or start blasting away.

"Boo!" Penelope said.

Burke jumped. "Dammit, Penelope, don't do that."

"Just testing your reactions," Penelope said, mildly disappointed that he hadn't taken a dip. It would have delayed the unpleasant, but inevitable, task. She took a deep breath and turned to confront the corpse of C.D. Masterly on the chaise longue.

He was on his back, hands and arms twisted beneath his body. His eyes were wide and protruding, gaping sightlessly at the night that had enveloped him so suddenly. A burlap bag had been carelessly discarded at his feet.

"What happened?"

"Near as we can figure it so far," Dutch said, "Vixen DeVaughn left him handcuffed to the bed while she took a shower and smoked a cigarette. When she came out, he was gone. She searched the house and then heard him scream. She got here in time to see a big rattlesnake under the chaise longue just before Masterly died. She took off hysterical. Naked, incidentally, except for some boots. Sam and Peggy caught up with her a couple of miles down the road."

"He looks like he was scared to death."

Dutch shrugged. "Maybe. Apparently, everyone knew he had a phobia about snakes."

"Was he bitten?"

Dutch pointed. Dried specks of blood clung to the fang marks on Masterly's left shoulder. Penelope pointed to another droplet of blood lower down on the arm. "What's this?" she asked.

"Rattlesnake with three fangs," Willie Stoner, the other half of the Robbery-Homicide Bureau, said. Tweedledum chortled.

"Hardly."

"Broke a fang the first time?" Burke said.

"Struck a second time with just one fang."

"Has anyone found a fang just lying around?"

"Probably took it with him," Burke said. "Didn't want to leave evidence behind. Who knows? Maybe rattlesnakes have dentists too. Get it stuck back in."

"I see this investigation is beginning at the usual low level of insight."

"Aw, Penelope, don't start," Tweedledee whined. "Could have been just a practical joke that went bad."

"Pretty sick joke."

Penelope turned to Sam Connors. "Did anyone drive by before Vixen appeared?"

He shook his head. "Everything was quiet until I heard the first scream."

"Whoever it was, he probably took the back road down," Tweedledee said.

"Or went back to bed," Dutch said. "Buffy Anne Mulholland was asleep in another bedroom. Claims she didn't hear anything. Slept through the whole thing."

"Or Vixen did it," Penelope said. "Running naked down the road, screaming hysterically, is a pretty good cover-up."

"That's occurred to me too."

"Or they're both in on it."

"But why would either of them want to kill their benefactor?"

"Good question. Let's ask them."

"Start with Vixen."

"Hey, boss, found some white powder in the bedroom. Looks like old C.D. did a few lines of cocaine."

Dutch shook his head. "That's all we need."

The nude jogger extraordinaire, now dressed — if a micromini leather skirt and a skimpy blouse was considered dressed — was puffing on her fifth cigarette of the day, having decided that a post-murder cigarette was in order. She had also traversed a gamut of emotions, coming down from hysteria through shock and disbelief to profound grief, going on to trembling nerves and mild fear, finally reaching nirvana in discovering she was the focus of attention for three men staring intently at her. Vixen immediately raised her ambitions. She slowly crossed her long, slender legs and smiled at Dutch Fowler, Larry Burke, and Willie Stoner, ignoring Penelope and Peggy Norton. Eat your heart out, Sharon Stone.

"All right," Dutch said. "Let's take it from the very tippy-tippy top."

The cameras were rolling. Vixen stubbed out her cigarette and smiled again.

After an hour's grilling, they knew just about what they had known before, which was to say, not much.

After they finished with Vixen, they went into the den, where Buffy Anne Mulholland waited with Sheila Tyler.

Buffy Anne Mulholland stuck to her story. "I had a headache and went to bed early," she said between sobs. Unlike Vixen, Buffy Anne demonstrated modesty, keeping her white fluffy bathrobe clutched tightly. "I took a sleeping pill. That's why I didn't hear anything."

"Did you and Masterly have an argument?"

"Of course not," she replied.

"Did you and Vixen have an argument?"

"No."

"You weren't jealous of her?"

"It wasn't like that."

"What was it like?"

"Not what you're thinking. We were all friends. We had separate bedrooms, for God's sake."

"Vixen and C.D. made love just before he was killed."

"Well, of course. Did you think we were kinky?"

While Dutch and the others went back to have another Q&A with Vixen, Penelope wandered off to the master bedroom. She had nothing against kinky. An occasional deviation from the norm was exciting, perhaps even healthy. Her own toy box consisted of a bondage starter kit (not unusual, since Laney had presented them to all of her lady friends one Valentine's Day), an additional pair of handcuffs (a souvenir from an earlier case), various lotions and oils, even a period costume or two from the days when she played Elizabeth Regina at the Elizabethan Springe Faire. So long as children and animals were not harmed, Penelope believed consenting adults were allowed to have a little fun. A ménage à trois, however, was beyond her experience, and she intended to keep it that way.

"But I'm not judging," Penelope said,

entering a massive walk-in closet in the master bedroom. A goodly portion of the space was devoted to what appeared to be the wardrobe department of a minor film studio specializing in bad straight-to-video dramas on the epic scale of Stormy's earlier films. Each costume was in duplicate, presumably in Vixen's and Buffy Anne's respective sizes. Penelope ignored the leopardskin cave girl outfits — she had one of her own — and pulled a golden metal breastplate from a hanger and held it up to her body. Too big, she decided, wondering if Andy would like her as Xena, Warrior Princess. She replaced it, pushing it aside to examine, in turn, a skimpy French maid's outfit, an even skimpier harem girl outfit with see-through pantaloons and diminutive halter (no ruby for the navel), schoolgirl apparel, leather corsets in black, red, and white, elaborate ball gowns (Louis XIV period, Penelope guessed), plain white cotton shifts of the sort Joan of Arc might have worn when she donned female attire. Farther along were several elaborate contraptions consisting mostly of silver-studded leather straps, the type of thing found in Laney's favorite mail order catalogue.

"C.D. liked to play dress-up," Buffy

61

Anne said, entering the closet. Big Mike was in her arms, clutched tightly to her chest. He was a sucker for a woman in distress.

Her voice startled Penelope, and she jumped guiltily, blushing, caught examining another's intimate secrets. "Did you?" she asked.

"Oh, I didn't mind. I liked pleasing him. We were going to be married."

Penelope's eyes widened in surprise. "Did Vixen know?"

"Sure. We hadn't announced it yet, but Vixie was going to be a scream queen when C.D. and I were married. We had it all planned. After *Ears of the Elephant* was in the can, C.D. was going into rehab. Afterward . . ." Buffy Anne plopped on the bed, holding Big Mike even tighter. He purred in sympathy. Tears welled in Buffy Anne's eyes and overflowed, streaming down her cheeks. "Who could have killed him?"

"I was about to ask you the same question."

"Everybody was envious of his success. He was a genius, you know."

"So he said."

"Dominique Anders was jealous. She wanted to marry him too."

"He seems to have been popular with women."

"He was working on that with his psychiatrist. He had a lot of things to work out."

"I can see that."

"And that creepy writer hates all of us. C.D. was going to bring someone in to do a complete rewrite."

Penelope was soon sorry she had asked the question. By the time she was finished, Buffy Anne had warmed up, eventually providing most of the population living west of the Mississippi with motives for killing C.D. Masterly.

During Buffy Anne's long recitation, Big Mike grew bored at the lack of attention, and hopped off her lap and went exploring.

The Fourth Estate was augmented by the arrival of Lola LaPola. She talked her way past Phil McCutcheon, but he insisted that her camera crew remain outside until the detectives finished their work, a task he was estimating might last until the arrival of the twenty-first century at their current rate of progress.

"Hello, everybody," Lola said. "What's up?"

"You got here fast," Dutch said.

"A neighbor called and told me the police were all over Paradise Regained. Naturally, I was curious."

"Naturally," Andy said grumpily. Although he quite liked Lola, Andy hated the electronic media and murderers who had no respect for community newspaper deadlines. If dastardly acts were to be committed in and around Empty Creek, they should be done before the *Empty Creek News-Journal* went to bed on Friday and Wednesday nights for the Saturday and Thursday editions respectively.

"Sorry," Lola said.

"Fill her in, Andy," Dutch said. "I'll make an official statement for both of you later. Okay?"

"Sure, Dutch."

"And, by the way, Andy."

"Yes, dear?"

"Don't even think about a ménage à trois."

"I never know what you're talking about."

Penelope smiled. She intended to keep it that way.

Dawn was breaking when Dutch sent Vixen and Buffy Anne to their rooms under escort by his two female police officers. Then they huddled in the living room.

"So, what do you think?" Dutch asked.

"Vixen," Tweedledee said.

"Nope," his partner said. "Buffy Anne. Never trust anyone who takes sleeping pills."

"Penelope?"

"Motive bothers me."

"Me too, but they both had opportunity."

"Vixen more than Buffy Anne. I can't see Buffy Anne racing around, forcing C.D. outside, tossing a rattlesnake in his lap, and getting back in bed before Vixen looked in on her. Besides, she suggested a number of other possible suspects. Too soon to judge."

"Vixen did the same after you left. According to her, nobody liked C.D. very much except her and Buffy Anne."

"What else would she say?" Tweedledee said. "Of course she's going to throw suspicion on some poor, innocent party."

"Ha!" Penelope said. "I haven't seen much evidence of innocence here in Paradise Regained."

"Toss a coin, then," Tweedledee said. "I'm going outside to commune with nature."

"Willie, go tell Peggy and Sheila to read

'em their rights. We can charge them with possession of a controlled substance."

"Don't forget that gossip columnist at the party," Penelope said. "He didn't seem to get along with Masterly very well."

"I remember very well, indeed. I was planning to see if he had an alibi."

"From what I've heard, we'd better check the alibis of everyone in the entire crew. Oh, and, Dutch?"

"Yeah?"

"Mikey found a needle in the bedroom."

Dutch's eyes widened. "Hypodermic needle?"

"More like the needle in the haystack."

"What's going on here?"

Penelope and Dutch turned to find Dominque Anders glaring at them. A pasty-faced Harry Duchette slunk in behind her.

Penelope looked at Dutch and raised an eyebrow.

Dutch responded by saying, "C.D. Masterly was killed this morning."

Blunt, Penelope thought, waiting to see how Dominque reacted, expecting shock, disbelief, a burst of tears, possibly even a flash of guilt in her eyes. The personal assistant to Mr. Masterly surprised her, however.

"He did it!" Dominique screamed, launching herself in a determined attempt to beat Harry Duchette into plowshares. The sudden attack threw Duchette to the floor, and Dominique pounced, sitting on his chest, pummeling him wildly with her fists.

"Not again," Dutch groaned, looking around for a punch bowl. "Norton, Tyler, somebody," he hollered.

"Get her off me," Duchette cried.

"I'll kill you," Dominique screeched, "dirty, lousy, no-good writer."

Peggy Norton raced into the living room. "Jesus, what's going on?"

"Get her off him," Dutch ordered.

Peggy threw an arm around Dominique's shoulders, yanking her off the cowering writer, dragging her across the floor. Dominque kicked at Duchette until she was pulled out of range.

"Dammit, settle down."

"Let me go. I'll kill him."

"Christ, cuff her."

The handcuffs clicking shut on Dominique's wrists succeeded in turning her wrath on Dutch. "What are you doing? Release me this instant."

"Oh, shut up," Penelope said, "and tell us why you jumped him."

"Arrest her!" Duchette cried. "Aggravated assault."

"Be quiet. You'll get your turn."

"He called me last night and read the most disgusting filth. All about me being tied naked to some cactus and begging to let me make love to him."

"I was drunk."

"You're depraved, and I'll thank you to keep me out of your perverted fantasies."

"I think I'm still drunk."

"And that's not all," Dominique continued vehemently. "He had poor C.D. tied to a cactus with a bunch of rattlesnakes trying to bite him."

Now, isn't that interesting? Penelope thought.

Chapter Three

Lola LaPola scooped the world on the death of C.D. Masterly, breaking the story on *Wake Up! Valley of the Sun*, a cheesy morning tabloid show co-anchored by Jennifer Sanchez, whose Spanish accent changed daily (her knowledge of the language was limited to ordering *cerveza* with a lisp, a skill acquired during a junior year abroad in Madrid), and Nolan Hardesty, who thought he was prettier than Jennifer (he wasn't, but his lisp was better). The show also featured Tiffany Sanders, a tap-dancing weather woman who went to bed each night praying for el Niño's return, Jack Bacon, a boisterous good ol' boy sportscaster who had 366 different bow ties (just in case he worked an entire leap year), and Ellis Walsh, an entertainment reporter who *knew* he was prettier than either Jennifer or Nolan.

As Tiffany clickety-clicked her way from weather map to satellite photo (Arizona weather was so boringly good), Ellis Walsh sulked, miffed that he hadn't been able to steal the Masterly story from Lola LaPola, but when she reported hard news she took on the demeanor of a cynical foreign correspondent, and Ellis had believed her when told she would use her elegant — and sharp — fingernails to rearrange the features on his face without benefit of anesthesia, local *or* general.

Even pretty faces knew when they had a major story, and they didn't interrupt Lola's long segment — complete with visuals of the now-handcuffed Vixen and Buffy Anne being escorted to different police cars — with vapid questions, allowing her to finish before the obligatory give-and-take, demonstrating to their tiny share of the market how familial the *Wake Up!* team truly was.

"Lola, this is Nolan."

As though I couldn't tell, Lola thought. "Yes, Nolan," she said.

"You say the rattlesnake got away? Do the police have an APB out on it?"

What a jerk. "The police are making every effort to apprehend the snake in question," Lola replied with a straight face.

"Lola, this is Jennifer. Good morning."

"Good morning, Jennifer." This ought to be good.

"Lola, do the police know if they're looking for a male or a female snake?"

"At this point, no, Jennifer," Lola replied, struggling to maintain composure. "They do plan to run DNA tests on the venom found in Masterly's body. Once those tests are completed, the police will send the results to the FBI for a profile on the snake."

"Oh," Jennifer said.

"Thanks very much, Lola, for a complete and concise report on a very bizarre incident."

"Well, there you have it," Nolan Hardesty told his viewing audience, "a serial-killer rattlesnake is on the loose in our Valley of the Sun this morning."

Fortunately, Lola did not hear his wrap-up on the story, or she might have swallowed her microphone. As it was, Lola lost it once the red light on the camera went off, laughing hysterically until tears ran down her cheeks. "What ninnies," she gasped when she was able to speak coherently again.

By the time Lola finished her report on the morning news segment, the word of C.D. Masterly's demise was spreading rapidly through the entertainment industry, causing more than one executive to reach for the Maalox.

Penelope missed Lola's report because, as the literary consultant to the E.C.P.D., she was appointed to follow Tweedledee, Tweedledum, and Hangover Harry Duchette to his room at the Lazy Traveler Motel to impound the manuscript that he readily admitted reading to Dominique Anders the previous evening. Andy remained behind to catch a ride back to his car with Lola, so it was just Penelope and Big Mike who entered the ground floor single — this screenwriter didn't rate a suite — after Tweedledee stuck his head cautiously through the door, perhaps expecting to find a ready supply of angry rattlesnakes.

But there was no evidence that a rattlesnake had ever been there. It would probably have been overcome by the fumes anyway. Duchette's room reeked of stale scotch, and an empty bottle testified that his hangover was real rather than feigned. The bed was rumpled and piles of dirty clothes were heaped in corners of the room. The top of the television was a depository for empty glasses. The only neat spot in the room was the small desk with a blue IBM Correcting Selectric II typewriter and a thick sheaf of manuscript pages and several bound copies of the script for *The Ears of the Elephant.*

"What were you and the Anders woman doing at Paradise Regained so early in the morning?" Tweedledee asked.

"C.D. wanted to go over the rewrite and Dominique was supposed to give me a ride up in the limo. He liked to start early so he could wake people up." He went into the bathroom and came back with a large bottle of aspirin. "You want some?"

When no one accepted his offer, Duchette gulped three down and grimaced.

"So why'd she give you a ride if she was mad over what you read to her?"

"She didn't hang up," Duchette moaned, pressing fingers against his temples, "so I thought she liked it."

"What did you do after you read to her?" Penelope asked.

"Fell asleep, I guess."

"Can anyone give you an alibi for the hours between eleven and, say, two? Room service waiter? Someone like that?"

"No, but I didn't do it. I put the herd of rattlesnakes in my novel only because C.D. told me to take them out of the script."

"I don't think they're called herds," Penelope observed.

"It sounded better than a bunch of rattlesnakes."

"It's still pretty damned coincidental," Tweedledum said. "Well, let's gather up your little story and go down to the station. We've got lots more questions to ask."

There was going to be a whole lot of questioning going on, Penelope thought, what with Vixen, Buffy Anne, and Dominique in custody, and Phil McCutcheon dispatched to rouse Hilly Hollander and inquire into his whereabouts during the post-midnight hours.

After copying the manuscript at the station, Penelope and Big Mike drove home, each suffering from sleep deprivation. Both were world class sleepers and tended toward grumpiness when they missed their usual ten or twelve hours in slumberland.

Still, Penelope couldn't resist delving into Duchette's tome. Her curiosity rivaled Mycroft's. She sat propped up in bed, reading Harry Duchette's novel aloud to Big Mike, just in case he had some thoughts on the matter. It was entitled *Death of a Director*, and she started with the last chapter. His prose was not going to make the world forget the great masters of crime fiction, but Penelope conceded that his imagination had a certain lurid but rather lyrical quality. Big Mike listened with interest, but seemed to be reserving his opinion.

" 'C.D. Masterly,' " she read, " 'the hack film director, and Dominique Anders, his evil assistant, are tied to a big skinny cactus, hanging by their thumbs. Dominique's naked body glistens with sunscreen, but nobody cares about Masterly's complexion. A herd of really big rattlesnakes slowly slithers toward them. Harry Duchette is sitting in the hot tub at Paradise Regained, his arms around the shoulders of Vixen DeVaughn and Buffy Anne Mulholland.

" 'Oh, Harry, you're so wonderful to rescue us,' Vixen said adoringly.

" 'Better than wonderful,' Buffy Anne said in her sultrier-than-thou voice that washed over him like the warmth of her hair dryer, which he also liked.

" 'Thank you, darlin's. Shall we make love again?'

" 'Oh, yes,' Vixen and Buffy Anne said in unison.

" 'Please, Harry,' Dominique cried. 'I'm sorry I called you a scumbag writer. Please, Harry, forgive me. Let me be your Constant Companion. I'll be ever so good to you.'

"Harry smiled, sitting back, reveling in the soft caresses of Vixen and Buffy Anne. 'I'll think about it,' Harry said, '*after* you write on the blackboard, "I will never insult writers ever again," five hundred times.'

" 'Yes, Harry darling, anything. I'm yours. Take me. Please, let me be your little sex slave.'

" 'Okeydokey.' "

While Dominique, now dressed in a schoolgirl uniform (Harry didn't seem to do well on logical transitions), wrote on the blackboard, Vixen and Buffy Anne did incredible things to Harry, reducing him to a whimpering specimen of manhood, before starting over — he seemed to have amazing restorative powers. And somewhere, poor C.D. seemed to have been misplaced.

Penelope leafed through previous chapters. Each started with C.D. Masterly and Dominique Anders being tormented — on the rack in a castle dungeon, about to be dipped in boiling oil, buried to their necks and used as tenpins in lawn bowling by a group of writers — but each time Harry seemed to encounter a beautiful woman or two or three, while poor C.D. was left dangling like the hero in an old Saturday matinee serial. Brynn Moore had a starring role in several chapters, including one memorable portrayal of a horny sorceress, as did one Amber Stark, whoever she was. Vixen and Buffy Anne had recurring roles. And Dutch was going to be really pissed when he read Chapter Nineteen, wherein Stormy made love to Harry on a trampoline while C.D. and Dominque huffed and puffed on a fast-moving treadmill. But Harry always took pity on Dominique, rescuing her at the end, losing C.D. in the transition. But there was only the one brief reference to the herd of rattlesnakes, which immediately disappeared for the greater good of Harry Duchette's sexual fantasies. Hardly something a murderer would commit to paper and then read to a woman with a featured role in the plot.

"That's it, Mikey, three hundred and forty-seven pages of one man's dreams, and I would venture a guess that Harry Duchette is in love with Dominique Anders."

Mikey yawned prodigiously. What Harry Duchette needed was a chapter featuring Murphy Brown, that cute little calico down the road who was the object of Big Mike's affections and the mother of his kittens.

Penelope tapped the manuscript into a neat pile and placed it on the nightstand. "I'm going to sleep," she announced, plumping pillows and settling back. Mikey turned around several times on her legs before finding a position that suited him. He sighed and closed his eyes. It had been a long day and night with a paucity of lima beans and nap times.

The parking lot of the Empty Creek Police Department was filled with trucks from a dozen or more television stations and even more cars rented by reporters who had arrived in Empty Creek while Penelope and Big Mike enjoyed their all-too-brief four-hour nap. Penelope parked down the street and picked up Big Mike when they reached the edge of the mob clamoring for entry and shouting questions at Harvey Curtis, who guarded the portals of the E.C.P.D. It wouldn't do for some reporter to step on a cat's tail, however inadvertently. Big Mike would shred Peter Jennings or Dan Rather just as fast as he would any vet wanting to take his temperature or a dog barking out of the wrong side of his mouth. Penelope took a deep breath and forced her way through the crowd.

"Hey, quit pushing."

"Excuse me, please," Penelope said. "Coming through."

Big Mike growled.

"Hey, what's going on?"

Big Mike hissed and spat — the feline equivalent of shouting, "Up against the wall!" — at a television reporter who pushed at Penelope with his microphone. It was fair warning. A second rude thrust of the microphone really ticked off Big Mike, and he cranked off the feline equivalent of a round from a nine-mm Sig Sauer, raking the reporter's hand with his claws. Never leave home without them.

"Ow, damn, that hurt!"

That parted the crowd. In another life, Big Mike had probably been with Moses at the Red Sea, although divine scripture had somehow failed to record his presence.

"Hi, Harvey," Penelope said, gaining the safety of the top step. "Having fun?"

"Welcome to Hollywood East." He scratched Mycroft's chin. "Good shot, big guy."

"How long has this been going on?"

"They've been coming in all day. Dutch has a joint news conference scheduled for four o'clock."

"Joint?"

"Studio honchos are here too."

"He in his office?"

"Yeah, go on in." Harvey bowed her through the doors.

"Who's she?"

"Nobody."

"Must be somebody. She's in there and you're out here."

"Damn cat."

Although not quite as loud and demanding as the mob outside, there was a pretty good crowd scene in the conference room adjacent to Dutch's office when Penelope and Big Mike entered. Brynn Moore was there with the Masked Madman, along with Stormy, Tweedledee, and Tweedledum, a bleary-eyed Harry Duchette, but he didn't appear to be in custody, and two men and a woman Penelope didn't recognize. One of the men was throwing a temper tantrum.

"You can't do this to me," he cried. "Don't you know who I am?"

"Don't you know who *I* am?" Dutch asked. Stormy stood behind him, massaging his shoulders and neck.

"You're the police chief of some hick department in some jerkoff town."

"You're not making a good impression here, Peter," the tall woman wearing a red

Chanel suit said. She turned to Penelope and held out her hand. "I'm Amber Stark, head of publicity for Century Cinema."

Ah, the mystery woman from Chapter Twelve, Penelope thought. Harry Duchette certainly has good taste in women. "I'm Penelope Warren," she said, "head floozy."

Amber grinned. "Good for you. Let me introduce you to my associates. The baby is Peter Benedict. He's the studio chief. He's not always like this, but then, he usually gets his way. This is James Stapleton. He's producing this abomination that will probably now gross a hundred million or more, thanks to C.D.'s unfortunate accident. And do you know Harry Duchette, our writer?"

"Very well, indeed," Penelope answered.

"And you can keep my fiancée out of your pitiful ramblings in the future," Dutch said.

"I thought it was sweet," Stormy said. "We really must get a trampoline."

Duchette groaned and took a not-so-surreptitious belt from a hip flask.

"And this is Big Mike. I wouldn't raise your voice anymore," Penelope told Peter Benedict. "He's not in a very good mood."

"Neither am I," Dutch said.

"He's stressing, big time," Stormy told

Penelope. "He really does need a trampoline."

"I don't care about your mood," Benedict said. Penelope noticed he kept his voice down. "I want my house. We've paid good money for it."

"It's a crime scene and you'll get it back when we're finished with it."

"But where am I going to stay?"

"Try the Lazy Traveler Motel."

"A motel? Here? In Empty Crick?" Benedict was aghast at the thought of mixing with the philistines.

"Creek," Penelope said. "Empty *Creek*. I recommend the Chrysanthemum Suite. It has a water bed and naughty movies on cable."

"It'll be just perfect for you, darling," Brynn Moore said. "I'd invite you to stay with us, but you know how jealous Bobby gets."

"Oh, I give up." Benedict snapped his fingers. "Take care of it."

"It's already done," Amber said. "Now, can we get on with the news conference? Where are we going to do it?"

"City council chambers," Dutch said. "It's the only place big enough."

"Where is it?"

"Burke, Stoner, show her."

"In bed, asleep. Unfortunately, alone, with no one to testify that I said my prayers before retiring."

"Why did C.D. attack you at the party?"

"Item," Hilly said. "What prominent film director was spotted shopping in a trendy bondage and discipline boutique on Melrose Avenue?"

"C.D. Masterly," Penelope said.

Hilly nodded. "He didn't like having his peccadilloes known to the world. He actually appeared at the *Millennium* offices, threatening physical harm. Security removed him. We have a lot of that sort of thing. He should have let his fingers do the walking."

"But there were no whips and chains at Paradise Regained."

"A home dungeon, I expect. It's so difficult to travel with chains. All that clinking and clanking, you know. And, dear lady, what do you do out here in rural America for entertainment?"

"We let our fingers do the walking."

"Wise," Hilly said, "very wise. We must get together for an aperitif."

"I'd like that," Penelope said.

They were interrupted by the principals filing in. They were led by a scowling police chief and they took places at the long, horseshoe-shaped table where the city council members and staff usually sat during what passed as representative government in Empty Creek. Dutch elbowed Peter Benedict out of the way and took the mayor's chair. Apparently, they hadn't taught Emily Post when he went through the police academy. Benedict was forced to settle for the mayor pro tem's chair. An arched eyebrow from Brynn Moore sent Stapleton scurrying to a lesser seat. Brynn motioned for Stormy to sit beside her. Amber Stark sat beside Stormy. With the hierarchy now firmly established, Harry Duchette slumped into a chair relegated for the parks and recreation director, the least powerful of the city positions, whose chair wasn't even padded and he had to share a microphone with the public works director.

In lieu of a gavel, Dutch banged the table with his fist. When the room quieted, he said, "I'm Chief of Police John Fowler. We are investigating the death of C.D. Masterly, which occurred at approximately twelve-thirty this morning. Pending autopsy results, the cause of death is uncertain. We are investigating a number of leads, but, at the moment, we have no suspect in custody. Any questions?" he concluded, the expression on his face saying, *There better not be.*

Fat chance.

"Chief, isn't it true that you arrested two women this morning?"

It was the only question he could hear over the hubbub as reporters shouted for recognition.

"Two women were charged with suspicion of possessing a controlled substance. They posted bond and were released. A third woman was taken into protective custody. She has also been released."

"Chief, Chief, Chief, rattlesnake!"

"There is some evidence that a rattlesnake played a role in Masterly's death."

Reporters hollered the same questions for fifteen minutes, eliciting only that C.D. Masterly was dead and that there were no suspects as yet. "I'll tell you more when I know more," Dutch finally said, and turned the news conference over to Peter Benedict, who praised C.D. Masterly as a great American and a film icon. His sentiments were echoed by James Stapleton, Brynn Moore, and Storm Williams.

Penelope was pleased that no one said, "The show must go on. C.D. would have wanted it that way."

The reporters had only two questions for Peter Benedict.

"Peter, will you shut down filming now?"

"Of course not. The show must go on. C.D. would have wanted it that way."

Oh, well.

"Who will replace C.D. Masterly?"

"Of course, no one can truly replace C.D., but Anthony Lyme-Regis, who actually lives here in Empty Crick part-time, will take over the helm of *The Ears of the Elephant*, which will be dedicated to the memory of C.D. Masterly. Ms. Amber Stark has a press release for you."

"Item," Hilly Hollander said, "which studio head who, by the bye, keeps a pet boa constrictor in his Beverly Hills home, is rather pleased that he no longer has to deal with C.D. Masterly?"

Chapter Four

An impromptu celebration for Anthony Lyme-Regis convened at the Double B Western Bar and Steakhouse immediately following the news conference. The Double B was an Empty Creek institution — a place where many a business or political deal had been cut, a social haunt where marriages often began (and sometimes ended), where a cat could belly up to the bar and get a saucer of non-alcoholic beer and a side of lima beans, where a children's charity unexpectedly benefited as the result of a ceremonious unveiling of a life-size nude portrait of Lora Lou Longstreet (Penelope immediately nominated her for president of the chamber of commerce), now hanging behind the long bar, and where tractor-pull aficionados coexisted with *Masterpiece Theatre* buffs with nary a harsh word. It was also as good a place as any for another spontaneous gathering, safe from inquisitive ears, where strangers, lacking a proper introduction, could be made to feel distinctly unwelcome, albeit in the friendliest of manners.

Such was the case when Penelope, Dutch, Tweedledee, and Tweedledum took a booth in the back. Nosy reporters were deftly intercepted by one or another of their friends and distracted — the old arm-wrestling contest ploy worked best on the men, and the prospect of entering one of the Double B's legendary wet T-shirt contests sent the women in search of a higher plane of drinking establishment — until even the densest among them got the point and either left or settled for an audience with Brynn Moore, who had been anointed an honorary Empty Creekian by Stormy and Big Mike (who deserted his customary bar stool long enough to make friends with the famed actress — one could never have enough laps designed for sleeping). Brynn, in turn, vouched for Bobby Danes, who carried a briefcase as carefully as the officer who always had the secret codes for the President should he need to start an atomic war, and Hilly Hollander. Amber Stark established her own bona fides when she was informed of the bogus wet T-shirt contest by going out to her rental car and lugging in a box of *The Ears of the Elephant* T-shirts. "Where do I sign up?" she asked Pete the bartender, who immediately fell in love and served her a drink on the house.

Dutch opened the meeting by requesting a bottle of the fiery beer brewed locally and seasoned with gigantic jalapeño peppers. Tweedledee and Tweedledum, their bellies insulated by a lifetime indulgence in jelly doughnuts, ordered the same. "Your usual?" Debbie Locke asked.

Penelope nodded. "I'm certainly glad I wasn't cast as a temperance union lady. I'd have to stop drinking to get in character."

Debbie laughed and went off to get their orders, humming "Onward, Christian Soldiers."

"Well?" Dutch said.

"A deep subject," Tweedledee cackled.

"Any more fourth-grade humor and I'll sic Mycroft on you," Penelope warned.

That shut him up. Tweedledee had been sicced, and good, on several occasions by Big Mike, who suffered fools even less gladly than Penelope — if that was possible.

"Let's start with your book report, Penelope."

"The book I read last summer was entitled Death of a Director by Harry Duchette, a compendium of rather imaginative tortures inflicted on the villainous C.D. Masterly and his diabolical assistant, Dominique Anders. In each chapter, Masterly gets lost when one beautiful woman or another —"

"Including Stormy," Dutch interrupted, "that jerk."

"Including Stormy and Brynn and Vixen and Buffy Anne and a host of others who make love to him," she continued, "but not myself or Daryl Hannah, two of the more notable exceptions. Dominique, after a suitable penance, is released to vow her undying love for Harry, and the other women also disappear." Penelope shrugged. "Harmless schoolboy fantasies of a lonely man mistreated by his director and the director's assistant, whom he secretly loves. And only one herd of rattlesnakes, and that inspired by Masterly's notes before the party."

"I ought to charge him with peddling pornography."

"Relax, Dutch. He wasn't peddling anything. You really do need a trampoline."

"He read it to the Anders woman over the phone. That's peddling."

"Is she pressing charges?"

"Nope. She probably liked it, but doesn't want to admit it."

"I thought it was pretty good stuff,

boss," Tweedledee said. " 'Course, I skipped Stormy's chapter," he added hastily.

"How would you like to see your wife in another man's sexual fantasies?"

"Hell, my wife ain't even in my fantasies."

"Three Empty Creek Special Ales and a glass of chardonnay for the lady," Debbie said.

"Put it on my tab, Debbie."

"Gee, thanks, boss," Tweedledum said.

"I expect some work out of you now."

"Aw, come on, Boss," Tweedledee whined. "It ain't easy to eliminate suspects when no one's got an alibi."

"It's called detecting. You're a detective. So detect something."

"Check out Peter Benedict," Penelope said. "He has a pet snake."

"How do you know that?"

"I have my sources," Penelope said with a smile. "It would also be interesting to get a look at Masterly's will. Who's his next of kin?"

"No family," Dutch said. "He was an orphan."

"I wonder who benefits from his death, then?"

"I got his lawyer's name from Amber,"

Dutch said. "I'll call him in the morning. I'm surprised we haven't heard from him already. Masterly must have been a big client."

"He probably hated him like everyone else," Penelope said, "and now I'm going to join the festivities."

Anthony Lyme-Regis entered the lofty heights of Empty Creek society when he arrived to direct Storm Williams in a series of well-received Super Bra commercials for television. He had gone on from there to direct any number of imaginative, witty, even intelligent spots for a variety of companies, including one that made its national debut during Super Bowl XXXII in San Diego. Tony had also endeared himself to Nora Pryor his first evening in town after a dinner hosted by Stormy and Dutch when he suddenly — under the influence of a very nice port — leaped to his feet, ripped off his old school tie, and started peeling off his clothes to the astonishment of all present, while bellowing a traditional rugby drinking song whose lyrics seemed to consist entirely of "Take it off, you Zulu warriors." Unfortunately, from Nora's perspective at the time, Penelope had intervened at the penultimate moment when Tony reached his red plaid boxer shorts by segueing into "The Marine Hymn."

It was an Empty Creek moment.

But if Reggie Pryor were present now, she would, no doubt, ground her mother — at least a week — for an excessive public display of affection. Nora was sitting on Tony Lyme-Regis's lap. Evidence of her well-wishing kisses smeared Tony's face.

"Congratulations," Penelope said, adding her own lipstick to his collection. "How did you pull it off, Tony?"

"I didn't. Stormy recommended me to Brynn, who then *suggested* to Peter Benedict that I was her director of choice. It's good to have friends."

"Isn't it great?" Nora said. "He's going to show me his casting couch later."

"Can we watch?"

Nora's blush-o-meter soared. "Absolutely not," she cried.

"Oh, darn. I was hoping to pick up tips for next time, if there is a next time, which I doubt, but while we're on the subject of casting, are you going to make any changes, Tony?"

"Bad for morale, old girl."

"I thought I was your old girl."

"You're my favorite old girl. Penelope is my next favorite old girl."

"You better not start collecting any more old girls."

"Have another glass of wine, Nora."

"Thanks, old girl. I think I will."

"No changes, then?"

"Everything remains the same," Tony said. He winked at Penelope. "Cooperating with the authorities in their investigations, don't you know? The indomitable Ms. Anders is now personal assistant to Mr. Lyme-Regis. Ms. DeVaughn and Ms. Mulholland remain on the payroll. And, although writers customarily disappear to wherever it is writers go when production starts, Mr. Duchette will remain for any last-minute rewrites that may come up. Dutch doesn't want them slipping off into the sagebrush. Quite a bad thing for suspects to disappear, I gather."

"Quite."

Despite a well-deserved and hard-earned reputation for hard partying, the death of C.D. Masterly cast a pall over the proceedings at the Double B, and the principals, some of whom had been up all night, headed off to their various dens. Stormy took a red-eyed Dutch home early.

Tweedledee and Tweedledum went to the tender mercies of their respective wives. Andy gamely tried to stay, but he was about to fall asleep in the chili fries, so Penelope sent him home with a kiss and a promise to introduce him to the pleasures of *her* casting couch on another occasion. Besides, it *had* been a long weekend, and his plants probably needed watering. As the guest of honor and his consort, Tony and Nora politely delayed departure for *their* casting couch, although they rehearsed for the momentous event by playing a little kneesies and footsies under the table. Brynn and Bobby, who didn't look at all like a Masked Madman with her in his arms, danced to a George Strait love song. Penelope, refreshed by her nap, however brief, and running on adrenaline, stayed on, chatting with Amber Stark, who was now personally attended to by Pete the bartender.

"I think you made a friend when you brought the T-shirts in," Penelope said.

"Well, I didn't major in public relations for nothing," Amber said, "and he is kind of cute. Is he attached?"

"He is now."

Amber smiled. "I may have to stay on awhile. Make sure we get some positive publicity, although Peter prefers the notoriety of murder. The gross keeps going up in his mind."

"You don't take any nonsense from him. I like that in a woman."

"He thinks he's in love with me, but I have no intention of becoming the fourth Mrs. Benedict. Besides, I like the third Mrs. Benedict."

"Did you like C.D. Masterly?"

"Of course not. No one liked C.D."

"What about Dominque, Vixen, and Buffy Anne?"

"Oh, C.D. had a certain boyish charm for women, but sooner or later, usually sooner, the real C.D. showed up."

"And who was that?"

"C.D. reserved all of his love for himself and his indulgences. Ultimately, a woman wants to be loved for herself." Amber glanced at Pete and smiled. "C.D. couldn't do that."

"And his indulgences included cocaine?"

"Hardly unusual in the Business."

"Buffy Anne said C.D. was going to marry her."

"Hardly unusual in the Business," Amber repeated. "It wouldn't have lasted."

"You're cynical. I also like that in a woman."

Penelope joined in the refrain this time. "Hardly unusual in the Business," they chorused, laughing.

They were still giggling when Brynn and her Bobby approached, walking hand in hand.

"We're going on to a place called the Dynamite Lounge," Brynn said. "I promised some of the crew I'd stop by. Do you know it?"

"It's a nice place," Penelope said. "A little different, perhaps."

"Stormy warned me everything was a little different in Empty Creek. I certainly haven't been disappointed. Would you and Amber like to join us?"

"Thanks, Brynn, but I think I'll stay here. Someone owes me a dance."

"Penelope?"

"Sure, I'd love to go."

"We'll follow you, then?"

"Just let me gather up Big Mike. He likes the Dynamite."

Unlike the Double B, the Dynamite Lounge was a sedate establishment that featured New Age and Andrew Lloyd Webber music exclusively on its jukebox, which was never silent for long. It also showcased a bevy of young beauties working their way through college as dancers and waitresses. For a topless joint, the Dynamite Lounge ranked pretty low on the naughty scale. Also unlike the Double B, where rowdiness was not only tolerated but often encouraged, the Dynamite had a strict code of conduct; even the slightest transgression could lead to a month's ban. As a result, the gentlemen and ladies — the Dynamite prided itself on being a family establishment — who frequented the little nightspot were always well behaved and well mannered. It was also a popular spot for lunch for a couple of homicide detectives who found inspiration and solace in the soft music and the double chili cheeseburgers.

They were playing Big Mike's song when they entered. A young woman on a small stage danced to "Mr. Mistoffelees" from *Cats*. She wore peach-colored shorts, matching tennis shoes, and a most excellent tan.

Another young woman, similarly attired, squealed, "Mikey," and scooped the big cat up, pressing him to her bosom, not at all worried that she might be scratched. This was definitely Big Mike's kind of place. Then she found herself staring into one of the most famous faces in the world. "Omigod," she cried. "You're Brynn Moore."

"Why, yes," Brynn said, smiling. "And you are?"

"Tiffany. I mean, that's not my real name, I'm really Sally Winston, omigod, it's really you."

"Tiffany is a very nice stage name," Brynn said.

"Thank you, would you, I mean, would it be an imposition, could I get you to autograph a napkin, or something?"

"I'll do better than that. We're joining that group down front. Stop by in a moment, and I'd be glad to give you my autograph."

"Omigod, that's my station. Wait until I tell my mother I waited on Brynn Moore."

Several tables had been pushed together front row center and two chairs reserved for Brynn and Bobby, who were greeted with a chorus of welcoming cries. As Penelope and Big Mike were introduced as Stormy's sister and favorite nephew to a host of lesser personages connected with the film — assistant cameramen, production managers, assistant directors, production assistants, makeup artists, hair stylists, the property master, the wrangler — a place of honor was created for Penelope next to Brynn. Penelope hoped there wouldn't be a pop quiz on the blur of names she'd just heard — the only ones she remembered were of the wrangler, who looked like he could play power forward for the Phoenix Suns (naturally with a height of six feet seven or so, he was nicknamed Shorty), and Brock Hackett, because he had been in no hurry to stop the fight between Masterly and Hollander. Big Mike skipped the introductions and scampered onstage, where he was deftly picked up by Jami, another old buddy. It wasn't the first time he had performed as an exotic dancer.

Bobby opened his briefcase and produced something more important than the president's secret codes — a stack of eight-by-ten glossies of Brynn Moore. He passed them over along with a pen, and Brynn autographed the first photo, inscribing it "To Tiffany with best wishes from your friend Brynn Moore." Handing it over to the waitress, Brynn asked, "Would your friends like one too?"

"Oh, would you, please, if it isn't too much trouble?"

"I'd be happy to. I'm delighted to find I have so many fans — for an old broad."

"Oh, you're not old, Ms. Moore, you could get a job here anytime," Tiffany blurted out. "Omigod, I'm sorry, I mean . . ."

"Don't be, my dear," Brynn said. "I take that as a very high compliment."

"They have an amateur night, Brynn," a third assistant director said.

"I lost my amateur standing long ago, Billy Joe."

Everyone laughed. Brynn continued to sign autographs, chatting comfortably with everyone. Penelope nursed a last glass of chardonnay and wondered at the easy familiarity Brynn displayed. It wasn't what Penelope knew of the caste system in Hollywood. By all rights, Brynn should have been off doing whatever stars did, leaving the crew members to find their own entertainment. But everyone at the table obviously adored Brynn.

"Is she always like this?" Penelope asked the man next to her.

"Yep. She's the greatest to work with."

"I heard that, Angel," Brynn said. "You just remember I'm the original bitch."

"Only when you need to be, Brynn. I heard you threw a hissy fit with Masterly, God rest his soul."

"That's different, of course."

"Why do they call you Angel?" Penelope asked.

Angel grinned. " 'Cause I'm so mean," he said. "I suppose we better drink a toast to the memory of C.D. Masterly."

"Aw, why? He was a jerk."

"Even jerks deserve a sendoff." Angel raised a bottle of beer. "To C.D. Masterly."

Beer bottles were raised reluctantly. "To C.D. Masterly."

"The big jerk," Angel added.

The group responded with much greater enthusiasm, even ad-libbing their own assessment of the late, great director's personality, son of a bitch and bastard being among the milder epitaphs.

"Hey, Brynn, is it true that Masterly died from a rattlesnake bite?" Shorty asked.

"Better ask Penelope. She's working closely with the police on the case."

Suddenly, everyone looked at Penelope with a wariness that had not been there before.

Penelope shrugged. "We're not sure about the cause of death yet, but, yes, someone apparently dumped a rattlesnake in his lap before he died. He appeared to have been bitten."

"I was afraid of that," Shorty said. "I'm missing a big ol' diamondback."

"And I'm missing a big ol' revolver," the property master said.

Chapter Five

Penelope was losing several tugs-of-war simultaneously. Her desire for additional sleep conflicted with a nagging sense of duty to be up and about her crime-solving obligations. She was also losing the battle with Big Mike for the covers. Every time she pulled the sheet up over her shoulders and face, Mycroft fought back, dragging it down again to the little nest he had produced at her feet. This somnolent conflict for covers supremacy lasted until Penelope finally decided she was tired of dreaming about rattlesnakes and revolvers dancing across a stage accompanied by Pat Boone singing "Love Letters in the Sand."

Ever so reluctantly, Penelope swung out of bed and planted her feet firmly on the floor. She might have fallen asleep again had Mycroft not been snoring so loudly. Ten minutes later, she opened her eyes. Five minutes after that she was on the way to the kitchen to wait impatiently while one of the twentieth century's better inventions — the automatic coffee machine with a thirty-second delay — brewed enough coffee for her to fill a cup and breathe deeply of its life-restoring properties. Right on cue, Big Mike, who couldn't stand to be left out of anything, even at the cost of having to wake up, padded into the kitchen to see what was happening. Finding nothing of interest, he promptly dozed off again with his face in the liver crunchies bowl.

It was a morning ritual that had lasted as long as they had known each other. Eventually, Mycroft roused himself enough to indulge in his second favorite activity — eating — which forced Penelope to get up and fill his bowl. With her ability to move firmly established, she took a second cup of coffee to the bathroom and hopped into the shower.

After she emerged from the shower, things progressed smoothly and quickly. She finished her coffee while brushing blond hair that was quite long now, falling to mid-shoulder, once again pleased that Andy had asked her to let it grow out. She dressed quickly, jeans and white cashmere sweater, and slipped into a pair of Gucci loafers, a birthday gift from Stormy.

By the time she returned to the kitchen

to fill her portable coffee cup, Big Mike was fortified and ready to rumble in any jungle that happened to present itself.

The rest of Empty Creek had been about its business for hours when Penelope and Big Mike entered the August portals of the Empty Creek Police Department and parted company, Big Mike heading for a bowl of milk and a visit with his friends in the jail — the keepers, not the inmates — and Penelope for Dutch's office. She found him indulging in his favorite workday pastime, leaning back in his chair, feet on the desk, and staring at the movie posters of Stormy in revealing and provocative costumes.

"Good morning, Dutch."

"It's practically afternoon."

"I'm aware of that. I assume your surly attitude means you didn't sleep well. Stormy should have given you a glass of warm milk."

"I slept okay, just not long enough, and I don't like warm milk. It's yucky."

"I always thought it vastly overrated myself. I prefer wine for my sleeping potion." Penelope plopped her feet on the desk. "So. What did you bring for show-and-tell today?"

"Preliminary autopsy report."

"Let me guess. No rattlesnake venom was found in Masterly's body."

"How in the hell did you know that? I just got the report myself."

"While you were blissfully sleeping in your beloved's arms — at least, I hope Stormy cuddled you — Mikey and I were out working. The snake had been milked for its venom Saturday morning."

"Give."

"You first. What *was* the cause of death?"

"Remember the third puncture wound?"

"The rattlesnake with three fangs. What a good title for a novel."

"It was a hotshot. Somebody filled Masterly with enough cocaine to kill an elephant. Maybe two. Your turn."

"I had a drink last night with Brynn and some of the crew. The wrangler was there and wanted to know if it was true that a rattlesnake had somehow been involved. He had six rattlesnakes ready for the shoot."

"Let *me* guess. Now he has five."

"You've got a flair for this, Dutch. Have you ever thought about taking up police work?"

"What else?"

"There's a revolver missing from the prop trailer. I think our list of suspects has definitely expanded to include everyone in the crew."

"Why didn't you tell me all this last night?"

"Oh, come on, Dutch. It was midnight. What were you going to do? Throw on some clothes, saddle your white charger, and gallop off, rousting everyone in sight. The snake and revolver were already gone."

"Fingerprints," Dutch said.

"Fingerprints, like warm milk, are vastly overrated. Any murderer, especially one handling even a milked diamondback, is going to wear gloves. Big, thick, heavy gloves."

"You still should have called me. I could have secured the scene. Scenes. Whatever."

"I'm not a total dunce. I took care of it. I called it in, and everyone agreed that they didn't want a grumpy old Dutch on their hands, barreling around all night. The night shift took care of it. We have a pristine crime scene waiting for us."

Empty Creek commemorated its frontier heritage each year with the Old Western

Days celebration, a glorious Labor Day weekend fest, when cowboys and cowgirls roamed the streets, epic gunfights were recreated — the shootout at Miller's Feed Store wasn't as glamorous as the OK Corral, but it was Empty Creek's own — and the saloons were filled with desperadoes cutting the dust of the trail with red-eyed whiskey.

For the tourist trade and the snowbirds who fled the blizzards of the East and Midwest for the sunny climes of Arizona, Empty Creek also had its own little authentic Frontier Town, circa 1880, where the good old days were memorialized year-round. The souvenir shops that flanked its dusty main street were carefully disguised as the sheriff's office and jail — deputies often arrested the prettier girls in town — the newspaper, *the* Miller's Feed Store, where a drunk Bad Bart Brown rolled off the roof into a horse trough to get his first bath in weeks, several working saloons and gambling dens, a supply store, a bawdy house for the town floozies, the eatery and boardinghouse run by the Widow Brown (no relation to Bad Bart), a one-room schoolhouse, even a white clapboard church for the pious. In short, the little theme park contained everything necessary for a film company to shoot an epic Western on location, which is how *The Ears of the Elephant* came to Empty Creek in the first place to surround Frontier Town with its trailers for equipment, props, wardrobe, hair and makeup, star dressing rooms, and the sundry other activities associated with filming on location.

"Where's the elephant?" Tweedledee asked, trudging along behind Penelope, Dutch, and Big Mike, looking rather longingly at the local bakery. He hadn't had a jelly doughnut for two hours.

"What elephant?" Penelope asked over her shoulder.

"If you're making a film with an elephant in the title, there ought to be an elephant."

"It's a metaphor," Penelope said. "In the old days, if you had seen the ears of an elephant, it meant you had done everything."

"Oh."

"The way I see it," Penelope said, "our perpetrator took the revolver and rattlesnake sometime after dark and hung around, waiting for the party to break up. When it did, he or she watched through the window until Vixen went into the bathroom . . ."

"Unless she did it," Tweedledee interjected.

"Let's assume for the moment she didn't," Penelope said, wishing she had a ruler to give Tweedledee a good crack on his knuckles. "When Vixen goes into the bathroom, he or she enters the bedroom through the sliding glass doors, threatens Masterly with the gun, releases him but only to handcuff his wrists behind him, forces him to the patio and the chaise longue, gives him the hotshot, and before he dies throws the rattlesnake in his lap. He screams in terror. The perpetrator takes off. Vixen rushes out in time to see the rattlesnake and watch Masterly die before she does her Jamie Lee Curtis imitation."

"That's a pretty good how," Dutch said, "but who?"

"I'm still working on that part."

"Yeah, and why the rattlesnake?" Tweedledee asked. "Why not just do him in the bedroom? Give 'im the hotshot and split."

"Vixen might have come out of the bathroom and interrupted. And, whoever did it wanted Masterly's last moments to be filled with terror. That's why the rattlesnake."

"Pretty damned mean when killing a guy isn't enough," Dutch said. "He's already terrified and then to scare the hell out of him even more. Somebody really hated Masterly."

A sign proclaimed that they had arrived at BASE CAMP ELEPHANT.

The corral of trailers looked like modern versions of the old Conestoga wagons that had carried settlers and adventurers west, following Horace Greeley's advice. They also looked like they had been pulled into a circle to defend against an imminent Indian attack. Penelope supposed the scowl on Dutch's face could be interpreted to mean he wasn't there to smoke a peace pipe.

Amber Stark met them and escorted the posse to the trailer where the guns were kept. Although dressed casually in faded designer jeans, red blouse, and suede loafers, the lack of a Chanel suit did not detract from Amber's elegance. Penelope skipped to fall in step beside her and asked, "Did you get your dance last night?"

"Oh, yes," Amber answered dreamily. "Pete taught me a step or two."

"Good."

"And we're going to the movies tonight."

"Double good."

The pleasure reflected on Amber's face

113

at the prospect of her date with Pete quickly faded, however, when they reached the props trailer and she went into strict business mode, introducing the official contingent to Claude Gilbert, a nervous gun wrangler.

They quickly learned too damned many people had keys to the various trailers, and those who didn't had access in one way or another, openly or clandestinely, even to the props trailer, where the door was double-locked along with locks on the glass-encased cabinets, holding a variety of period weapons — rifles, revolvers, derringers, and shotguns. The crew had enough weapons available to repel a pretty good-sized force.

"How'd you discover it was gone?"

"After Shorty told me he was missing a rattlesnake, I got a bad feeling and thought I'd better come over here and check things out. One of the holsters was empty."

"What was it?"

"A forty-four."

"Loaded?"

"We don't have live ammunition. Just blanks, and we don't pass that out until the very last minute before a take."

"If my scenario is correct," Penelope said, "the gun didn't necessarily have to be

114

loaded. The bedroom lights were dimmed for romantic purposes. Masterly would have no reason to believe the gun was unloaded."

"Damned if it makes sense to me," Tweedledee said.

"Well, let's go see the rattlesnakes."

"I've seen enough snakes. You go ahead. I have to go to wardrobe and then Mikey and I are going to pay a visit to Dominique Anders. I want to ask her about the twenty-four hours before Masterly died."

"We've been through all that," Tweedledee said. "He pissed off everyone he met that day. You're just afraid of rattlesnakes."

"And you're not?"

"Not if they're in cages. They *are* in cages?"

"Dutch, do you have a ruler in your office? A big wooden ruler?"

"Sure, why?"

"I may want to stop by and borrow it later."

Stout Mrs. Finney in wardrobe had nimble fingers and a mouth full of straight pins as she directed her assistants in minor adjustments to the rather provocative and revealing red gown that Penelope now wore. It wasn't a custom fitting by any means, and it was accomplished mostly with masking tape and safety pins.

"Aren't you afraid you'll swallow a pin?" Penelope asked.

Mrs. Finney smiled maternally, standing back for a final appraisal. "I find them relaxing. Some people chew gum. Some smoke. I like my pins." She stood back and appraised Penelope. "I think something in blue for your second dress. You'll look good in blue."

In his room at the Lazy Traveler, fortified by coffee and Danish from room service, Hilly Hollander worked on his column for *The Millennium*, typing even faster than Harry Duchette, who was in the room next door, working on the latest installment of his tome, a chapter involving Dominique Anders, of course, and Penelope Warren — the police chief had issued no prohibitions against using his future sister-in-law. Poor Dominique was now chained to a rock and threatened by a giant fire-breathing gila monster. While Dominique clanked her chains and pleaded for her knight to rescue her, Harry and Penelope picnicked on cucumber sandwiches and Dom Pérignon.

Harry sat back and smiled down at the

116

sheet of paper in his typewriter and contemplated whether to free Dominique now or later.

With no real need for contemplation or creativity, Hilly's fingers danced across the keyboard of his laptop computer typing in his head and byline because he had never figured out how to make the computer do it automatically.

Hollywood Hollerings
by
Hilly Hollander

GREETINGS FROM THE HINTERLAND: The rustic little community of Empty Creek, Arizona, established 1870, was rocked in the Sunday a.m. when the body of C.D. Masterly was found poolside at his rented villa here. We are told there is absolutely no truth to the rumor that he was wearing naught but a red garter belt at the time, but the local cowboys and cowgirls, unaccustomed to the vagaries of Hollywood, were shocked anyway with the scandalous buzz of rattlesnakes, drugs, and kinky behavior wafting through the clear desert air.

ITEM: Anthony Lyme-Regis should do quite well in taking over the directorial reins on *The Ears of the Elephant* from the late, unlamented C.D. Masterly. The English-born helmster has created many commercial critical successes for the small screen. His sixty-second gems have delighted many. Now all he has to do is put his talents to fashioning one hundred and twenty such gems and, *voilà,* a two-hour movie. After all, how hard can it be? Masterly was considered a genius.

ITEM: It was the delicious, delectable, always delightful, Brynn Moore who *recommended* Lyme-Regis to the redoubtable head of Century Cinema, Peter Benedict. We are told there is also no truth to the rumor that Brynn threatened to take *her* red garter belt elsewhere if Benedict did not comply with her wish.

ITEM: Our sources reveal that the local constabulary is augmented by beauteous Penelope Warren, sister of none other than our own Storm Williams, who has graduated from those titillating costume dramas to co-starring with our ever sultry, seductive, sexy Brynn, and a Mycroft Holmes (Sherlock's elder and smarter brother) namesake, the biggest damned domestic cat one could ever hope to see. We're told this dynamic pair has a flair for crime fighting that should worry whoever sent poor old C.D. to that director's chair in the sky.

Hilly added several more items until he had exactly 1,200 words. After all, they weren't paying him for 1,201 words. He had nearly completed the computer mumbo-jumbo necessary to send the column to his miserly masters at *The Millennium,* when there was a sharp rap on the door.

When he opened the door, Penelope said, "I'm sorry to disturb you. I was looking for Dominique Anders."

"Next door," Hilly said.

"It's always next door in China," she said cryptically.

"Dear lady, you know the Goons?"

"Doesn't everyone?"

"Not in my circles, unfortunately."

"I fell into bad company in Africa. Entire dinner conversations were carried on in Goon." She paused, took a breath, assumed the Peter Sellers role in *Bridge on the River Wye* and barked, " 'Sergeant Major!' "

Big Mike had heard all this many times

before and scooted into the room. It wouldn't hurt to search for a clue or, better yet, a stash of lima beans. Since the screen on Hilly's laptop was a pastel green and almost the color of lima beans, Mikey started there.

" 'Sar!' " Hilly responded instantly, snapping to attention in the British fashion with a good stomp of his foot. Since he was barefooted, he ad-libbed, "Ow."

Penelope ignored his deviation from the script. " 'Know anything about trees, Sergeant Major?' "

" 'Born in one, sar!' "

" 'Yes, well, you see those wooden ones across the river . . .' "

During this exchange, Big Mike inadvertently clicked the mouse, changing the address destination, and sent Hollander's column winging through cyberspace, where it arrived at the e-mail address of one Emily Horster in Akron, Ohio, who had mastered the intricacies of her computer in order to better coordinate the activities of her sewing club. As an avid reader of *The Millennium*, Miss Horster was delighted to find Mr. Hollander's column in her computer mailbox. She also perceived its mysterious arrival as a sign that her many e-mail fan letters to Mr.

Hollander — he had answered a number of times, which explained how Mikey happened to find her e-mail address in the computer — had at last had the desired impact and that her love for him was no longer unrequited. It was too bad about C.D. Masterly, but . . .

Miss Horster managed to stave off the vapors long enough to send a brief but passionate reply, concluding with the words "Wait for me, darling, I'm yours. Emily." She then scurried off to pack *her* red garter belt and call the Greyhound station to inquire about their schedule to Empty Creek, Arizona, wherever that was.

Quite unaware that there had been the teeniest little hitch in his cyberspace gitalong, Hilly politely offered to call room service for refreshments.

"Nothing for me, thanks," Penelope said, "but I'll take you up on lunch soon. All my friends are tired of Goon talk."

"What a pity."

"Isn't it?"

"By the time we have lunch," Hilly said, "I'll have your dossier for you."

"What dossier?"

"Why," Hilly said with a perplexed expression, thinking that perhaps the poor woman spoke *only* in Goon. "Everything

The Millennium has compiled on Masterly over the years. It's quite extensive. Let the record show that I am cooperating completely with the authorities in order to remove suspicion from my fair name."

Harry Duchette had finally decided to show compassion for his captive princess, who was in grave danger of getting her beautiful tootsies toasted by the fire-breathing gila monster, when there was a knock on his door.

"Good God," Penelope said, "it's still next door. Do you know the Goons?"

Harry blushed and stammered, "I wasn't doing anything. Honest. And the only goons I know are producers and directors."

"I was referring to *The Goon Show*, the great BBC radio comedy show starring Peter Sellers and Spike Milligan, among others."

"Never heard of it. Sorry."

"Too bad, but never mind. I was looking for Dominique Anders."

"Second door down."

"Thanks, and keep writing. There's such a paucity of good salacious literature. I must remember to introduce you to my friend Laney. You really should exchange notes."

★ ★ ★

"Finally," Penelope said when Dominique Anders answered her door. "I've come to invite you to lunch."

Chapter Six

The moment one person dies at the hands of another marks the exact midway point in the most important forty-eight hours in a murder investigation. The last twenty-four hours of life may reveal activities of the deceased that provide valuable information, leading to an arrest and subsequent prosecution. The twenty-four hours following a murder are equally crucial. With the passage of time, the trail grows as stale as leftover popcorn.

Already, a voluminous amount of information and paper had collected in the crime file — photographs of Masterly's body and the patio from every conceivable angle. The same camera had recorded every detail of the master bedroom and the hallway leading to the grand living room and the patio. Measurements were taken. Sketches, too, had been drawn. Tweedledee, surprisingly, had a flair for detail, although his sketches often looked like they should be placed on the refrigerator door by the proud parents of a first-grader rather than in the file for future reference. Statements had been taken from Vixen, Buffy Anne, Harry Duchette, Dominique, Hollander. Their subsequent interrogations were recorded. Even now more interrogations were under way — of Shorty and Claude Gilbert — and the investigation was expanding to include those with access to keys.

All of which had gotten them precisely nowhere to date. With Masterly's uncanny ability to irritate everyone he came in contact with, even a pedestrian on the other side of the street might have been angered by the director in a moment of sidewalk rage, although such a confrontation would have been instantaneous — like Masterly's attack on Hollander, and Dominique's on the walking Lonely Hearts Club — rather than meticulously planned to involve a stolen rattlesnake and revolver. Penelope recalled her own momentary desire to throw Masterly through the window. It seemed Stormy had been right. Masterly could have been murdered by anyone he knew from the fourth grade on.

Still, all the best textbooks dictated the same forty-eight hours as the way to go. And since Masterly's next to last daytime hours had been spent largely in the company of Dominique Anders, she was now seated across from Penelope in the Double B, sipping a glass of chardonnay. Instead of skin-tight jeans and a too-small T-shirt, Dominique wore a simple peasant skirt and blouse with sandals replacing stiletto heels. She looked almost demure, if a tough, six-foot Amazon beauty could be described as demure. Big Mike was on his bar stool next to Red the Rat, commiserating with the old prospector on his latest failure to find the lost gold mine he had been seeking for upward of thirty years now. With the lunch rush over, Pete the bartender was polishing glasses and, Penelope would have bet the farm, mooning over Amber Stark.

"I know it's more like thirty-six hours," Penelope said, "but let's start with Friday morning. When did you see Masterly first?"

"The limo picked us up at five a.m. exactly, and Harry and I arrived at Paradise Regained about five-thirty."

"Why so long? It's a ten-minute drive."

"We stopped to pick up coffee and doughnuts."

"No coffeemaker at the house?"

"C.D. didn't always share. It depended on his mood."

126

"What was his mood?"

"The usual."

"Which was?"

"Not good. He didn't like Harry's latest rewrite on the notes from Thursday. So he gave more notes and sent Harry off to write 'something decent for a change.' Those were his words."

"Did Harry take offense at that?"

Astonished, Dominique said, "He's a writer. No one cares what a writer thinks."

"Yes, well, I like writers. Most of them anyway."

"He's a creep."

"Does he call you often and read to you?"

"Every night."

"Why do you take his calls?"

Dominique reddened slightly. It softened the Amazonian facade, and for a moment she looked vulnerable. "It was always interesting to see what he was doing to C.D. in the latest episode."

"And you?"

"Hell will freeze over before I make love with him."

"What was your relationship with Masterly like? You weren't always his personal assistant."

"We were lovers," Dominique answered matter-of-factly, "but I didn't last the usual six months. C.D.'s attention span for a relationship was exactly six months."

"What happened with you?"

"You saw his closet?"

Penelope nodded.

"I wasn't a good role player, for one thing. I had no ambition to be an actress. I also refused to be on his bimbo team. I told C.D. from the beginning that I was either his only girlfriend or not. After three months, I wasn't."

"But you stayed on to work for him."

"There were no hard feelings between us, and it was a good job."

"Buffy Anne said you wanted to marry C.D."

"Hardly."

"What about Vixen and Buffy Anne? Where were they in the six-month window?"

"Vixen was going to be the next great scream queen after we finished location shooting here. Buffy Anne had another month before going into the scrapbook."

"She also says C.D. was going to marry her."

"Wishful thinking. C.D. already had his eye out for a replacement."

"Well, let's go on. Who else did C.D. see that day?"

Penelope quickly learned that between the hours of nine and five-thirty, Masterly had managed, in one way or another, to alienate or otherwise anger someone in every meeting he attended, starting with Peter Benedict's brother-in-law (a worthless executive producer, according to Dominique), including Penelope and Laney at the casting call, and ending with Mrs. Finney in wardrobe, with a whole bunch of other people in between who might have wished harm on Masterly.

"He wanted buckskin dresses for Vixen and Buffy Anne. I guess he was planning to play cowboys and Indians. Mrs. Finney kept pointing out there were no Indian maidens in the film, but she went off looking for buckskin anyway."

"She must have found some. There were two dresses in the closet." And that would explain the needle Mikey found, Penelope thought. Mrs. Finney must have dropped it during the fitting, although it wasn't a leather needle. She probably wouldn't use masking tape and safety pins for Masterly's costume desires.

Dominique's account of Saturday clearly indicated that Masterly's talent for offending people continued unabated, abusing Harry Duchette with some more notes, snapping at assistant A.D.'s, the caterer, and assorted waiters and waitresses until he turned semi-gracious host for the party. He certainly hadn't learned to play nicely in kindergarten. Whether he was in heaven or hell, Masterly was probably providing the management with extensive notes on how the place should be run.

"What happened after the party broke up?"

"C.D. disappeared with Vixen and Buffy Anne, leaving me and Brock Hackett to make sure everything was taken care of. He'd been sniping at Brock all day, and so I told him to leave. There wasn't that much to do except make sure the caterers didn't slip off with the silver."

"What time did Brock leave?"

"Oh, about eight, eight-thirty, something like that."

"And you?"

"An hour or so later. The caterers were actually very efficient."

"Did you see C.D. before you left?"

"No. I assumed he was otherwise occupied. I locked the door and left."

After lunch Penelope offered to drive Dominique back to the Lazy Traveler.

"Thank you, but I'd rather walk. It'll be good for me."

"Thanks for coming and thanks for your help."

"I didn't kill him."

After Dominique's departure, Penelope remained at the table, swirling the remnants of her wine slowly. Debbie had seen Penelope in her contemplative trances often enough and left her to her thoughts, skirting her table when she served other customers. Big Mike, however, took advantage of her thought mode and deftly hopped into her lap for a little quality contemplation time of his own, knowing from long experience that while meditating, she was unlikely to be squirming and disturbing him.

Dominique's exit line was good, but Penelope wasn't entirely sure of its veracity. The woman obviously had feelings for Masterly, or she wouldn't have stayed on. It was certainly possible that she was jealous of Masterly's other girlfriends. It was also possible that Masterly had, indeed, intended to marry Buffy Anne, and the knowledge of that caused Dominique's jealousy to crest like a flood and drive her to murder. Her vehement attack on

Duchette could have been part of her cover-up and an attempt to shift suspicion. But if Dominique *was* right and Buffy Anne and her dreams for saving the rain forest while anchoring the Rodeo Drive economy were about to become mere memories in Masterly's photograph album, Constant Companion Number Two might have decided to take the old "if I can't have him, nobody can" route. Jealousy provided motive for two suspects, possibly three, if Vixen had ambitions loftier than blood and gore scream flicks. And all three had access to keys and enough of Masterly's cocaine to mix up the potent overdose shot into his veins. But any one of them, certainly Vixen and Buffy Anne, could just shoot him up while he was sleeping and be done with it. Did one or another of them hate Masterly enough to go through with the elaborate plan to make his last moments so miserable? Who could loathe a man so much?

Despite bringing the missing rattlesnake and revolver to the attention of the police, both Shorty and Claude Gilbert had moved up on the suspect list simply because of ready access to the props used in Masterly's murder. Probably, both men had a motivation for killing Masterly —

everyone else seemed to. And Harry Duchette might have reached the saturation point of public defilement. Hilly Hollander had been embarrassed by Masterly in a room full of people. Item, Penelope thought, Hollywood people are too weird. Strong words from a resident of Empty Creek which were almost immediately revised when Penelope was shocked from her reverie by the arrival of George Eden, Empty Creek's very own version of Gerry Spence, and his two latest clients.

"Good God!" Penelope exclaimed. "Did you and Sheila have a fight?"

"No, why?"

"You clash."

When police officer Sheila Tyler had taken the criminal defense lawyer to her heart, the first thing she did was number all of his clothes and accessories so George could dress himself and not look like the creation of a mad artist flinging paint haphazardly at a canvas. But he was now attired in gleaming yellow pants that wouldn't be allowed on the Geezer World golf course, a wool red and green plaid lumberjack shirt, and gleaming brown wingtips.

"It's my independent streak," George said, "and I think I look very nice."

Penelope shook her head. "You'd better not let Sheila see you in that outfit. Hello, Vixen, Buffy Anne."

The Constant Companions looked at George, who nodded.

"Hi, Penelope," they said in unison.

"I told them not to speak to anyone unless I told them it was all right," George explained.

"That must make it very difficult if they want to order a cup of coffee and you don't happen to be there."

"I like clients who can keep their mouths shut."

"Well, can I ask them a few questions?"

"Sure. We have nothing to hide."

It took a few moments for everyone to arrange themselves at the table, order drinks from Debbie, and for Mycroft to change position in an effort to find a lap that would remain still. He settled on Buffy Anne, which was a good sign for the young woman. Big Mike had only once sat in a killer's lap. But, then, anyone can make a mistake. Just look at Tweedledee's record.

"You survived jail," Penelope said.

"I thought it was a very valuable experience," Vixen said, "in case I ever make a women-in-prison film. I felt just like Linda Blair in *Caged Heat*."

"I felt just like a woman in jail," Buffy Anne said.

"Well, that's the whole point, silly."

"And she kept screaming the whole time."

"I was rehearsing. I don't like to waste time sitting around."

"I was ready to throw her in the box, or the hole, or whatever they call it, myself. What kind of jail is it that doesn't have solitary confinement?"

"I'll speak to Dutch about it."

"They took a drug test voluntarily," George said. "They're clean. I'll get the charges dropped. Dutch just wanted to keep them around."

"What did you and C.D. do Friday night after Dominique and the others left?"

"We had drinks on the veranda," Vixen said.

"It's a patio," Buffy Anne corrected her.

"Well, you never know. I might make a woman-in-Africa picture someday. Anyway, after drinks on the veranda, we went to dinner at a place called the Dynamite Lounge. Do you know it?"

"I've been there."

"Dinner was fine, but afterward we got thrown out because C.D. made a pass at Tiffany. She was our waitress person."

"I hope her boyfriend wasn't there. He's very big."

"Oh, no. The bouncer convinced C.D. he should leave. And so we went home, but C.D. was pouting — he could be such a baby — so we just spent the night in our own rooms."

"Screaming?"

"Jiggling," Vixen said. "That's important too. Would you like to see?"

"No thanks."

"I would," George said. "It might help in your defense."

"Hi, Sheila," Penelope said.

George jumped and turned around. No Sheila. "That wasn't fair, Penelope."

She smiled. "No, but effective. What did you do, Buffy Anne?"

"I was writing a letter to the President, expressing some concerns about his environmental policies. We're pen pals."

Penelope nodded sagely. Just too weird for words. The fact that she had a cat who lusted after lima beans, an Arabian mare who doted on peppermint candies, a boyfriend who greatly resembled illustrations of Ichabod Crane, and a best friend who gave presents from an adult bookstore and marital aids mail order catalogues apparently didn't occur to her.

★ ★ ★

With suspects in the Masterly case multiplying like the rabbits who awaited their daily handout of largess from the kitchen, Penelope devoutly hoped that Tweedledee and Tweedledum were having better luck with *their* twenty-four-hour period of investigation. Chardonnay whinnied in greeting when she saw Penelope and Big Mike ambling down the path from the house.

"Hi, Char," Penelope said, stroking the horse's neck. She unwrapped two peppermint candies and left Chardonnay munching contentedly while she went off to toss carrots and lettuce scraps to the bunny rabbits. Then it was time to mix up a healthy concoction for Char's dinner. Big Mike stretched out to watch the bunnies chow down. After they had eaten, they might, depending on their moods, have a good game of stalk and jump, an exercise the cat and rabbits both enjoyed.

With the chores accomplished, Penelope sat down in the lawn chair — *after* checking beneath it to ensure that Clyde the rattlesnake, who hung out in the neighborhood, hadn't taken up residence. She sat there watching Big Mike stalk bunnies, ears flat, butt twitching, staring intently at his target. When he pounced, the rabbit calmly leaped straight up in the air and came down behind Mycroft. He could have caught the rabbits easily, but who needed a house full of rabbits? Penelope decided it looked like a whole lot more fun than what she had been doing all day, and joined the fray, quickly mastering butt twitching and staring, but failing miserably at flattening her ears and pouncing. Still, the bunny rabbits indulged her politely. After all, she was the lady with the goodies. She was on her third stalk, hunkered down on all fours, concentrating hard, wiggling her backside, when Andy asked mildly, "I like it, but what *are* you doing?" He held two glasses of wine.

"Trying to forget how strange Hollywood people are."

"Oh."

Her prey hopped calmly away.

Penelope jumped up, brushed her knees off briskly, and kissed Andy. "Hi, cutie," she said, taking her wineglass, "want some candy?"

"I'd rather play skin the rabbit."

"Shh, they'll hear you."

"Sorry." His apology was directed to the rabbits. They seemed to accept it.

"But hold the thought until after dinner." Penelope took his hand and they walked to the banks of Empty Creek, which was, indeed, empty of water — at the moment. The creek bed was dry for much of the year, filling only during prolonged rains, but it could become a wild, raging river in one of those hundred-year storms that seemed to be occurring more and more often despite the name — Penelope blamed atomic fallout from the fifties rather than an angry Ma Nature. But now it was just good old Empty Creek, a deep ditch in the desert floor.

Mycroft said good-bye to his buddies and bounded after Penelope and Andy, sitting next to them on the bank. Together, man, woman, and cat watched the deepening red over the western horizon. Since she rarely saw sunrise — at least, not since the Marine Corps — Penelope appreciated the evening light show provided by Ma Nature in a placid mood. It was a habit acquired in Ethiopia, where she took a gin and tonic and sat on her little stoop (not everyone in Africa had a veranda), watching the magnificent sunsets over the vast expanses. It was just as good in the Arizona desert, maybe even better, with the addition of Andy to squeeze her hand and provide some cardiovascular stimulation. Although a slow starter — it had taken him forever to work up the nerve to ask Penelope out, and even longer to kiss her for the first time — Andy's dormant qualities as a world class necker quickly surfaced, much to Penelope's delight. All in all, hanging out in the desert, smooching, sipping wine, and watching the sun set was a pretty good way to end the day and ease into the evening, to say nothing of forgetting dark thoughts of murder — for a moment or two.

It was nearly dark when the trio finally headed back up the path to the house.

By unspoken agreement, they did not speak of Masterly's murder while they prepared dinner together, ate, and washed the dishes afterward. Sometimes it was just better to let the subconscious do its own thing. Instead, they engaged in a spirited discussion over which was more boring, opera or ballet.

"You just like full-figured women," Penelope said. "I know what you're watching with the opera glasses."

"It's better than ballet," Andy retorted. "The only thing there is to hope somebody's tutu falls off."

"Face it, we're both philistines at heart, and this little philistine is really bored now." She pushed her chair back and stood up.

With the bunny rabbits safely tucked into their warrens and the stars in the heavens, it was time to play a little skin the rabbit. Penelope suddenly thrust her arms straight up in the air.

Andy smiled and ever so slowly pulled Penelope's sweater up, revealing the smooth warm skin of her belly and the fact that she was an innie.

"Hey, where is everybody?" Dutch shouted.

Damn!

"In the kitchen," Penelope said.

"Why do you have your arms in the air? Are you being held hostage?"

Penelope dropped her arms. "I was just wondering if I could slam-dunk."

"No way." Dutch poked around in the refrigerator and came out with a bottle of beer.

"So what brings you by?"

"Just wondering if you discovered any great clues today?"

"Nope. You?"

"Nope. I counted them up though. We have one hundred and four suspects, and not one decent alibi among them. What's wrong with these people?"

"Good question. What about Masterly's will?"

"I called, but Stanley M. Barkingham, Esquire is on safari in Kenya and cannot be disturbed, according to Miss Matilda Grimes."

"And she is?"

"The old shrew who guards Barkingham's august gates. He'll be back next weekend. I suppose it can wait until then. Whoever is the beneficiary will have hated him too."

When they finally got back to skinning the rabbit, Andy had just pulled Penelope's sweater over her head, when the telephone rang.

"Now what?" Penelope asked.

It was Stormy. "Don't forget I'll pick you up at four," she said gleefully.

"What for?"

"You have a four-thirty call for wardrobe and makeup. I checked."

"I thought they'd shut down filming for a decent interval out of respect for Masterly, even if he was a jerk."

"They did. One day. Time is money."

"Oh, all right, I'll see you tomorrow afternoon, then. I'll be at the bookstore. Pick me up there."

"Four in the morning, sis."

Penelope groaned. "They make movies in the middle of the night?"

"That's why they pay us so well. It's not our talent, but our ability to function when everybody else is asleep, or supposed to be."

Just like a murderer, Penelope thought.

Chapter Seven

When Penelope wished to arise at a certain hour (not often), she set Alarm One on the clock radio to an oldies but goodies station which, after half an hour or forty-five minutes or so, managed to penetrate that part of her brain in charge of wakey-wakey. When she really *had* to get up (very infrequently), she set Alarm Two, which brooked no nonsense from the sleeping party of the first part, sounding as it did like the warning Klaxon on a submarine about to dive.

Penelope, who had been in the midst of a pleasant dream having something to do with Andy in a bunny suit tickling her cheek with his whiskers while offering to share his carrot, groped for the alarm, managing to turn the volume full blast on some station playing the national anthem as the prelude to another broadcast day. So much for easy listening.

Mycroft, the sleeping party of the second part, not having been forewarned of an early departure time, leaped into the air and came down in a defensive position, ready to protect home, hearth, and lima beans from whatever alien invaders were making such loud, rude noises amid the rocket's red glare and the bombs bursting in air.

"It's time to get up," Andy said rather smugly from beneath a pillow.

"Mumph," Penelope replied, banging away at the clock radio. It wasn't fair. The men all had a later call because they were supposed to report in the required garb and didn't need as much time in makeup. Floozies had to look good for the camera.

Just before a concerned witness might rush to dial 911 to report her for clock-radio abuse, Penelope managed to unplug the whole damn thing prior to learning whether or not the flag was still waving.

Even in the now-deafening silence, Big Mike searched for the offending source of that hideous noise. Someone or something was going to get a good what-for as soon as his weapons system fixed on a target.

"Interesting," Andy said.

"Bumph?"

"Life with Penelope Warren. I don't know what I did for amusement B.P." He poked her gently in the back. "Are you up?"

Penelope fell back.

Andy pushed her upright. "If you get in the shower, I'll fetch coffee."

Penelope mumbled something that sounded like "Thank you, sweetie," and managed to maintain an upright position while she stumbled to the bathroom.

When Andy returned with coffee, Penelope was not only showered, but dressed. Sort of. "Your shoes are on the wrong feet," he said.

"Oh." She grabbed the coffee cup with both hands and sipped. "Ah."

"And your sweater's inside out."

Andy pulled the sweater over her head and helped her slide her arms into the sleeves, although he much preferred un-dressing her. Then he allowed her to sit on the edge of the bed, taking the risk that she would fall asleep again, and managed to get her loafers on the proper feet. "I'd be a lousy shoe salesman," he said.

"God, I hate being a movie star." It was her first coherent statement.

"You're an extra."

"Whatever."

Precisely at four a.m., a ghostly white limousine glided to a stop in front of Casa Penelope and John, Stormy's favorite local driver, hopped out and rushed to open the door. "Death follows Penelope Warren," John intoned solemnly. He had once been present when Big Mike discovered the body of an Empty Creek city council-woman, ironically, also on Crying Woman Mountain. That unnerving experience had convinced him to take precautions when-ever he was in Penelope's company.

"It's nice to see you, too, John," Penelope replied. "How have you been?"

"In love," John said.

"What's his name?"

"Stevie, but I call him Slats. He's kind of skinny."

"Everyone should have a boyfriend named Slats."

"I think so."

When Penelope got in the limo next to her sister, Big Mike was already in Stormy's lap, sound asleep, needless to say.

"Good morning," Stormy said cheerily.

Penelope winced when John closed the door behind her. "You're half right. It's morning," she said.

"Aw, come on, sis, be happy. We're going to make a movie."

Despite herself, Penelope felt a tinge of excitement. "I'll have to get a new dress for the premiere," she said.

John pulled out and turned away from town.

Where are we going?"

"To get Laney, and then Samantha and Leigh," Stormy said. "I want to make sure all my floozy friends and dance hall girls get started right."

"That's sweet of you," Penelope said.

"Aw, shucks, ain't nothing."

The headlights caught Laney and Wally kissing passionately.

"Well, that's one way to wake up," Penelope said. "I should have thought of it."

Laney jumped in and waved fondly at Wally until he was out of sight. Then she settled back and said, "Dare we talk?"

"Oh, I'm awake," Penelope said.

"Well, good morning, then. Isn't this fun?"

"On scale of one to ten, I'd rate it about a two, slightly ahead of fishing and malaria and behind just about everything else I can think of at the moment."

"You're just an old grump."

"Someone has to do it."

It seemed to be contagious. Samantha and Big Jake were necking in the front doorway of her house. Samantha jumped when the headlights flashed over them and quickly smoothed her clothing. "And all I got was a peck on the cheek," Penelope complained.

"Hi, everybody," Sam said. "This is going to be fun."

"That wasn't?"

"Just a little something to remember me by until later. We're going to play pirate."

"Who gets to walk the plank?"

"Oh, we haven't decided yet. Spontaneity is better, don't you think?" Samantha Dale had certainly left her bank president persona at home.

Whatever it was in Empty Creek's water supply that sent hormones careening out of control was working overtime. The centerfold for *Library Journal* — as soon as they relaxed their rather stodgy editorial stance — and her husband were also engaged in a bit of early morning dalliance. Penelope, however, was willing to give them the benefit of the doubt. Leigh might have been looking for new ways to increase library patronage and circulation.

"I think you're on to something, Leigh," Penelope said. "Take a memo to the American Library Association. Item: We have discovered that the pucker factor is underutilized in the modern public library . . ."

"Exactly," Leigh said. "Statistics show . . ."

"Oh, never mind."

Frontier Town was not exactly bustling when they arrived. Union regulations apparently required crew members to stand around in groups while drinking coffee poured from urns and eating assorted pastries from laden folding tables. Tweedledee had obviously missed his true profession. Despite the early hour, Penelope wondered who among them might have killed C.D. Masterly.

Stormy guided them to a large hand-lettered sign reading, EXTRAS REPORT HERE. Nora and a bubbling production assistant awaited them. "Hi, everyone," Stormy said brightly. "This is Kimberly Ferrell, your assistant babysitter."

"I want to stay up and watch television," Laney said.

"I want to play strip poker," Samantha said, and immediately blushed. "Sorry. That just popped out."

"No," Leigh joined in. "Monopoly. I want to play Monopoly."

"I want to go back to bed," Penelope said.

Big Mike rubbed against the P.A.'s leg. "Meow?" he said. He was probably asking where they kept the liver crunchies and lima beans.

Kimberly looked at her charges uneasily. Apparently, her film school hadn't offered a course in dealing with a group of strange women impersonating extras.

"You're all grounded," Nora broke in. "Be nice to Kimberly. It's her first job."

"Don't worry, Kimberly," Stormy said. "They're actually worse than this when you get to know them."

"Thank you, Ms. Williams."

"Well, I'll see you all later."

"Where are you going?"

"My trailer," Stormy said. "I *am* going back to bed. They won't need me for hours yet."

"That figures," Penelope groaned. "All right, what do we do now?"

Kimberly looked at her clipboard. "First, I check you in and then give you your pay vouchers. You have to give them back at the end of the day or you won't be paid. Fill them out completely, including the back of the top copy. Then we're going to wardrobe and makeup and hair. Wardrobe will tell you where the atmosphere changing rooms are. Then we wait here."

151

Penelope had heard that one before.

Kimberly consulted her clipboard again. "There's coffee, doughnuts, and bagels over there. Don't use craft services. I assume you're all virgins."

"Are you?" Nora asked sympathetically. "We should find you a nice young man, although I still think it's perfectly all right to wait for marriage, especially in this day and age."

"I don't think it's any of your business," Laney huffed.

"Perhaps you should define virginity," Samantha said. "Maybe we could stretch the rules."

"If chastity is a requirement," Penelope said, "we're all in trouble. This is the most unlikely group of virgins you'll ever see."

Kimberly blushed. "I meant to the Business."

"Well, why didn't you say so, then?"

"I look like a tart," Penelope said after everyone had been to hair, makeup, and wardrobe, and were all back in the holding area. "We all look like tarts."

"We're supposed to," Nora said. "I hope Tony likes my costume."

"What's not to like? Pretty hot stuff."

"I don't know," Nora said, looking down

at her décolletage. "I really may ask for a referral."

"Why don't you get your nose pierced at the same time? They probably have some sort of two-for-one sale."

"Listen up, everybody!" a man wearing a headset yelled. "Last chance to hit the honey wagons."

"What a charming greeting," Penelope said. "And you are?"

"I am Milan Penwarden and I am your leader."

"Ah, the head baby-sitter."

"Please don't leave the area. We'll be ready for you shortly."

Big Mike took advantage of the moment to yawn and stretch prodigiously.

"Oh, dear," Penwarden said, consulting his clipboard. "There is no cat in this scene. Or any other, for that matter. Lose the cat, please."

"Are you sure?" Penelope said. "I distinctly heard Mr. Lyme-Regis giving notes to the writer that he should include a cat. I believe he said something about cats being good for the gross," she added, expanding her little white prevarication.

"Oh, dear, oh, dear," Penwarden said. He spoke into his headset. "Jerry, do you know anything about a cat in this scene?"

Penwarden waited while Jerry, a third assistant director, talked to the second assistant director, who consulted with the first assistant director, who approached the director. Tony's answer then traveled back down the chain of command to Penwarden.

"He's a bar cat," Penwarden announced dubiously. "Someone should have told us."

"I did."

Penelope smiled, thinking that she perhaps had a future as a casting director although, with as much time as Big Mike spent in the Double B, it was pretty much a no-brainer.

With the baby-sitters engaged in earnest conversation about Big Mike's pay voucher and the necessity of ordering cat food from catering, Penelope and Mycroft slipped away unnoticed from the holding area — or tried to.

"Where are you going?" Laney hissed.

"Sleuthing," Penelope said, putting a finger to her lips. "Not a word to anyone."

Penelope wanted to be inconspicuous, but all hussied up in her tart uniform, wearing bloomers for the first time in her life, her face caked in about ten pounds of makeup, complete with beauty mark on her left cheek, and accompanied by Big Mike, she felt like several sore thumbs throbbing in the crowd. Among the many valuable rules of life Penelope had learned during her service in the Marine Corps, however, was the clipboard rule. *Never* stand around aimlessly. Someone of higher rank will always find some task — usually boring and unpleasant — that needs to be accomplished. *Always* carry a clipboard and pencil, creating the illusion of a mission vitally important to national security. A ladder and hammer achieved the same purpose, but they were heavy and unwieldy. A necessary corollary of the clipboard rule was to walk with a purpose.

"Look industrious, Mikey," Penelope said in lieu of the essential equipment.

But members of the film crew were accustomed to seeing all sorts of creatures in their midst, and saw nothing but an extraordinarily pretty extra in costume and an ordinary, if rather large, house cat, although such a disparaging thought would be better left unvoiced in his presence. Compared to apparitions wearing cabbage heads in *Attack of the Vegetable Monsters* (a straight-to-video epic Stormy had once thankfully rejected), Penelope and Big

155

Mike might have been the invisible woman and cat. So much for the clipboard rule and a determined stride.

"Good morning," Amber Stark said from the boardwalk in front of the saloon. She held Pete the bartender's hand tightly.

At least, *they* weren't necking — yet.

"Good morning, Amber, Pete." Penelope replied pleasantly, seeing no reason to inflict her views on early rising on innocent parties. "What are you doing up so early?"

"I wanted to show Pete around and, believe it or not, I love all this."

"I'm a prospector," Pete said.

In some mysterious Hollywood process, Pete the bartender was a prospector while Red the Rat, who had spent much of his adult life searching for lost gold mines in the desert, was the assistant bartender. The real-life newspaper editor had been designated Bad Guy Number One, while the real-life cowboy, albeit unemployed in the normal course of events, became the crusading newspaper editor. Big Jake Peterson, absolutely the worst poker player in Empty Creek, naturally played a slick town gambler. Penelope was only mildly surprised that Big Mike hadn't been asked to play a dog.

"Well, you've seen Red sit at the bar

often enough. You should have picked up some pointers."

"Look grizzled and mutter a lot."

"Exactly."

"Have you found any suspicious characters out here?" Amber asked.

"I'm still looking."

"It's hard to believe that one of us killed him. That's a bit harsh, even for Hollywood." Amber sighed. "Well, I better take Pete over and then I have to deal with the Fourth Estate."

"Where are they?" Penelope asked.

"Up the street."

She watched Amber and Pete walk off, still holding hands, and wondered if there had been a plot to kill Masterly for the publicity value alone. The bizarre nature of the crime guaranteed tabloid publicity forever, especially if the crime went unsolved, but that, too, was a bit harsh, even for Hollywood.

"Come on, Mikey, let's visit Lola."

Amber Stark had taken good care of the press corps even if they were grumpy about having to stand behind ropes. They had their own coffee urn and a long table covered with breakfast goodies. There were at least a dozen camera crews supplemented by still photographers and print reporters.

Lola waved cheerfully. "Wow," she said, "I'm impressed."

"With what? My early appearance or my appearance."

"Both. I'll do a feature on you. How it feels to be an extra in an important film."

"Better wait until I've done something. All I can tell you right now is that work starts too damned early for me, I'm covered in goo, and I should have brought a coat. I'm getting goose pimples."

A flash bulb went off in Penelope's face.

Blinking through the colorful stars that obscured her vision, Penelope saw a shadowy figure approach. "And very nice goose pimples, they are," Shadowy Figure said. "I should like to photograph all of them. My card."

Still blinking, Penelope took a grubby, well-worn card and read: Brendon Mack National Talent Search, Inc.

"You need new cards," Penelope said, holding it distastefully between thumb and forefinger.

Mack snatched the card away and stuck it in his breast pocket. "I shall make you famous," he said. "I represent a number of national and international magazines and newspapers. If you have your calendar, we'll set up a photography session and by this time next week, fame, fortune, glamour, perhaps even a Page Three Girl."

Lola snickered.

"And for you," Mack said, "I'm compiling a portfolio of working newswomen for *Playboy.* Dear Hugh suggested it the last time I was at the mansion."

"The last time I was at the mansion," Penelope said, "dear Hugh told me to stay away from scum buckets like you. Buzz off."

Mack buzzed.

When Lola managed to stop laughing, she asked, "Anything new on the case?"

"My investigations are continuing," Penelope said solemnly. "How about you?"

"Zilch. Lots of file stuff."

"Everybody has files, but none of it makes any sense whatsoever."

By the time Penelope and Big Mike returned to the holding area, having found nothing more sinister than a rapidly climbing cholesterol level among the crew members, the male extras had arrived and assumed their various screen personas.

"Where have you been?" Andy asked anxiously. "They're almost ready to start."

Penelope kissed his cheek. "You're sweet, but so anal retentive. I'll give them another hour. Maybe."

An hour and a half later, Milan Penwarden clapped his hands briskly. "All right, ladies and gentlemen, we're ready for you now."

Finally. Penelope hoisted her skirts and led her bevy of floozies, dance hall girls, bad guys, gamblers, and editors down the main street of Frontier Town to the saloon.

Inside, it was evident that not everyone had spent the morning hanging out near the refreshments. The focus of attention was a card table already dressed with whiskey bottles, glasses, piles of assorted chips, and a deck of cards. Surrounding the set was a mass of equipment — cameras, lights, screens, cables.

Tony had promoted Vixen and Buffy Anne to stand-ins for Brynn Moore and Storm Williams respectively. The Masked Madman was standing in for Craig Halliday. They were already seated at the table.

If Tony was nervous, it didn't show. He placed the extras himself while Dominique Anders hovered, ready to record the slightest pronouncement in her notebook, although it was empty at this point. Andy, Big Jake, and Wally took their seats at the card table. "Penelope," he said, "stand behind Andy and lean into him just a little."

Penelope couldn't resist. "What's my motivation?" she asked, almost bringing a smile to the face of the indomitable Ms. Anders.

Tony grinned. "Exude sex."

"Too easy."

Nora and Samantha were to come down the stairs in the background. Laney was at the bar with Pete. Red the Rat polished glasses. Big Mike listened to Tony explain his role and promptly fell asleep on the bar — method acting at its best. Eat your heart out, Marlon Brando. Except for the role reversals, costumes, and a whole bunch of strangers around the periphery of the scene, it might have been just another average night at the Double B.

Even the shouting fit in. With all the bellowing that went on while lighting was adjusted, measurements were taken from the various cameras to the stand-ins, and Tony conferred with various people, Penelope decided that strong lungs and a good voice were prerequisites for moviemaking.

After several rehearsals with the stand-ins and extras, another call went out. "First team, step in."

In due course, the principals appeared and took their places after a brief conversation with Tony.

Looking cool, sis, Penelope thought, not wanting to disturb her. She was working now and already in character as Annie Two Guns, who had returned to her hometown after traveling the world and seeing the ears of the elephant.

Stormy wore jeans and chaps. Spurs on her boots jangled. The holsters were tied down around her thighs in gunfighter style. Her hat hung down her back. Her shirt was unbuttoned to reveal the provocative swell of her bosom.

Claude Gilbert and his assistants distributed revolvers to all the heretofore empty holsters. Brynn Moore took a double-barreled shotgun casually, breaking it open expertly to ensure for herself that it was unloaded.

They ran through the scene twice more with the principals.

Just when everything seemed ready and Penelope figured the fat lady was about to shout, "Action," Tony took a last look through the monitor. "Oh, dear," he said. "Head Floozy. Your breasts are hot."

"They certainly are," Penelope said, "but is this the proper place and time?"

"No, I mean your breasts are *hot*. There's light reflecting from them. Makeup."

The first assistant director bellowed, "Makeup!"

The cry was taken up by second and third assistant directors. "Makeup!"

Just in case makeup hadn't gotten the word yet, the production assistants joined in. "Makeup!"

Makeup rushed to a blushing Penelope and dusted the swell of her breasts, careful not to smudge her bodice.

"Perfect," Tony said after looking into the monitor.

"I certainly hope so," Penelope said.

After some more shouting, the first A.D. said, "Lock it up."

"The set is up," Second A.D. shouted.

"Rolling!" everyone and his or her cousin cried.

"Sound speed."

"Sound."

"Mark camera A."

Clack! went the clapper on the slate.

"Mark camera B."

Clack!

"Background," Tony said to cue the extras.

Penelope leaned into Bad Guy Number One.

Nora and Samantha flounced down the stairs.

At the bar, Laney slugged back her rye whiskey, grimacing at the taste of the tea. She hated tea. Next time she was going to bring a flask. Pete put his arm around her waist and squeezed. That wasn't so bad.

A stone-faced Stormy watched Craig Halliday deal the cards. Big Jake peeked at his cards looking much like W. C. Fields discovering he held five aces. Wally, the crusading frontier newspaper editor, fanned his cards. Andy dropped his.

"Action!"

Brynn Moore pushed through the swinging doors of the saloon, the double-barreled shotgun over her shoulder.

She paused dramatically, looking over the saloon before walking to the table, hitting her mark perfectly.

Stormy dropped her cards on the table and slowly pushed her chair back. When she stood up, her hands rested lightly on the butts of her revolvers. Everyone on the set stared at the two women, waiting for the confrontation.

"I heard you were back," Brynn said.

"I heard you were in trouble," Stormy said.

Mother and daughter embraced.

"Cut," Tony said. "Very nice. We'll do one more just to make sure."

"Back to one!"

Everyone returned to their places. The litany was repeated with a great deal of hollering. The dialogue went perfectly. Mother and daughter hugged.

"Cut. Very, very nice. Check the gate."

Cameramen opened their cameras and checked to ensure that there was, indeed, film and that the lens had remained clean throughout. Thumbs-up.

"Print it."

The crew applauded Two-Take Tony.

That's it? Penelope thought.

"Moving on," Tony said.

And the whole thing started over from another angle.

Chapter Eight

Unlike the legitimate theater, where the performance on the stage unfolds sequentially from beginning to end, continuity is not a concern in shooting movies. The first scene of *Elephant* shot — the reunion of mother and daughter — was not the opening scene of the script. It occurred on page seventeen of the script after the back story of the classic conflict, a feud between two families, cattlemen and sheepherders, had been established. The second scene shot that morning began on page forty-seven of the script and continued on page forty-eight, when the cattlemen came into town for a Saturday night revel. It was here that the head floozy took Bad Guy Number One's hand and led him up the stairs — sixteen times before Tony was satisfied and said, "Print it." Penelope took solace that she and Andy had not been responsible for destroying Two-Take Tony's reputation. They had played their parts perfectly in each tedious trip up the stairs. Big Mike had been the consummate trouper, snoozing away gallantly on the bar and jerking awake each time blanks were fired into the ceiling to herald the arrival of the cowboys. Stormy knew her lines and hit her mark exactly during each take. Not so with some of the other minor actors rushing into the saloon.

Take one reminded Penelope of her first day — it lasted thirty-six hours before beddy-bye — at Parris Island, when her platoon of fifty-six frightened women, wondering what had ever possessed them to enlist in the United States Marine Corps, could not even manage to put their toes on a white line to the satisfaction of their drill instructors. These actors didn't even have to do it in unison. How hard was that? It wasn't as though they hadn't rehearsed the damned scene. The stand-ins and extras had managed to get it right.

Things were a little better on the second take — until one clumsy cowboy stomped on Laney's toes, eliciting a howl of protest and a good elbow to his ribs. Laney confided later that she didn't care if he was a former member of the Brat Pack and she was naught but a lowly extra in the hierarchy of Hollywood.

They almost had it on the third take, but

a helicopter flew overhead, and since the flying machine had not yet been invented during the time frame of the feud, a chorus of "Cut!" rang out from sound personnel. Penelope even shouted the command in her best parade ground voice just to see what it felt like.

Takes four, five, and six were spoiled by a revolver that went click instead of bang. An extremely nervous Claude Gilbert crossed his fingers for take seven and sighed gratefully with the resounding blast. Unfortunately, a cowboy tripped over his spurs and took a pratfall across the poker table, landing in Stormy's lap, which she and Tony took calmly enough, but it necessitated a delay while all the props were restored.

Take eight was a disaster.

"Ten-minute break," Tony ordered. He sat in his director's chair. Without being asked, Dominique massaged his neck and shoulders, which set Nora to fuming.

Take nine might have been a keeper had a couple not entered by the back door. "Excuse me, we're from Minnesota. Can anybody tell us where the rest rooms are?"

Ever the gentleman, Tony calmly provided directions to the loo.

"Whatcha doing here?" the man from Minnesota asked.

"Attempting to make a movie," Tony said, "but never mind, you just go on and spend your penny. There's a good chap."

"We never go to movies," the woman from Minnesota said. "Too much violence, nudity, and swearing. Hope you ain't doing that here." She looked dubiously at the floozies lined up along the bar.

"Madam, the Reverend Jerry Falwell personally approved our script."

"That's good. I seen him on TV."

When the couple exited, Tony turned and asked, "Who, I pray, is in charge of locking the doors around here?"

Everyone in the crew was suddenly busy with important tasks.

Brock Hackett sheepishly raised his hand.

"Unless you are planning to join the French Foreign Legion on the morrow for assignment to Djibouti, where I devoutly hope you will be assigned to cleaning piss pots in the officer's club, please lock the door. There's another good chap."

Hackett scurried to the offending door.

Tony sat down for back rub number two.

Nora restrained a sudden urge to use her gold card to purchase Ms. Anders a one-way ticket to Djibouti and settled for glowering at her sweetie pie's personal assistant.

Good spirits restored, Tony called for take ten.

And eleven, twelve, thirteen, and fourteen.

After take fifteen he said, "Very nice. I think we've got it, but let's take one more, quickly now."

Take sixteen was a carbon copy of fifteen.

"Check the gate."

Affirmative.

"Print it."

Cast, crew, and extras broke for lunch.

Milan Penwarden and Kimberly Ferrell gathered their charges and hovered, ensuring that their virgins, still unwise in all things Hollywood, did not join the buffet line ahead of their allotted place in the hierarchy. Crew members generally ate first because they would go back to work sooner than the others in the film company. The director, cameraman, principal actors, and actresses — Brynn Moore, Storm Williams, and Craig Halliday among them — could eat in their trailers or take their repast in an egalitarian fashion at the simple folding tables set up by craft services. In this case, both Brynn and Stormy chose to eat with the troops. Lesser personages among the players followed along the buffet line until it was finally time for the extras to hit the outdoor mess hall.

There were exceptions, of course. Tony Lyme-Regis, having no desire to irritate his lady further, plucked Nora from the clutches of the baby-sitters. Peter Benedict, James Stapleton, and Amber Stark showed for lunch. The studio muckymucks, having apparently survived their time among the plebeians at the Lazy Traveler, jumped to the head of the line. Amber democratically joined the extras and waited with Pete.

Not so Milan Penwarden. After making sure once again the virgins understood the dire consequences that would befall them should they transgress the natural authority, he joined the other production assistants in line.

All of this was fine with Penelope despite her training in the Marine Corps, which dictated that officers and noncommissioned officers did not eat or sleep until the marines under their command had eaten and bedded down. Always take care of your marines first and they will take care of you was the theory. And a good theorem it was, especially when people are shooting at you with intent to kill.

Unfortunately, broccoli was on the menu. Unlike some notable politicians, Penelope dearly loved broccoli — properly steamed broccoli, like her mother made. Boiled broccoli, however, was an abomination usually not to be tolerated under any circumstances. This was broccoli mush, deleted of all its nutritional value by over-cooking. Penelope looked at the tepid goo with the same disdain Big Mike would exhibit if she presented him with a plate of lima beans all mooshed up, but broccoli, in any form, sounded good to Penelope's palate, so she scooped some on her tray and went on to decide among the entrees, choosing hot turkey and dressing (with an extra portion for Big Mike, who had passed on a can of tuna cat food procured by the baby-sitters), skipping the cranberry sauce.

Penelope and Big Mike waited for Andy, and together they went to a long picnic-style table set for sixteen. It was occupied only by Milan Penwarden and two P.A.s.

"Is anyone sitting here?" Penelope asked politely, unwittingly violating extra rule number one — never speak to anyone above you unless spoken to first. It was

172

then permissible to prostrate oneself before one's betters, all the more convenient to kiss their shoes and worship the ground they happened to be standing on at the time. But Penelope didn't think the rule applied to common courtesy.

A production assistant waved disdainfully.

The trio of extras settled in. It was then that Penelope noticed that the production assistants had generous portions of sumptuous steamed broccoli on their trays.

"Excuse me," Penelope said, violating extra rule number one again. "Where did you get steamed broccoli? All we got was boiled broccoli."

"They must have run out of the good stuff," Penwarden said.

Penelope nodded. The scene was right out of Orwell's *Animal Farm.* "All animals are equal, but some animals are more equal than others." The thought sent her hackle tachometer racing dangerously close to the red line. Still, she might have held her spoon had Big Mike not taken that moment to demonstrate his opinion of boiled broccoli. He dipped his paw into Penelope's serving, perhaps attracted by its similarity in color to lima beans. Having tasted it, however, he flipped his paw, flinging the gook across the table, striking Penwarden in the face. Horrified by his action, Big Mike — always a gentlemanly cat — would have apologized had he been given the opportunity. Penelope, too, would have been a willing translator, but, alas, neither was given an opportunity.

The Great Broccoli War was about to start.

Penwarden threw his broccoli across the table. It spread much like the pellets in a shotgun shell and struck all three extras in various places.

Normally a mild-mannered woman, this was too much for Penelope. Retaliation was definitely in order. She scooped up a spoonful of her own broccoli and flipped it expertly across the table. It landed with a splat on Penwarden's face, and he wiped it off and pitched it back. "You're fired!" he shouted.

"Good." Penelope fired a fast ball concocted from turkey stuffing, ending any hopes for a mediated peace.

P.A. Number Two threw the remains of her soft drink in Andy's face, although he had not yet committed a hostile act. No slouch with a spoon himself, he saw to it that green gook soon dripped off her chin.

The other extras, still in the buffet line,

rushed to protect their own, and the production assistants were peppered by a variety of foodstuffs. They dove for cover under the table.

Kimberly Ferrell — Penwarden had left her in charge — looked at her wards with dismay, her baby-sitting life passing before her eyes.

Attracted by the commotion, Stormy saw her sister being assaulted in a food fight. Although she had cleaned her own tray, Stormy grabbed a roll from a handy basket and heaved it in the general direction of Penelope's assailant. Not having Penelope's athletic ability, however, Stormy's aim was wide and struck Brynn, who had gone back for a second cup of coffee, in the back of the head. Never a spoilsport, Brynn returned fire with a handful of black olives, peppering everyone at Stormy's table, including Dutch, who had shown up late for a visit.

The melee was brief but furious, with everyone joining in the Great Broccoli War, except Big Mike, who took the opportunity to eat his ammunition, tucking into the turkey and what was left of the stuffing.

Celery stalks and radishes filled the air like Scud missiles. Shorty opened a bottle of soda, shook it vigorously, and sprayed

Claude Gilbert. Amber popped Peter Benedict in the back of the head with a handful of congealed gravy and giggled with satisfaction.

Order was restored by Tony, who leaped to an apple crate, his face covered in salsa, and shouted, "In the name of Her Majesty, the Queen, I order you to stop this rioting." He wiped salsa from his cheek and licked his fingers.

As the director, Tony felt it imperative to find the cause of the altercation. He jumped down and rushed to Penelope's table.

"It was our fault," Penelope admitted, trying not to laugh. "They gave everyone else steamed broccoli and all the extras got was boiled broccoli. Big Mike was just doing what any good marine officer would do, making sure that his men had good food."

Tony nodded wisely, although he didn't have the foggiest notion of what Penelope was talking about. What was wrong with boiled broccoli? *His* mother had boiled everything, including beef. Still, he made a mental note to have someone speak to craft services and then peered under the table. "Come out from there," he said.

Penwarden crawled out. "I fired her for insubordination," he cried. "And the cat."

Tony whispered in his ear.

Penwarden paled. "But, of course, I'm willing to give them a second chance."

Although Penelope hated to trade on Stormy's influence, she realized her place in the pecking order had just climbed several notches. She offered her hand to Penwarden. "Friends?" she said.

"Friends," Penwarden replied. He solemnly took Penelope's hand and laughed when she came away with a fistful of cranberry sauce. "Gotcha," he said.

Kimberly Ferrell sighed. She might live to baby-sit another day.

"And, old boy, do speak to craft services about the broccoli problem."

"Right away, Mr. Lyme-Regis." He hurried away to do his master's bidding.

While it had all been fun and a lively climax to luncheon, Penelope did feel guilty about the wasted food and determined to make another contribution to Save the Children.

For the second time that day, Penwarden turned his back and Penelope and Big Mike escaped the holding area and headed for Stormy's trailer, knocking loudly in warning. God only knew what that pair might be up to.

But when invited to enter, Penelope found Dutch helping Stormy learn her lines, cuing her from the script in his lap.

A little tuckered out from a long day of creative endeavors and straightening out the food situation, Big Mike went straight to Stormy's lap and settled in for a brief nap. Certain rights and duties came with being his favorite aunt.

"Well," Stormy said, "you certainly provided a little excitement."

"You know how Mikey feels about boiled broccoli."

"I do now." She scratched his chin. "Maybe you can look into my leaky faucet." Big Mike yawned. I'll check into it after my nap, he seemed to say.

"Have you found out anything?" Dutch asked.

"Oodles of things about moviemaking, but nothing useful. You?"

"The boa constrictor died two weeks ago. Something he ate disagreed with him. And Peter Benedict was nowhere near Empty Creek until after Masterly was killed. Makes me wonder about a certain Hollywood columnist."

"It would have been difficult for Hilly to get the snake and revolver."

"Unless he had an accomplice."

"That would apply to Benedict also."

"Why kill your director just before starting the movie? Benedict would more likely kill the writer," Dutch said, indicating the script. "This is dreck."

"It'll get better," Stormy said. "Tony's trying to restore all the good stuff C.D. took out. Harry Duchette really is a good writer."

"He'd better be."

A harried Brock Hackett rushed around the corner of Stormy's trailer and nearly knocked Penelope over, narrowly missing Big Mike, which was a good thing. Big Mike might not have been so gracious as Penelope in accepting Hackett's apology.

"No harm done," Penelope said. "Actually, I was hoping to bump into you, although not quite so literally. I wanted to ask about your relationship with Masterly."

"I didn't kill him," Hackett said.

"No one said you did. I'm just trying to get a picture of what happened that night, and you were one of the last people to see him alive after the party."

"Dominique stayed later than I did."

"So she said. Where did you go after you left Paradise Regained?"

"Back to the motel. I had a couple of

drinks in my room to calm down and then went to bed. I've already told the cops all this."

"I know," Penelope said patiently. "As I said, I'm just trying to get a feel for Masterly. What kind of person he was to work for?"

"Horrible," Hackett said. "Everyone knew that. He was a petty tyrant and totally lacking in talent. The people around him made him look good."

"Including you?"

"Yes," Hackett said bluntly. "Including me, but I'm sorry he's gone. Now I won't have the chance to kill him."

The climactic plot point of *The Ears of the Elephant* happened on page ninety-one of the script, where Brynn Moore, searching for her daughter, came into the saloon and had the misfortune of being overcome by a band of vigilantes intent on lynching her after a bogus trial.

A stunt woman dressed exactly like Brynn fought furiously through seven takes until, finally overpowered each time, she was thrown to the floor and her wrists tied behind her back. When the vigilantes hauled the stunt woman to her feet, Brynn stepped into the scene, after a crew member ensured that the ropes on Brynn's wrists were exactly like those on the stunt woman's.

Penelope's role in the background during the last five takes was to hold Big Mike firmly, since he had gone to the assistance of the stunt woman in distress, adding a very realistic scratch to a vigilante's face. After Big Mike sent the vigilantes scurrying for cover in the second take, Tony said, "Let's try it without Mikey this time."

Hissing and spitting and puffing, although her greatest exertion had been to cross the room, Brynn faced her captors defiantly, chest heaving, providing very credible evidence that she had been the woman in the very carefully choreographed fight.

"Gawd damn, she's a pistol, ain't she?"

"It took ten of you this time. You're going to need more than that to hang me."

"Cut." The cry, taken up by damned near everyone, echoed through the set and rolled across the desert.

Between takes, Brynn leaned against the bar and chatted with Penelope. A professional, Brynn shook her head at her keeper, who offered to untie her. "No sense wasting time," she said.

Brynn's keeper, a prissy young man,

glared at Bobby Danes, who had pretty much usurped his duties of tending to the star's every need or whim.

Bobby filled a glass with distilled water and held it to Brynn's lips.

"Thanks, darlin'."

"Anything else you need?"

"Better lines for the gallows scene. I will not say, 'You'll never get away with this.'"

"I don't blame you," Penelope said.

"Should I have word with the writer?" the Masked Madman asked.

Brynn shook her head. "Poor Harry's working hard to fix it, I'm sure. You could scratch my nose though."

Bobby obliged. "Anything else itch?"

Brynn smiled. "Not at the moment, unfortunately."

"We're ready, Brynn."

"Excuse me, please." The actress closed her eyes, took a deep breath, and when she came up from wherever she had gone, Penelope swore she could see sweat on Brynn's face, the result of the fight. That was acting.

"Rolling!"

"Sound speed!"

"Mark camera A!"

Clack!

"Mark camera B!"

Clack!

"Background!"

"Action!"

Brynn delivered her line. "It'll take more than that to hang me." Then she delivered her boot right into the groin of Vigilante Number One. "Ow, goddamn, hold her," Vigilante Number One cried, grabbing his goodies but staying in character.

"Damn," Brynn ad-libbed. "That felt good."

"Cut!" Tony shouted. "Very inspired bit of business, Brynn. Let's keep it in."

"Let's not," Vigilante Number One groaned.

At the end of a remarkably long day, Penelope was ready to submit her resignation from the movie business. Standing around while various people shouted incomprehensible instructions was very tiring, extremely boring, and not very lucrative for a lowly extra. Penelope calculated that when she received her check for this day's work, it would be somewhere in the vicinity of the minimum wage. She could accomplish that on a slow day at Mycroft & Company while having a lot more fun.

On the other hand, it was kind of neat to cruise the not-so-mean streets of Empty Creek in the back of a stretch limousine with the girls, drinks in hand, courtesy of the limo's well-stocked bar.

But, despite having been in proximity to any number of suspects for more than twelve hours, she still didn't have the foggiest notion of who might have killed C.D. Masterly.

Chapter Nine

Praise all the deities in the pantheon for a call sheet that didn't have her name on it. Penelope and Big Mike didn't have to be on location for several days — plenty of time to get a little work done at Mycroft & Company and perhaps even do a little productive sleuthing before again reporting for work on *The Ears of the Elephant.*

They hadn't been in the bookstore since the Friday before Masterly's death, which necessitated a brief tour for Penelope to check on the well-being of her friends the books. For someone who was in the honorable profession of selling books — as many as possible during the course of a fiscal year — Penelope was notoriously reluctant to do so, parting with each one a little sadly, hoping that the customer would give it a good home, use a bookmark rather than dog-earing its pages, not crack its spine, not read it in the bathtub or otherwise endanger it, always treating it as a trusted and valued friend. Her longtime assistant, the vivacious Kathy Allen, was surprised that Penelope did not demand a signed affidavit testifying to the customer's suitability and good character before allowing a book off the premises.

"Everything's fine," Kathy said. "I dusted first thing and no one's been abducted yet today." That was good for Penelope but bad for the profit margin. Over the course of their friendship, Kathy had accepted Penelope's eccentricities and adopted many of them herself. If Penelope posed nude for a calendar, by God it was all right for Kathy to do so. If Penelope suddenly dyed her hair purple, Kathy would probably not even hesitate before following suit. She even peeked over Penelope's shoulder when they filled out their extra applications, indicating special skills and whether or not they were willing to do semi-nudity or nudity. When Penelope absentmindedly checked yes next to semi-nudity, Kathy did the same, although she doubted a woman would go to a lynching half clothed. "I think all our customers are out making a movie," Kathy added.

"Quite likely," Penelope said.

"Did you have fun?" Kathy was torn between pursuing a doctoral degree in

English literature — like Penelope — or her own star on the Hollywood Boulevard Walk of Fame, like Stormy, who ranked only slightly below Penelope in Kathy's heroine-worship department.

"If you like getting up at four a.m., standing around all gussied up like a frontier trollop while a whole bunch of people do mysterious things with equipment and talk to one another on headsets, it was simply oodles of fun. It did have its amusing aspects, but it was really more interesting than festive. There's too much standing around waiting for something to happen, but I have new respect for Stormy and Brynn Moore. They've succeeded in a tough business."

"I can hardly wait."

"Take a book," Penelope said. "You'll have time to read the complete works of Charles Dickens."

Although Penelope usually enjoyed her work in the fictional world of mystery, especially reading reviews and going through publishers' catalogues, keeping up with favorite authors and discovering new talents, eagerly poring through the titles in each new shipment, when real violence intruded upon Empty Creek she was always saddened at the inherent cruelty in the human condition. Even considering her rather slightly off-center personal life — her mother had once observed that she was destined to go through life with a suitcase that always needed repacking — Penelope liked order and harmony in the external world and was offended when the oddball symmetry of Empty Creek was upset. She would have been quite content to pursue her normal activities — making a modest but comfortable living, seeking perfection in various Olympic necking events with Andy, treating Big Mike and other animals of her acquaintance as intellectual equals — more so than some people she knew, and otherwise gliding through life peering at the unfolding adventures around her through slightly distorted rose-colored sunglasses.

Alas, the arrival of C.D. Masterly and the film company of *The Ears of the Elephant* had upset the Empty Creek Apple Cart. The E.C.A.C. was now lurching down the road aimlessly in search of the dastardly villain who took it upon himself or herself to be judge, jury, and executioner.

In short, Penelope Warren was not only frustrated at her lack of progress in solving the murder of C.D. Masterly; she was pissed, a fact she announced to Big Mike, who, sensing her discontent, was sleeping in front of the fireplace in the bookstore property. It was a wise cat who knew when to stay out of Dodge.

Her words unheeded, like Cassandra of Troy, her sister's namesake, Penelope was left to make order out of chaos.

"All right, Penelope Warren, look at the indisputable facts logically. A famed film director is murdered by the unlikely combination of rattlesnake and cocaine overdose while alone in the house with two girlfriends, the one sleeping in a separate bedroom, the other discovering the victim and succumbing to a hysterical jog through the night. The property master discovers a missing revolver and the snake trainer is missing a diamondback, recently milked of its venom."

Penelope sighed mightily. "Now what?" she asked.

If Kathy heard Penelope mumbling to herself, she gave no indication and busied herself with mounting a display of Laney's latest romance novel, a steamy tome entitled *Savage Vixen*, an irony not entirely lost on Empty Creek's book mistress, considering a suspect in the case was named Vixen DeVaughn.

"Now what, indeed." There were just too damned many people with a grudge of one kind or another against C.D. Masterly with his pattern of verbal abuse of the writer, all and sundry assistant directors, and production assistants, and violent confrontation with a Hollywood columnist. And precious few of the film company had any sort of decent alibi, a truth that further irritated Empty Creek's foremost amateur detective.

"My head hurts."

"Mr. Dee and Mr. Dum are here," Kathy announced.

"I'll be right out."

Mycroft gazed up at them suspiciously. Always beware visitors who came sans gifts.

"Guess what?" Tweedledee said.

"You've lost the E.C.A.C.?"

"The what?"

"The Empty Creek Apple Cart. I have it on good authority that our apple cart is missing."

"What apple cart, for Christ's sake? You need a vacation."

"Now, that's the first sensible idea I've heard in recent weeks."

"Come on, Penelope, guess."

"You've given up jelly doughnuts for Lent."

"Lent's over."

"Dammit, Penelope, guess," Tweedledum said. "This is good."

"I feel faint."

"You're no fun at all."

"You want a hint?"

"Unless you plan to spend the rest of the day irritating me . . ."

"V.D."

"I told you to use protection."

"Not that kind of V.D."

"I assume, then, you refer to Vixen DeVaughn."

"Yep. Guess what?"

"Please, not again."

"We've been running names through the computer. Mostly everybody connected with the film has come up clean. Unpaid parking tickets, that kind of thing. Craig Halliday beat up a guy in a bar. Couple of guys arrested for soliciting prostitution."

"Hardly unusual in Hollywood. I have it on good authority that Malibu is the courthouse to the stars. Would you, pretty please with strawberry jelly on it, get to Vixen?"

"She was busted for cocaine possession."

"So?"

"Don't you see? She had opportunity, knowledge of drugs. She'd know how to mix up a hotshot."

"Rattlesnake? Motive?"

"We've got a couple of details to figure out yet."

"Let me know when you do."

"You got a better idea?"

"Not at the moment, but I'm working on it. What about personnel records?"

"It ain't like a real business," Tweedledee said. "For the actors, it's mostly social security number, agent of record, that sort of thing. Eight-by-ten glossy with credits listed on the back. The crew is more straightforward. Rate of pay, lots of documentation to provide, prove citizenship, forms they have to sign to show they understand safety regulations. Don't play with the animals without permission of the trainer. Nothing there unless you want to see Vixen's eight-by-ten."

"You filched it?"

"There were two, one with and one without, and it's just until we can ask her for autographed copies."

Penelope didn't think the with and without referred to the starlet's smile. "Is this before or after she sues you for false arrest?"

"Better do it before, I guess. Wanna see?"

"If it will hasten an end to this inane conversation."

Penelope took the photograph and examined it critically. Vixen's plastic surgeon was certainly skilled. "Well, she doesn't need a Super Bra, does she?"

"I kinda hope she didn't do it."

"I sincerely doubt there is a correlation between a woman's figure and her propensity to commit murder." Penelope turned the picture over and read Vixen's brief credits. Twice she had played topless dancers — roles she was well qualified for — but mostly the résumé indicated that she was a member of SAG and AFTRA, that she had played one of the Pigeon sisters in Neil Simon's *The Odd Couple* in a community theater production, and had studied acting with Paul Mantee.

"You better return this to her file before someone misses it."

"It's evidence," Tweedledee said.

"The only evidential value in that photograph is that you are both dirty old men. Where are Vixen and Buffy Anne, by the way?"

"Back at Paradise Regained. Masterly gave them a sublease."

"I'll bet that pleased Dutch."

193

"We were through with it. Peter Benedict wasn't so happy, though he went back to Hollywood with Stapleton."

After Tweedledee and Tweedledum left, Penelope complimented Kathy on the artistic display of *Savage Vixen*.

"I'm looking forward to it," Kathy said. "I can't wait to read the sex scenes to Timmy."

"I'm not sure he's ready for this one, but take a copy along to read on the set."

Laney had treated Penelope to a preview in manuscript of some of the juicier scenes. She particularly liked the chapters where the fictional Vixen, an Eastern heiress to a newspaper fortune sent to Arizona for her health, found her new environment anything but healthy, and was abducted, in turn, by a wealthy rancher intent on matrimony, an Indian chieftain intent on a beautiful bauble for his campfire, and a mustached bandito intent on knowledge of her person in the biblical sense while holding her for ransom. The rancher kept Vixen imprisoned in the stables wearing a ball and chain until she would consent. The Indian chief's betrothed in the tribe was irritated by his lack of interest in her own worthy charms, and Vixen came within one of Big Mike's whiskers of being barbecued at the stake by the Indian maiden. The bandito thought he might teach the aptly named heroine some manners with a horsewhip. She was rescued from each perilous situation by a handsome if rather laconic gunfighter who seemed bemused by his lady love's propensity for winding up bound and disheveled. I really must get Laney and Harry Duchette together, Penelope thought.

"And take the rest of the day off."

"I don't mind staying."

"I insist. You need to be properly rested for the beginning of your acting career."

"What are you going to do?"

"Pursue justice."

That said, Penelope stuck a copy of *Savage Vixen* in her purse before posting a hand-lettered sign in the window and closing Mycroft & Company for the afternoon.

GONE FILMING, the sign read.

The Empty Creek Video Theatre was conveniently located next door to Mycroft & Company, and the display of movie posters that had disappeared into her subconscious because of familiarity now caught Penelope's eye again. In honor of

195

C.D. Masterly's august presence in town, the video store had stocked up on copies of his previous five films. Penelope stared at the poster for *Starbright*, a film so bad that *ShowGirls* now invited comparisons to *Citizen Kane*. After a moment's reflection, Penelope said, "Come on, Mikey, let's have a C.D. Masterly Film Festival."

Kathy Allen shrieked and nearly fell off Timothy Scott's lap when Penelope and Big Mike entered the Video Theatre. "What are you doing here?" she cried.

"I can see what you're doing," Penelope said, "but, never mind, I approve of hormone stimulation. It's good for the psyche. Still, the question is what the two of you are doing here. Besides necking, I mean?"

"It's my new job," Timmy said.

"I forgot to tell you," Kathy said, "but I've hardly seen you."

"It gives me lots of time to write," Timmy said despite considerable evidence to the contrary in the form of lipstick on his lips and cheeks. Although he had abandoned *The Kathiad*, an epic poem in twelve books after Homer's *Iliad*, devoted solely to singing the praises of Kathy's breasts, once described as "yon dangling alabaster orbs," young Scott still qualified as Empty Creek's somewhat deranged poet laureate. He was now working on sonnet number twenty-seven, a celebration of Kathy's right earlobe.

Penelope produced her membership card. "Well, give me the complete works of CD. Masterly and I'll let you get back to *writing*."

"They're all out," Timmy said.

"Damn. I suppose that was to be expected with the sudden notoriety."

"Except the set I put away for you in the back. I thought you might get around to watching them."

"Isn't he smart?" Kathy said.

Timmy quickly brought out a stack of five videos. "*Passion*," he said, "good, but overrated. *Killers*, not bad. *Brothel*. A turkey. *Lack of Rapport*, two turkeys. *Starbright* gives turkeys a bad name. Without the use of the F word, its running time of one hundred twenty-two minutes would have easily been cut in half."

"I believe you may have a future as a film critic," Penelope said.

Penelope and Big Mike arrived at Frontier Town in time to trail behind a group of extras and their baby-sitters heading for the set. A strange thought passed through Penelope's mind. She was actually a little sorry she wasn't working. Good God, she thought, am I beginning to like this nonsense?

Shorty was sitting on the boardwalk, his chair propped back against the wall of the saloon, a book in his lap, when the extras arrived.

Kimberly Ferrell paused. "Hello, Shorty," she said, smiling shyly.

"Hey, darlin', how you doing? See you tonight?"

Kimberly nodded, blushing. She rushed through the swinging doors of the saloon.

Penelope, always wanting to be in tune with the bookish public, lagged back and asked, "What are you reading, Shorty?"

"*Oedipus.*"

"Poor Oedipus, destined to kill his father and marry his mother, rushing headlong to find the truth, only to be destroyed. Certainly, one of the greatest plays ever written."

" 'A tragedy is the imitation of an action that is serious and also, as having magnitude, complete in itself . . . with incidents arousing pity and fear, wherewith to accomplish its catharsis of such emotions.' "

"I don't know many cowboys who go around reading Sophocles and quoting Aristotle's *Poetics*," Penelope said.

"I majored in theater for two years until I discovered I couldn't act worth a damn. But I could still ride, horses like me, and I love the Business anyway. I started out as an extra, and one thing led to another. So here I am, the best damned wrangler in Hollywood."

"And it's a good way to meet pretty girls."

"It is that. You won't blow my cover, will you? Kimberly likes cowboys better than intellectuals."

"I'll keep your secret."

"We'll be at the Dynamite tomorrow after work if you want to stop by. It's amateur night. I've got a bet with Kimberly that she won't get up there and dance."

"What do you get if you win?"

"She has to buy me a nice romantic candlelight dinner."

"What if you lose?"

"I have to buy her a nice romantic candlelight dinner."

"A sure thing."

"Best kind."

Penelope pushed through the saloon doors and took roll. All but one of the suspects were present and accounted for. Only Vixen DeVaughn was missing. Buffy

199

Anne was standing in for Stormy while assistant directors placed the extras and whispered instructions. Dominique Anders, pad and pen at the ready, stood behind Tony Lyme-Regis, who was peering intently through a monitor. Harry Duchette sat in a corner sipping coffee and staring at Dominique. Brock Hackett had a laptop computer on a folding chair in front of him. Even Hilly Hollander was present, making notes in a reporter's notebook.

Penelope tiptoed to Tony and looked over his shoulder. There was trouble on the monitor. Big Mike was sitting on a sawhorse and clearly in the shot. "I'll get him, Tony."

"Oh, hi, Penelope. How are you this fine day?"

"I'd be better if Mikey weren't sitting right in the scene."

Tony glanced at the monitor. "Don't worry. As long as he stays there, he'll be fine. He's in the safe area."

"What's that?"

"The camera actually sees more than will be in the scene. Everything on the periphery will be cut out."

"Oh."

In the safe area on the other side, Penelope saw Duchette wave tentatively.

She looked up in time to see Dominique stick her tongue out at him. Considering some of the other gestures Dominique might have made, Penelope thought that was progress. The writer, however, hung his head disconsolately.

"Still feuding, I see."

"You should have heard what he read to me last night."

"I'll probably see it."

"If it were ever published, I'd have to leave the country."

"That good?"

Dominique blushed. "Disgusting," she said.

For Penelope, her reply lacked the proper degree of conviction for true outrage. Methinks the Amazon doth protest too much.

Penelope called Big Mike, who decided to respond — this time, probably because he found film making boring too — and together they slipped out before the shouting started. Outside, they discovered that the media frenzy had dissipated, leaving only Lola LaPola and her camera crew behind the ropes in the designated area. The murder of C.D. Masterly was moving steadily away from page one to small paragraphs on page thirty-three, reporting the lack of progress in solving the case. On television, the story no longer led the evening news, having been reduced to the category of "In other news, there has been no progress in the C.D. Masterly case." Lola LaPola had managed to stick close to the filming by doing a series of features. The making of *Elephant* still had some local news value. When Penelope and Big Mike arrived, the reporter was just finishing an interview with the missing suspect about her duties as a stand-in.

"And I understand you have other ambitions as well," Lola said.

"Oh, yes, would you like to hear?"

"Yes, indeed." Lola pointed her mike at Vixen.

Amber Stark waved frantically. Too late.

Vixen took a deep breath and emitted the mother of all screams, popping two buttons on her blouse to the delight of the cameraman.

A dozen voices in the saloon shouted, "Cut!"

Production assistants stampeded through the saloon doors in search of the offending ambient noise.

"Oops," Lola said.

A disgusted Tony Lyme-Regis stood on

the boardwalk and said, "This might be a good time to break for lunch." It wasn't the mother of all understatements, but it was close.

Amber hurried over to apologize. "I didn't know she was going to scream."

"See you later." Lola hastily retreated to the news van, leaving her cameraman still filming as Vixen attempted to repair the damage to her blouse.

"I need safety pin," Vixen said.

Penelope thought she needed a larger blouse, but produced a safety pin from the recesses of her purse anyway.

"Thanks."

"I thought you weren't supposed to talk without your lawyer present."

"Only about the case."

"How about the time you were busted for possession?"

"I don't think I should talk about that."

"It's public record."

"Do the police know?"

"They told me."

"I have to go now."

"Vixen, wait."

But Vixen scurried away, looking very much like a woman with something to hide.

"What do you make of that, Mikey?"

"Meow," he said, watching Vixen break into a trot. Nice tush.

"Me too," Penelope replied, translating erroneously. "I think we should go visiting."

Chapter Ten

When it came to cat burglary, Penelope naturally deferred to Big Mike's greater expertise. Her own experience was limited to sniffing out hidden Christmas presents as a child and later, when she had read every book in the children's section of the library, to finding the more erotic novels in her parents' library. However, in breaking and entering (or escape and evasion, for that matter), Big Mike had no rival. He was adept at getting into or out of some incredible places, especially when his instincts told him that Murphy Brown, that cute and sexy little calico who lived down the road, would not be averse to a little fooling around despite the elaborate precautions taken.

After the first litter of Little Mikeys and Murphys, Josephine Brooks always warned Penelope when her Murphy Brown was in season. Penelope locked every window and door in the house — to no avail. Big Mike simply learned to open the window clasp.

When she tied the windows shut in addition, he gnawed through the rope. Chains on the windows and doors were no deterrent and led to a classic locked room mystery that still baffled her. If Big Mike had built a secret trapdoor somewhere, Penelope had been unable to find it.

There was another solution, of course, but neither woman wanted to take it. For her part, Penelope wasn't about to have Big Mike meowing soprano. And Murphy Brown (no slouch at escape and evasion herself) was such a beautiful cat (if a bit of a slut) that Josephine wanted to breed her with a male who possessed a better pedigree than Big Mike's.

Penelope attributed Big Mike's intelligence to a superior gene pool. His parents, grandparents, and great-grandparents had survived the rigors of life in the African bush, which took cunning, sound judgment, and courage. Natural selection dictated that dummies will be eaten, and Big Mike was no dummy. Perfecting his bear imitation, he had ruled fearlessly over a domain that included packs of wild dogs, predatory hyenas, jackals, and various slithery creatures packing poison (without a permit to carry a concealed weapon, it might be added). A yowling Big Mike, skittering along on his hind legs, front claws unsheathed and ready for action, was an awesome sight few critters cared to challenge.

So when a good cause dictated a little breaking and entering, Penelope, of course, turned to Big Mike for advice. He was also pretty good at covering her six. She had checked the call sheets to ensure that both Brynn and Stormy were working, also necessitating the presence of Vixen and Buffy Anne as their stand-ins. Paradise Regained would be empty for the day. Thus, Penelope believed a few quiet and reflective moments in Paradise Regained without the clamor of a murder investigation might yield some valuable insight into the mind of the murderer. It might also allow her to see something she had missed on the night of the murder. It was worth a try. Nothing else was working. An "Ah-ha!" was definitely needed.

Although she had not developed her psychic powers to any degree, Penelope did not discount her ability. She thought she would make a pretty good witch if she put her mind to it. After all, she already had a devoted familiar in Big Mike, and some of the stuff he got up to was downright uncanny, even spooky. Nor did she discount alternative medicine, astrology, sooth-saying, the tarot, aliens, or any other paranormal activities. Just because she hadn't had any personal encounters with aliens didn't mean they weren't out there. In fact, she rather hoped they were. Laney had once come up with a pretty sexy fantasy, to be played by consenting adults, which involved the abduction of a beautiful earth woman and her subsequent physical examination by a handsome alien doctor. Once Andy got the hang of the rules — there were none — Penelope was quite happy to schedule another appointment. The roles could be reversed, of course, but Penelope soon discovered that she preferred being the abductee rather than the abductor.

Only slightly distracted by the possibility of another close encounter of the third kind with Dr. Gordo, Penelope took the back road up Crying Woman Mountain, believing she was taking the same route as Masterly's killer. At the top of the mountain she stopped the Jeep, turned the engine off, and then switched the ignition to on, put it in neutral, and coasted down the hill, gliding silently to a stop some seventy-five yards above the circular driveway. Despite an intensive search on the night of Masterly's death, the police had been unable to find any trace of the killer's route into Paradise Regained. Penelope contended, then and now, he would not simply drive up and park in front of the house. Too much chance that a passing witness might remember at least the make and model of a car parked there, although a canvass of the exclusive neighborhood had found no witnesses to anything until Vixen went keening down the hill. That little episode attracted attention.

While poetic license had its place, Penelope was a great believer in authenticity and so donned a ski mask "Look nonchalant," she told Mikey, as though anyone would believe a woman wearing a ski mask and a twenty-five-pound cat skulking along a six-foot wall were there to read the meters.

They reached the gate in the wall. It was locked, just like the night of the murder. Penelope had briefly considered borrowing a rattlesnake and a gunnysack, but that was taking authenticity a little too far, and there was no use in discounting poetic license altogether. She passed an imaginary gunnysack containing a big and equally make-believe diamondback through the gate.

While Penelope pondered the problem

of what the killer did with the revolver while scaling the wall, Big Mike hunkered down, measured the distance, and leaped effortlessly to the top of the wall. He could have easily stepped through the grates in the gate, but what fun was that? He looked down at Penelope and seemed to say, Come on. What are you waiting for?

Penelope put the revolver issue aside. Since no gunshot wounds had been treated of late at local hospitals, the killer had obviously gained entry without shooting himself in the process. Penelope stepped back and took a short run, leaping and grabbing the top of the wall. Big Mike watched with some amusement as she struggled to pull herself up and hoist a leg over the top. She was puffing a little when she finally got herself situated on the wall. It had seemed a lot easier when she was eighteen, running the obstacle course at Parris Island, singing about how much she loved the Marine Corps.

Sitting on the wall, Penelope realized this exercise was all a great waste of time if it was an inside job, but she could not bring herself to believe that either Buffy Anne or Vixen — despite the revelation about Vixen's drug bust — were killers. "Let's do it, Mikey."

She jumped down, remembering to take the imaginary gunnysack and revolver, and crept to the sliding glass doors. The draperies were back and the glass doors were open. She looked through the screen and saw the bed was neatly made, but there was nothing else in the room to suggest that anyone had been there recently. Penelope tried the screen door.

Locked.

She took her Swiss Army knife, sawed a slight tear in the screen, and easily popped the flimsy latch. Stepping into the master bedroom, she listened intently, but there wasn't a sound in the great house. Big Mike headed for the kitchen, perhaps hoping that either Vixen or Buffy Anne had left a snack out for visiting cats. Penelope stopped in Vixen's bedroom. The former Constant Companion wasn't exactly a neat freak. The bed was unmade. Clothes and underwear were strewn about the room. In the adjoining bath, panty hose hung over the shower door and the vanity was cluttered with what appeared to be one each of every cosmetic known to woman. The medicine cabinet revealed nothing more mind-altering than a large bottle of generic aspirin. A stack of trade paperbacks on the nightstand attracted

Penelope's attention. They were all devoted to filmmaking in one form or another — acting, writing the screenplay, directing.

Well, she's intent on learning the Business, Penelope thought before turning her attention to the chest of drawers, where she discovered, to no surprise, that Vixen appeared to have one each of everything in the latest Victoria's Secret catalogue — lacy bras in 36D (wow!), frilly panties, garter belts in assorted colors. Penelope rummaged through the drawers and found nothing more incriminating than a well-worn copy of *The Joy of Sex* beneath a pile of corsets.

Penelope repeated the process in Buffy Anne's bedroom and learned that the former Junior Constant Companion was also well stocked for the courtesan's trade with a lifetime supply of frilly doodads (a modest 36C), cosmetics, and an illustrated monograph on the art of spanking as denoted in the *Kama Sutra*, although in Buffy Anne's case everything was in its proper place and neatly folded or arranged. And, when Buffy Anne wasn't poring through naughty literature, her reading tastes were devoted solely to environmental issues. Her vial of sleeping pills was almost full.

Despite Tweedledee's excitement over Vixen's earlier drug bust in Los Angeles, there was no drug paraphernalia anywhere, although Penelope believed that with the heat on, Vixen was smart enough to get rid of anything like that — if it existed, which Penelope still doubted.

Having discovered nothing more interesting than Vixen was messy and Buffy Anne was fastidious, Penelope went back into the master bedroom, followed by Big Mike, complaining bitterly about the lack of hospitality around here.

"Hush," Penelope whispered. "We're supposed to be murderers."

Penelope stretched out on the bed and put her arms over her head, approximating the position Vixen left Masterly in when she went into the bathroom to smoke her cigarette and take her shower. Penelope closed her eyes and breathed deeply, clearing her mind, waiting for the revelation that would send Masterly's killer to jail. Penelope knew there was something to be learned in Paradise Regained, if only she could recognize it.

When nothing came, she turned and stared at the doors opening to the patio. It had been a warmish night, and the doors were open. All the killer had to do was slide the screen open and step into the bedroom. Vixen had left the key to the handcuffs on the nightstand. With a revolver stuck in his ear, Masterly would offer no resistance when his killer freed him from the bedpost, only to cuff his hands behind his back and prod him through the open door to the patio. The killer would have left the rattlesnake in his gunnysack outside, if only to facilitate freedom of movement. The killer knew exactly when to enter the bedroom, which meant he must have been outside for some time, listening and watching while Vixen made love to Masterly.

Imagining the scene, Penelope shivered, feeling the chills run up and down her body. God, the poor bastard, she thought. And what if Vixen hadn't decided to smoke her cigarette and take a shower? Would she be dead too? And Buffy Anne's sleeping pill. We might have had a triple homicide.

Big Mike's ears perked up.

Penelope listened.

Mikey's ears swiveled, his tracking system hard at work.

Penelope heard it then. The front door banged shut and someone said, "Shhh!"

Damn. Busted.

Penelope got up and quickly smoothed the bedspread. "Come on, Mikey," she whispered, tiptoeing into the closet, secreting herself between the metal breastplates and the French maid's outfits. Big Mike hid behind the ball gowns.

A number of thoughts stampeded through Penelope's mind, foremost among them was that the murderer — possibly in the plural — might have returned to the scene in search of something, which opened up a whole new area for investigation. What if Masterly had stiffed his drug dealer, for example? Dope dealers were notoriously lacking in humor when they weren't paid. The rattlesnake might have been a variation on the old Colombian necktie school of revenge. Which brought a second, equally unpleasant, thought to mind. If the killer — or killers — *had* returned to the scene, she was unarmed except for her Swiss Army knife and, as Sean Connery had pointed out so astutely in *The Untouchables*, it wasn't a good thing to bring only a knife to a gunfight. Damn poetic license anyway. Penelope had broken her own rule number one for conducting murder investigations — never leave home without her AR-15, the civilian version of the military M-16 rifle, or at least the snub-nosed thirty-eight she had borrowed from Tweedledee and forgotten to return. She would have bought her own handgun long ago, except for one little problem. She couldn't hit the wall of her living room — from inside — with a hand-gun. Not so with the rifle (she had quali-fied Expert in the Marine Corps), but it was unwieldy to carry the rifle everywhere. Besides, it made liberals nervous.

Oh, well, a little late to run out to a gun store, which meant it was definitely time to review a few principles of hand-to-hand combat.

Penelope had gone through eye gouging (ugh!), ripping his nose off (double ugh!), and was progressing to knee breaking (much better), when a familiar voice said, "Come on, no one's here. Let's start looking."

Penelope was mildly disappointed that she wasn't going to wrap the case up in the next fifteen minutes or so. "Up against the wall," she hollered from the safety of the closet. She would have preferred to leap out and scare them out of several lifetimes, but that might have been a little dan-gerous. Tweedledee had a tendency to be trigger happy.

"Penelope, is that you?"

"Yep," she replied, pushing her way through the costumes.

"Jesus Christ, don't do that. You nearly gave me a heart attack. What are you doing here?"

"Recreating the mise-en-scène."

"Nearly made a messy scene of my own. We didn't see your Jeep. Thought the place was empty."

Penelope immediately regretted not taking a chance. Tweedledee would never live down wetting his pants. "I parked around the curve like any respectable villain would do."

"Well, let's toss Vixen's room and get out of here."

"I've already done it," Penelope said.

"No drugs?"

"She's clean. Let's have lunch. I'll treat."

"The Dynamite?" Tweedledee said hopefully.

"I'll spring for your lunch, but I will not underwrite your ogling bare-breasted maidens. Sushi."

"Toss you for it." Tweedledee handed her a quarter. "Odd man chooses."

"Don't be sexist. Odd person chooses."

They flipped. Tweedledee and Tweedledum showed heads. Penelope had tails.

"Double or nothing? Rock, paper, scissors?"

"Sushi," Penelope said firmly.

"Okay, but you better take off the ski mask."

"Oh, yeah. I forgot."

Hiroshi Ishii greeted them enthusiastically from behind the bar of the Empty Creek Reformed Sushi Bar. The name of the little establishment was not a reference to religion, but, rather, testimony to Hiroshi-san's conversion from Yakuza gangster and dealer in illicit fossils to respected restaurateur.

"*Konichiwa,* Penerope-san," Hiroshi-san cried, bowing formally. "*Konichiwa,* Mycloft-san."

Penelope bowed twice, once for herself and once for Mycroft, who was already on the counter, salivating over the fish delicacies behind the glass.

"Tweedredee-sans, welcome."

"How's it hanging, Hiroshi?" Tweedledee-san said.

"Hot sake for all." It was not a question.

"We're on duty."

"Just tea for me," Penelope said, remembering an unpleasant experience when Hiroshi-san had once showed up on her doorstep with a bottle of sake under one arm and a harakiri attitude under the other.

Hiroshi-san ignored their protestations, and three large sake containers and matching cups appeared on the counter before his guests.

"Oh, what the hell, we've already broken about half a dozen laws today," Tweedledum said. "Cheers."

"What if we're looking in the wrong places?" Penelope asked. The thought of a Colombian necktie still bothered her. Drug dealers were vindictive to the max. "What if Masterly was killed because of a dope deal gone bad?"

"Empty Creek ain't exactly high on the international drug cartel's point of entry list."

"Yeah," Tweedledum agreed with his partner, "and how many dope dealers would know about Masterly's snake phobia?"

"What's wrong with Vixen? Everything points to her."

"Except the evidence."

"That's the trouble with you, Penelope, you always want everything neat and tidy."

"I'm fussy that way."

"I don't know," Tweedledum said.

"Sometimes I think that Dominique babe's good for it. She's a cold one."

"Nah, the only one she wants to kill is the writer. I wonder what Duchette's doing with her in his latest chapter?"

"Don't start. I'll have to take another cold shower."

Hiroshi-san served up Arizona rolls for three and some tuna sashimi for Big Mike. Arizona rolls were California rolls concocted to Empty Creek standards — the wasabi contained a subtle hint of jalapeño.

Penelope nibbled at her Arizona roll, still feeling there was something at Paradise Regained, but she hadn't been able to recognize it. The Osmosis School of Detection was a failure.

Now what? she wondered.

After lunch Penelope decided to check in and set up a lunch with Hilly and see if the dossier on Masterly had arrived. It wouldn't hurt either to see what Harry Duchette *was* up to in Chapter Whatever. It might be better than Earth Woman Abducted by Aliens.

At the Lazy Traveler, Hilly Hollander answered the door clad in garish plaid Bermuda shorts, loafers — no socks — a red cashmere sweater, sleeves stylishly pulled up to his elbows, and a quizzical expression on his face. He held a piece of paper in his hand. "This is very strange," he said. He handed the e-mail message to Penelope.

She quickly scanned it, noting it had been sent three days earlier. "Don't you pick up your mail every day?"

"Of course not. It's usually complaints about my expense account."

Penelope nodded. She approved that the author wrote in the standard style rather than the e-mail manner without capitalization and sloppy punctuation. E-mail was further deteriorating the state of the English language. She read the concluding sentence aloud. " 'Wait for me, darling, I'm yours. Emily.' Who's Emily?"

"One of my many fans. We've corresponded occasionally."

"Interesting address: emilynewlife.com. It seems you have a groupie intent on wreaking havoc upon your bod."

"Good God, I hope not. Women are so complicated."

"Are you gay?"

"Of course not. I just prefer simplicity in my relationships. When I feel the need for female companionship, I have a special friend — a professional, if you must know, working her way through graduate school.

221

We go dining and dancing and afterward get naked and sit in bed, talking. She doesn't nag me about cleaning up my office or taking out the garbage or doing the dishes. It's quite satisfactory. Much better than my ex-wife, who was compulsive about such things. She ironed my socks, for God's sake. I mean, really."

"Well, perhaps emilynewlife.com won't arrive."

"If she does, I shall flee to Africa and search for the source of the Nile."

"It's already been discovered."

"No! When?"

"Some time ago, actually. In the nineteenth century."

"Damn the luck. What's left?"

"Well, you could go to Ethiopia and ferret out the Ark of the Covenant. That's where it's reputed to be. No one's done that yet. I'd start in Lalibella."

"Good. I'll make arrangements with Abercrombie and Fitch. Or is it Holland and Holland?"

"Both are quite reputable and probably experienced in mounting safaris."

"It's settled, then. Ark of the Covenant, here I come. Now, how can I help you, dear lady? Besides, the dossier, I mean."

"You have it?"

"Indeed." Hollander handed over a thick folder.

Penelope opened it and leafed through quickly. Much of it consisted of clips of "Hollywood Hollerings" by Hilly Hollander, but there were clips from the trade papers, the *Los Angeles Times* and the *Daily News*, and a sheaf of legal papers indicating that Masterly had been sued on more than one occasion for allegedly stealing story ideas from others.

"Thank you," Penelope said. "I'll go through it tonight. Lunch tomorrow?"

"Delighted. And duly noted how cooperative this little suspect has been?"

"A matter of record. Of course, you can't leave for Ethiopia until this case is solved."

"Work fast, dear lady. The Emily clock is ticking."

So is the Masterly clock, Penelope thought. If we don't make some progress soon, the killer might get away with it.

Penelope knocked on Harry Duchette's door.

"Go away, I'm working."

Penelope banged louder. "So am I."

The door opened and Harry peered out nervously. "I thought it was Peter Benedict, back to give me more notes. I'm sick of notes."

"The suits have left town, but I have some notes for you too."

Duchette groaned. "I should have listened to my mother and gotten a real job at the post office."

"Too late. What's up with the perils of Dominique today?"

Harry Duchette grinned. "Old favorite of mine. The beautiful Dominique Anders is tied to the rail road tracks."

"And the 4:52 is thundering down on her." That would be a little hard to recreate in the bedroom at Casa Penelope. But, with a little ingenuity . . .

"How did you know?"

"It's always the 4:52. And whom are you consorting with today?"

"I'd rather not say. Tony will kill me."

"Be gentle with Nora. She embarrasses easily."

"Not in my story, she doesn't."

"We'll have to give her a copy. She's entirely too shy for her own good. Most of the time anyway."

"You wouldn't?"

"I would. By the way, did you know Vixen is studying screenwriting?"

"Everybody thinks they're a writer."

"She ever ask you for advice?"

"Wish she had."

"Better stick with seducing Dominique."

"How'd you know?"

"I recognize love letters when I read them, even if they are weird and perverse."

"She hates me."

"Just keep writing. Where did you get the idea for *The Ears of the Elephant?*"

"Masterly. Why?"

"I wonder where he came across the Pleasant Valley War?"

"What war?"

"Ancient history in Arizona," Penelope said. "But Masterly was accused a couple of times of stealing stories. Settled out of court."

"That happens all the time. Even to somebody like Spielberg. Somebody's always looking to make a few bucks. Most of it's a scam. And it's less expensive to settle than go to court. But there are scumbags in the Business who *do* steal ideas. I'm surprised the writers haven't shot everyone in Hollywood above the rank of mailroom clerk."

Chapter Eleven

Penelope stared at Harry Duchette. "Or used rattlesnakes as the weapon of choice?" she said coldly.

"I shouldn't have said that, I guess."

"Probably not."

"I'm sorry. It just slipped out. I didn't kill him."

"But you've thought about it often enough."

"Idle fantasies to counteract the frustrations of working with the man. I swear I'm innocent. You believe me, don't you?"

"I'm not sure." She turned and walked abruptly away, looking back once to see Duchette slumped against the door. Let him worry, Penelope thought. She didn't think he was a killer, but whenever someone went on a rampage, the neighbors usually told the television cameras, "He was such a quiet man. I can't believe he would do something like this." Rarely did they say, "He was a dirtbag. I figured he'd do it a lot sooner."

Penelope was also surprised that Harry Duchette didn't know about the Pleasant Valley War since *The Ears of the Elephant* was loosely based on the great feud. The Pleasant Valley War was storied in Arizona history, the last great range war fought between cattlemen and sheepherders, and the destruction of two families, the Tewksburys and the Grahams. It had been a vicious conflict, fought over a period of years, ending only when the last of the Grahams was shot and killed from ambush. Many a book had been written about the feud, including Zane Grey's *To the Last Man*, an apt title. Masterly had apparently come across the tale somewhere and adapted it for the nineties, making one of the families a matriarchy. It was strange that Masterly hadn't shared the source material with Harry. But then, everything about Masterly was exceedingly weird, Penelope thought. She tapped her fingers impatiently against the steering wheel.

"Got any great ideas, Mikey?"

"Meow?" Frozen yogurt?

"Well, this day has been a complete failure." Penelope started the Jeep and headed for the police station. Harassing Dutch was always a good way to cheer herself up.

It wasn't Route 66, but for Miss Emily Horster, late of Akron, Ohio, embarked on the first great adventure of her life — if she didn't count her brief marriage to Jack the Jerk Horster — it was quite satisfactory. Traveling by bus was really quite luxurious, providing expansive views of the passing scenery by day and ample opportunity for the imagination to work by night. The bus roared down Interstate 71 to Columbus, where it picked up Interstate 70 to Indianapolis and went on to cross the Mississippi River at St. Louis. There she changed buses for points west on Interstate 44 through Missouri and into Oklahoma City, where she again changed buses and headed south into Texas and Big D.

Along the way, Miss Horster amused herself by reading — there were only so many corn fields that one could admire before they became tedious — watching for Arizona license plates, chatting with fellow passengers, and consulting her road atlas to mark her progress on the journey to Empty Creek.

Rest stops were numerous, and Miss Horster picked up each new edition of *The Millennium* to ensure that Hilly Hollander's column was still datelined from Empty

Creek, Ariz. Should the dateline suddenly revert to Los Angeles, she simply planned to extend her one-way ticket into that evil city where she had been born but had left at the age of two. In either case, she expected no difficulty in finding the man of her dreams. Empty Creek was but a speck on her map of Arizona, and it shouldn't be difficult to find him there. After all, Empty Creek couldn't compare to the metropolitan area of such a big city as Akron, population 223,019 at the last census (now diminished by one), and if he had returned to Los Angeles, it would be a simple matter to present herself at the editorial offices of the tabloid — after a good night's rest, of course. She wanted to be at her best when dear Hilly saw her for the first time.

Excitement growing, Miss Horster followed her southerly route carefully on the atlas from Fort Worth to Abilene and Big Spring and Odessa and up again into El Paso to cross the Rio Grande into New Mexico. Only one more state to traverse before the momentous meeting. Hilly Hollander's number one fan smiled at the thought of his tender greeting when she finally arrived. She closed her eyes, tilted her head upward, parted her lips, and awaited his first kiss.

"Don't you ever knock?"

"Nope," Penelope replied with good humor, "unless the door is locked, and then I usually pick the lock." It was good to see that Dr. Gordo was not an aberration. If there was one constant in Empty Creek, Penelope believed, it was the water supply and whatever mysterious property it contained that kept libidos hovering at 212 degrees Fahrenheit. How else could modern medical science explain Cackling Ed, for example, a Geezer World resident who had apparently landed with the Pilgrims and still chased after any woman younger than himself — which consisted of the entire female population of Empty Creek.

"Pretend she's not here," Stormy said.

"How can I do that?" Dutch asked, trying to disentangle himself from the web she had spun while sitting in his lap.

"Why aren't you working anyway?" Penelope asked. "Even the Tweedles have shown more initiative of late."

"I know."

"You do?"

"Who do you think sent them to Paradise Regained?"

"In violation of the Fourth Amendment?" Penelope said despite having walked all over it herself. But at least she'd had the good sense to wear a ski mask.

"*They* had a warrant."

"Oops. They forgot to mention that."

"You're lucky I don't toss your pretty little butt in jail."

"Good idea," Stormy said. "Then we can get back to business."

"Sis!" This is not going well, Penelope thought.

"Serve you right. Mirandize her, Dutch, and let's get on with it."

"Later. She might have found something she forgot to share with the Empty Creek Police Department."

"I wouldn't do that, Dutch."

"Want me to count the number of times . . ."

"Never mind."

"So. What did you find?"

"Unless they're better actresses than I think, Vixen and Buffy Anne are clean. An old possession charge is not evidence of murder."

"It's the best thing we've got at the moment."

"Motive, motive, motive."

"Opportunity, opportunity, opportunity."

"I know, I know, I know."

"Stuck, stuck, stuck."

"I wish that damned lawyer would catch amoebic dysentery and cut his safari short."

"Patience, patience, patience."

"Does anyone care what I think?" Stormy asked.

"Of course, honey bunches. What do you think?"

"It's simple enough. You've been looking at the obvious. Try concentrating on the obscure instead. When you make the obscure obvious, why, *voilà,* you have your creep — or creepess."

"Huh?"

"Really, Dutch. It's not that hard. Forget Vixen and Buffy Anne. Too obvious. The same with Shorty and Claude."

"Too obvious?"

"Exactly. Ditto Hollander and Duchette."

It was memory-lapse time. Penelope decided not to share Harry Duchette's statement of less than an hour ago — yet.

"You've eliminated all our best suspects."

Stormy smiled. "See how easy it is."

"She's right, you know," Penelope said, "in a loony sort of way."

"Okay," Dutch said. "Who's the least obvious person?"

"Me," Stormy said.

"You have an alibi. You were with me."

"See. You're making progress already."

"All right, who's after you?"

"Sheesh," Stormy said. "Do I have to do everything?"

"Well, you guys get back to whatever it was you were doing. I've got a doctor's appointment."

"Finally," Stormy said.

Penelope didn't risk a smart-assed comment. It wouldn't be the first time she'd been behind bars in the local hoosegow, and she didn't want Earth Woman to miss her appointment with Dr. Gordo.

"Close the door behind you."

Entering the house, Penelope went directly to the kitchen, depositing the Masterly dossier and his complete filmography on the kitchen table, opened the refrigerator, poured a glass of wine, took a sip, and set it aside for later. With a plastic bag of lettuce and carrots and a peppermint candy for Chardonnay, Penelope and Big Mike set off to feed the various critters.

On their return, Penelope filled Big Mike's bowl with liver crunchies, set out some celery stalks and radishes for her own hors d'oeuvres, and settled in to kill a little time while awaiting the arrival of Dr. Gordo and his evil minions. She sipped wine and munched on veggies while leafing through the thick folder that followed Masterly's career. He had been one of the few lucky ones, anointed by that movie mogul in the sky for success while hundreds and thousands of others labored unsuccessfully, toiling in obscurity, eight-by-ten glossies or scripts under their arms, hoping for that one elusive break. No apprenticeship as a clerk in a video store, a waiter, a cabdriver for Masterly. In film school, Masterly's student film had won several awards which, in turn, led to unlimited access to the one ingredient vital for achievement in Hollywood — money, lots and lots of money.

As the writer-director of *Passion*, Masterly's comet had blazed across the Hollywood night sky, gathering Golden Globe and Academy Award nominations, although Masterly did not win. That critical and box office success led to *Killers*, a film that, given the success of *Passion*, could be described only as a great disappointment. The critics turned on Masterly with the release of *Brothel*. *Lack of Rapport* sent film noir back to the early talkies. But in film land, nothing begets success like failure. The devastating reviews of *Starbright* and its box office failure simply led Peter Benedict to green-light *The Ears of the Elephant.*

There were pictures of Masterly on sets, at the Academy Awards with one or another beautiful woman on his arm, including Dominique Anders with a frozen smile on her face. There were photos from black tie charity events and film premieres. Items from "Hollywood Hollerings" were highlighted. Hollander had praised Masterly in the early days of his career, although he had stopped short of calling him the reincarnation of Orson Welles, as some critics did. But then Hollander had turned, sniping at Masterly's personal life, his drug use, sexual peccadilloes, his extravagant lifestyle.

Penelope read through feature stories from newspaper Sunday magazines. Each extolled his genius early, but quickly slipped to the tone of "What Happened to C.D. Masterly's Talent?"

Closing the Masterly dossier, Penelope felt there was something missing. It was really just a clip file, but dossier sounded so much more professional and secret agentish.

I have the Masterly dossier for you, the

director of the Central Intelligence Agency said.

Thank you, Agent Penelope Warren replied. Agent Mycroft and I will make good use of it.

Remember, the clock is ticking. You have less than twenty-four hours to save the world.

We're on the case.

We're counting on you. Do you have your invisible ink?

And my poisoned bubble gum wrapper.

Good. Now, kiss me before you go.

Never. You are the evil Dr. Gordo from the planet Burp. Where are your evil minions?

Waiting for you, Earth Woman, like all good little minions should do. There is no escape. You and your puny planet are doomed.

What have you done with the director of Central Intelligence?

He is awaiting the 4:52.

Not the 4:52?

Yes, Dr. Gordo cackled. The 4:52.

A.M. or p.m.?

P.M., of course.

"Hi, sweetie," the real Dr. Gordo said, leaning over to kiss his beloved, blissfully unaware of the danger he was in.

Agent Warren pounced. "You'll never take me alive," she cried, stuffing the last radish in her mouth. "Bleeth," she added.

Dr. Gordo and his evil minions abducted the earth woman with some degree of difficulty since, by the time he had tickled her into submission, he was wishing he had some handy railroad tracks and Penelope almost relented. That Dr. Gordo sure could kiss.

During the struggle, Dr. Gordo and Agent Warren managed to skin a rabbit or two, leaving a trail of clothing from the kitchen to the bedroom. By the time Dr. Gordo had flung Agent Warren to the bed and fastened her — that bondage starter kit came in handy on occasion — both were in a bit of a state, but rules were rules.

Agent Mycroft yowled and scratched at the door, demanding entry to no avail. An unfortunate incident had occurred when Sam Connors and Penelope had been an item, and since then Big Mike was banned from the bedroom during amorous moments despite all his protests — it *had* looked like a scratching post.

"You'll get nothing from him," Penelope said, eyes blazing, fingers fluttering.

"Perhaps not, but *you* will talk."

"Fat chance of that, skinny alien doctor."

"What are these for?" Dr. Gordo asked, caressing her breasts.

"Mmm," Agent Warren said.

"Speak."

"If you must know, females from my planet give milk to their babies from them."

"Nice packaging," Dr. Gordo said. "But shouldn't the nutrition content be specified?"

"The FDA . . . hasn't . . . gotten . . . around to that . . . yet . . . you beast . . ."

The physical examination of the helpless and whimpering earth woman continued, with Dr. Gordo calling out each new discovery to be recorded by one or another of his faithful minions.

"Interesting reaction when one blows in her ear. Heavy breathing is induced."

"Oh, God," Agent Warren cried.

"And here. See how her stomach muscles ripple when the tongue is applied to the belly button."

"I surrender. Please, I'll tell you anything."

"What is your recipe for spaghetti sauce?"

"Except that."

"Then I have no alternative."

"What are you going to do?"

"Lick you to the point of insanity."

"Not that. Anything but that."

"Ah, we have found her weakness. Let the licking commence."

"Mmm, no, wow, yes . . . take one small can of tomato paste . . ."

By the time the dreaded licking torture ended, the 4:52 had come and gone — oh, well, he hadn't been a very good CIA director anyway — and Agent Warren had given up the recipes for her spaghetti sauce, flaming curry dish, boom-boom hot dogs, and her social security and driver's license numbers, as well as admitting to any number of licentious thoughts while simultaneously forcing the evil Dr. Gordo to beg for a little mercy of his own.

Not bad, considering she was doing it no hands.

Much later, snuggled warmly in Andy's arms, Agent Warren said, "Well, that was fun. Are you Burpians all alike?"

"I'll never burp again," Andy sighed.

"You'd better."

"God, I love you."

"I love you too, darling."

"Wake me up in a week or so."

"Oh, no. We've got lots to do yet."

"What?"

"Over dinner we're going to watch old Masterly movies, and after that we're invited to the Dynamite. It's amateur night."

"Are you entering?"

"That perked Dr. Gordo up, I see."

"I'll vote for you."

"Some other time perhaps, when I'm not on the job."

Eating spaghetti — the earlier activities had whetted her appetite for pasta — in front of the television, Penelope used the fast forward to accelerate the viewing time through *Passion* and *Killers.* During the credits of *Lack of Rapport*, Penelope froze on the writing credit.

"That's interesting," she said. "Masterly wrote *and* directed his first two films. Here, he takes on a collaborator, and by *Lack of Rapport* he had become a big-time director. Probably didn't have time to do everything himself."

Penelope ejected the cassette and plugged in *Starbright.* Again Masterly had collaborated on the screenplay, although he took sole credit for the story, the same as with *The Ears of the Elephant,* but each cowriter was different. Masterly and Perkins, Masterly and Devonshire, Masterly and Crookhauer, and now, Masterly and Duchette. None of them would rival the great writing teams of Hollywood.

"He should have continued to work alone," Penelope said.

Tiffany, AKA Sally Winston, was onstage, dancing slowly, dreamily, to a haunting piano concerto, oblivious of her audience, when Penelope, Andy, and Big Mike arrived at a crowded Dynamite Lounge. Amateur night was a popular feature, attracting adventurous couples who sought just the slightest tinge of wickedness in their relationship. Men, if only they would admit it, were excited by the prospect of their wives or girlfriends being slightly "bad."

Andy fogged his glasses and wiped them carefully with a napkin he grabbed from the bar.

"My, what big eyes you have, Dr. Gordo," Penelope said.

"Only for you, my dearest, only for you."

"Ha!"

Amber Stark waved to them. She was seated with Pete in a booth against the wall. "Join us."

Big Mike accepted the invitation by jumping into Amber's lap.

"Are you dancing?" Penelope asked, slipping into the booth.

Amber laughed and patted Pete's knee. "He has to wait for coming attractions," she said.

"She's in training for the wet T-shirt contest."

"How do you train for someone dousing you with water?"

"It's all in the breathing and muscle tone."

"Of course, I should have known that." Penelope turned to Amber. "In between your training sessions, would you do me a favor and contact Masterly's cowriters?"

"Sure, why?"

"I want to know where the story lines came from on his later films."

"I'll do it first thing tomorrow."

"Did we miss anything?" Andy asked.

"Define miss."

Waiting for drinks, Penelope surveyed the room, taking roll of her suspects, both obvious and obscure. Shorty and his friends were down front, but Kimberly Ferrell wasn't there, having apparently changed her mind, allowing modesty to overcome her bet. Vixen DeVaughn was at another table with Brock Hackett, the second assistant director. Buffy Anne was absent, presumably at Paradise Regained writing to one or another of her pen pals on the state of the rain forest. Harry Duchette and Dominique Anders were also on the missing list. They were probably shouting at each other about the 4:52 over the telephone. Hilly Hollander was with Brynn Moore and Bobby Danes.

The music ended and Tiffany bowed to a round of enthusiastic applause.

"And now, ladies and gentlemen," the bartender said over a microphone. "It's amateur night. Our first contestant is from Los Angeles, California. Let's all welcome Kimberly Ferrell."

Wrong again.

Everyone at Shorty's table stood and clapped wildly to the overture from *Man of La Mancha*.

Andy quickly polished his glasses again.

"You need some defogger," Penelope said.

"You'd think the Dynamite would sell it. They'd make quite a nice profit."

"We want Kimberly," Shorty chanted. The others at his table took up the cry. "We want Kimberly."

The backstage curtain ruffled, but Kimberly appeared to be having serious doubts about this aspect of show business.

243

"Kimberly, Kimberly, Kimberly."

She peeked through the curtains.

The applause rose to a crescendo.

Kimberly's blushing face emerged. She clutched the curtains tight around her.

She disappeared.

"Shorty's going to win," Penelope said.

Kimberly pushed through the curtains, arms crossed over her chest, and began to sway with the music.

"Good old baby-sitter," Andy said.

At an appropriate place in the music, Kimberly flung her arms in the air and hit the afterburners.

Everyone at Shorty's table went daft.

"I'm buying a case of defogger tomorrow," Andy said.

Two more young women — both locals — danced, but they didn't have a chance against the applause meter as measured from Shorty's gang.

"Our final contestant is also from Los Angeles. Let's have a big Empty Creek welcome for Vixen DeVaughnnnnnnnn!"

Vixen stood and flung her tank top across the room.

"No fair," Shorty shouted.

The audience disagreed, clapping wildly as Vixen jiggled to perfection. All of those hours rehearsing would have paid off had

Shorty not hurriedly consulted with the bartender, pointing out that Vixen had given up her amateur status by performing as a topless dancer in two different major motion pictures. Vixen took her disqualification gracefully, even joining in the applause for Kimberly, who returned to the stage to accept her trophy from Belinda Baxter, a former dancer at the Dynamite, but now the manager.

And that might have been that, except for a congratulatory nightcap for the winner, had not a flashbulb lit the room.

Kimberly shrieked and pulled the trophy to her for protection from the photographer.

Belinda searched for the offender. Photography was strictly forbidden at the Dynamite.

Shorty leaped across two tables and grabbed Brendon Mack, National Talent Search, Inc., by the scruff of the neck, shaking him until the camera fell to the floor. Shorty took the camera and rewound it expertly before removing the film canister.

Mack was not lacking in courage despite his height and weight disadvantage, and he went after Shorty, hitting him hard in the mouth. Shorty shook his head and went into a serious case of paparazzi rage, pummeling the photographer until he was pulled off by his friends, still struggling to get at the fallen Mack, his face contorted by uncontrollable anger.

It wasn't until Kimberly jumped off the stage and placed herself between Shorty and the photographer that the wrangler relaxed.

But Penelope could not forget the look of uncontrollable fury on his face. He might have killed the hapless photographer if others had not intervened.

That was not very obscure at all.

Chapter Twelve

Not yet having booked tickets to go in search of the Ark of the Covenant, Hilly Hollander, dapper as always, arrived at the Double B precisely at the appointed time to join Penelope. Big Mike, of course, was at his usual vantage point at the bar, taking note of this portion of his kingdom. Penelope offered her cheek for the customary Hollywood greeting.

"Dear lady, I have been so looking forward to this."

Penelope smiled. "Nice cologne."

"Oh, just a little something I picked up at Chanel."

"I hope you have a sufficient supply. At the rate we're going, you may be away from Rodeo Drive for a while."

"The dossier was of no help?"

"It was very inclusive of his career, but lacking in details of his earlier life."

"A vision approaches."

"Must be the best cocktail waitress in Arizona."

"Indeed," Hollander said, rising to bow and kiss Debbie's hand.

Although it was the first time a customer had greeted her in such a debonair fashion, Debbie accepted the gesture as though it happened every day. In the normal course of Empty Creek events, she had to slap pawing cowboy hands away. "Nice cologne," she said.

"I shall replenish my supply and bathe in it if it will make you happy."

"I think the subtle aroma is better."

"Whatever pleases you, dear lady."

"Is he always like this?"

"I'm not sure," Penelope said, "but probably."

"Only when confronted by two beautiful women."

"Well, this beautiful woman would like a glass of wine. What would you like, Hilly?"

"A Manhattan, please," Hollander said, staring into Debbie's eyes, "stirred with your sweet finger in lieu of the maraschino cherry."

"Sam could be in trouble if this keeps up."

"Sam?"

"Her boyfriend. He's a cop."

"A noble profession."

"You were telling me about Masterly's early life before your poetic attack."

"I was?"

"Most assuredly."

"Such a delightful interruption. Ah, well, to business and the boyhood of C.D. Masterly. It's mostly rumor. Masterly himself was never very forthcoming."

"Did you ask him directly?"

"Oh, yes, when we were on more amicable terms and before he promoted himself to master of the universe. His stories varied. He seemed a pathological liar, but one unable to spin his tales with any degree of consistency. Once, he told me his father was missing in action in Vietnam. On another occasion, his father worked for the CIA in Germany. He spoke only once of his mother — a beautiful woman who would have been a great actress had she not died during his complicated birth. All balderdash."

"You didn't believe any of it?"

"With the aid of the Freedom of Information Act, not for a moment."

"And what *do* you believe?"

"A more mundane version of the facts, although very Horatio Alger–like. He was born to a most dysfunctional and broken family and lived in a series of foster homes."

"His parents?"

Hollander shrugged. "Deserted by his mother and his father, a mean drunk, drank himself to death."

"That might explain his later excesses, the indulgences in women and drugs. They were the family he never had."

"Quite likely."

"Unfortunately, it doesn't explain who killed him."

"Perhaps, I should write a book. The Mysterious Life and Death of C.D. Masterly. We might never know who killed C.D., like the Black Dahlia. As a mystery maven, you know the crime, of course."

"Elizabeth Short. Her body was found in a field near downtown L.A. in 1947, cut in half."

"A demented magician, no doubt, unskilled in his craft. That's always been my theory."

"I wonder if the police pursued that angle?"

"A would-be actress, she could have taken up with a magician, volunteered to be the beautiful assistant in the box, not knowing that the saw would be real. I suspect the police of that era were too unimaginative to consider magicians, demented or otherwise."

Penelope was grateful for the arrival of the drinks. There had been a transformation, albeit ever so slight, in Hollander's eyes as he expounded on the Black Dahlia. It could have been no more than a morbid interest in a long-ago murder, like people still fascinated by Jack the Ripper more than a century after brutally killing Mary Kelly, his last victim, and disappearing into the London fog. Or it might be that the thought of sawing a woman in two appealed to Hilly Hollander. Did that extend to preparing a hotshot and dumping a rattlesnake in Masterly's lap?

"Thanks, Debbie."

"You're welcome. And, for the gentleman, a Manhattan stirred with my very own little finger and two maraschino cherries on the side."

"You anticipate my every wish. You're much too kind to a poor wordsmith."

"I'll be back in a minute to take your orders."

"Shall we drink to unsolved mysteries?" Hollander asked, raising his cocktail.

Penelope frowned. "I don't like unsolved mysteries," she said finally. "Robert Stack notwithstanding, I intend to find whoever killed C.D. Masterly."

"To a tidy solution, then."

"A tidy solution."

After lunch, Penelope decided she would settle for even a messy resolution to the case of C.D. Masterly. As for a book, Penelope wondered how a mystery novelist would go about plotting this one. Over the years, any number of authors had visited Mycroft & Company for readings and book signings. A devoted coterie of mystery aficionados always attended, and during the question and answer periods, Penelope learned a great deal about the work habits of writers and how their books came to be. Some did extensive outlines, plotting each chapter in detail before beginning to write. Others simply took a situation or a character and started writing, each new workday bringing revelations and surprises.

If, and it was a mighty *if,* Penelope ever determined to write a mystery novel herself, she knew she would probably subscribe to the free-form style of creation, letting her characters have free rein to get themselves in and out of trouble, while she sat back, applauding each zany move and each new surprise and twist in the story. Of course, she would warn her heroine — a fearless and intrepid woman very much like Penelope named Elfrida Fallowfield — of impending danger. "Elfie, don't open that door." Naturally, Elfrida would pay no attention whatsoever — she resembled Penelope in that respect also — and would get herself into a world of hurt. "Elfie, I warned you," Penelope said, watching Elfrida battle a host of bad guys — she could take *and* give a punch — emerging victorious with the solution in hand. Natch. "Well, if it's that easy, Elfrida, who killed C.D. Masterly?"

"Who *are* you talking to?" Nora Pryor demanded.

Penelope blinked. She had managed to cross the street from the Double B and enter Mycroft & Company — Big Mike in her arms — completely oblivious of her surroundings. But she recovered quickly. "Why, Elfrida Fallowfield, of course."

"And who is that?"

"Elfrida Fallowfield, P.I. She wears a black leather cat suit." A nice touch that Big Mike would appreciate, Penelope thought. What's so hard about writing? This is coming along very nicely. Just need a few surprises — and that damnable solution. *That* could get to be a bit of a sticky wicket or a googly, whatever that was. Penelope had once watched an entire cricket test match between England and Australia and never quite recovered from the experience. But she firmly believed any sport that gave the score at tea time had redeeming social qualities.

"I see," Nora said, slipping into maternal mode and putting her wrist against Penelope's forehead. "You don't seem to have a temperature."

"She was fine when she left," Kathy said, "but there are days when she needs a keeper."

"I'm fine. Don't you ever just let your imagination run?"

"Not with people named Elfrida Fallowfield."

"It's a perfectly nice name. What are you doing here anyway? I thought you'd be on location."

"I was. That's why I'm here. Shorty was bitten by a rattlesnake and Brock Hackett gave him a shot of antivenom even though the snake had been milked. And he did it quite expertly, I might add."

"Now, that's the kind of surprise Elfie would appreciate. Come on, let's go."

"I'm supposed to be grounded."

"What did you do now?"

"Reggie found my copy of *Tattoo*, and when I grounded her for reading it, she grounded me for buying it in the first place — and underlining certain passages."

"Whole pages, chapters even, I'll bet."

"It is pretty erotic. I wish Dale Banks would write the sequel. He, or she, set it up for one."

"Oh, come on, I'll put in a word with Reggie on your behalf."

Penelope, Nora, Big Mike, and Elfie Fallowfield piled into the Jeep and headed north out of town and back in time. The beginning of the nineteenth century was marked by the end of the paved road and a caution sign warning of a javelina crossing. Beyond that point, men were men, women were women, cats were cats, and the trappings of twentieth-century civilization diminished considerably so long as the ubiquitous tour jeeps that took snowbirds and tourists into the back country and the occasional ugly satellite dish were ignored — no problem for this particular quartet. Despite intimidating bulldozers and construction crews intent on taming the desert for young upwardly mobile families, the desert was the desert, fighting back, yielding each encroachment grudgingly.

Penelope was rooting for the desert. She liked being able to go back and experience what it was like in 1870, when Empty Creek had first appeared on the territorial map. How dreary to live in a place like Los Angeles — where she had grown up on the Palos Verdes peninsula — with its freeways and ever-changing city skyline and strip malls and huge warehouselike stores filled with the latest in technology. For Penelope, the answering machine and the cell phone heralded the impending downfall of America. She did accept television (for football season), the VCR (renting movies was definitely good, even for Masterly's bombs), an automatic coffeemaker with a pause feature, the computer (for some unknown reason), and the electric can opener (more for Big Mike's sake than her own — if he had a fault, it was his impatience to get at the lima beans).

"You can take the rest of it and chuck it," Penelope said.

"I agree." Nora, too, felt the kinship with the past, evidenced in her history of and guide to Empty Creek.

There was a special place on the corrugated dirt road, where Penelope eased the

Jeep to a stop. It was unlikely Masterly's killer was waiting at Lonesome Bend to confess. "Come on," she said. "I want to show Elfie the view."

"There is no view," Nora pointed out, but she jumped out of the Jeep anyway.

"That's what's so nice," Penelope said, leading the way into the desert.

A hundred yards off the road, they were atop a slight rise in the midst of a quiet primeval beauty. After an initial wariness at the intrusion, birds resumed their chirping and flitting about through the desert scrub. Stately saguaros lifted their arms to the heavens, lonely guardians of their threatened domain. There were scattered homes out there, little ranchettes, much like Penelope's own, but they were swallowed by the vast desert. It was the reason people lived in and about Empty Creek. They were the descendants of the hardy pioneer stock, free-spirited and fiercely independent men and women who had settled in this harsh and forbidding landscape, recognizing their need to be away from crowded cities, to live in manners of their own choosing.

Big Mike sat between the two women, peering intently into the desert, his ears swiveling, taking in the sounds and sights that escaped Penelope and Nora. This was his territory more than theirs. On many a nocturnal stroll through the desert, he had learned its wonders and its dangers, absorbing the subtle nuances that meant the difference between life and death. He had stayed atop the food chain through courage and cunning and he had no intention of changing, even on a brief nature walk on a bright spring afternoon.

A small lizard darted from behind a barrel cactus and froze when Mikey stared him down. The big cat almost smiled and seemed to say, Good afternoon, Mr. Lizard, releasing him to go about his day. A lizard's work was never done.

No one spoke. They were unwilling to break the natural solemnity of the desert. Penelope had visited the great cathedrals of Europe — in Venice, Paris, Seville, London, Canterbury, and Durham — all chilled and hushed with the weight of time and countless knees bent in supplication. None were so majestic as this desert cathedral. It was her church of choice.

A soft breeze ruffled Penelope's hair. She brushed a strand away from her eyes. "We'd better go," she said reluctantly.

"Did she like the view?"

"Oh, yes."

"Who is this Ms. Fallowfield anyway?"

"My new friend. She's beautiful, with an excellent figure, like me, naturally."

"Naturally."

"Elfrida is also fearless, intrepid, trustworthy, loyal, and brave. She would be an excellent role model for Reggie. In short, Elfrida Fallowfield is one pretty hot babe."

"Like you?"

"Naturally." Penelope smiled. "Exactly like me."

"And where did Elfrida come from?"

"Now, that's an interesting question, and perhaps too illustrative of my warped personality, but I'll tell you anyway."

"Goody."

"Did you watch *The Avengers* when you were a girl?"

"Of course. Diana Rigg was my heroine."

"Me too. Well, anyway, Harry Duchette had Dominique tied to the railroad tracks with the 4:52 barreling down on her, and when I was wondering what a good mystery writer would do in solving Masterly's murder, Elfrida appeared."

"What does that have to do with Emma Peel and *The Avengers*?"

"I didn't realize it until now, but there was an episode where Mrs. Peel was tied to some railroad tracks. I think it was called 'The Gravediggers.' You see? It's really quite logical. Elfrida is Diana Rigg's successor."

Nora shook her head. "Definitely warped."

"Yes, isn't it nice?"

"Andy's so lucky to have you *and* Elfrida."

"Oh, I don't think Andy is ready for Elfrida. Sometimes, he can't handle me."

By the time they got to Lonesome Bend Ranch, where the second unit had been shooting rattlesnake scenes, the excitement was over and they had moved on to shooting horses in the corral scenes. The second unit, a small secondary crew, was responsible for the mundane shots unworthy of the director's attention — inserts, crowds, scenery, diamondback rattlesnakes.

Cricket, a pretty and petite woman with the silken hair of Rapunzel who would have been a refugee from the sixties had she been old enough, waved from her perch on the corral. Big Mike galloped over to say hello, hitting his mark perfectly, jumping to the top rail of the corral in a single mighty bound. Take that, Superman. Cricket was an old friend and he had once saved her life while dozing on her belly. She gave him a big hug.

Elfrida probably could have imitated Big Mike's leap — supple leather cat suits were good for that sort of thing — but Penelope and Nora wisely decided to restrain their enthusiasm.

"I was wondering when you'd get out here," Cricket said. "It's good to see you."

"You could come to town occasionally."

"You know how I am. I like it here."

Penelope nodded. "How's Noogy."

A dreamy smile appeared on Cricket's face. "That man sure can kiss, can't he, Nora?"

Nora also smiled, along with a deep red blush. After her divorce and when she had resumed dating, she, too, had once been an item with Noogy. *That man* knew how to treat a woman with respect and graciousness, among other things.

Not to be left out, and remembering the deep black pools that passed for *that man's* seductive eyes, Penelope felt the weakness in her knees again. She had once been tempted to leap in and swim a few laps with Noogy herself.

Juan-Carlos Estavillo was a short, fat, mustached reference librarian of Mexican descent who had recently given up his charter membership in the Señorita-of-the-Month Club for a more permanent relationship with Cricket. But so far as Penelope knew, he had not relinquished his fondness for the caramel nougats that provided his nickname.

Still, she wasn't there to discuss the sex life of Cricket and Noogy, although it would certainly be interesting. Cricket didn't work her way through Berkeley as a dominatrix named Mistress Juliana and writing XXX-rated novels on the side for nothing. "You girls compare notes while I go talk to some people about a rattlesnake bite."

"Penelope!" Nora wailed, her blush deepening. "You're impossible."

"Yep. Keep a record for me."

Shorty tipped his cowboy hat to Penelope. "Howdy."

"Are you all right?"

"Sure. No big deal. This kind of stuff happens."

"Shouldn't you go to the emergency room, just in case?"

"Naw," Shorty drawled. "This ain't the first time I've been bit. All they'd do is give me an antivenom shot, and Brock already did that."

"So I heard."

★ ★ ★

Penelope immediately sensed that Brock Hackett didn't want anything to do with her — he knew her only as one of many lowly extras and a meddling amateur detective — but the presence of Nora, the director's significant other, altered his mind set considerably, not necessarily for the better. "I thought we'd see you out here," Hackett said, "as soon as Tony's little spy rushed off."

"I don't know what you're talking about."

"Have it your way."

"Tell me what happened."

"The snake got frisky and Shorty didn't move fast enough. That kind of stuff happens sometimes," Hackett said. "No big deal."

Penelope wondered if Hackett had written Shorty's dialogue too. "Where'd you learn to give shots?"

"My mother was diabetic. I knew how to give her the insulin, just in case."

"Ever do drugs?"

Hackett backed away, raising his hands in denial. "Hey, don't try to lay that stuff on me. The only time I experimented, I didn't inhale either."

"Just asking."

★ ★ ★

"What were you doing out here today?" Penelope asked when they were back in the Jeep and heading for town.

"Making notes for the third edition of my book. If *Elephant* is a big hit, which I'm sure it will be, it would be nice to include a chapter on the making of the film. I wanted to learn everything I could, including how the second unit works. That's all. Why?"

"Just curious."

"So, what did *you* learn today?"

"I don't know, really." Shorty had been bitten by rattlesnakes before. That was certainly an interesting revelation. Brock Hackett knew how to administer a shot and thought Nora was a spy for Tony Lyme-Regis. But all of that, a half-off coupon, and a buck fifty would get you a Bloody Mary at the Double B on half-off night. It didn't mean either one of them had murdered Masterly. "I'm just gathering information," Penelope added. "That's what I do."

Information Acquisition Specialist. It wasn't a glamorous role like that of Elfrida Fallowfield, P.I. Penelope Warren, I.A.S., lacked that certain flair, but they also serve who only sit and analyze. Penelope wondered how many bytes were still available in her brain before the system overloaded and the hard disk crashed. *That* would be a useful bit of information to have.

"I'm definitely getting a cat suit," Penelope said. "I don't know why I've waited this long."

Elfrida Fallowfield wasn't going to have *all* the fun on this caper.

Penelope, Nora, and Big Mike arrived at Mycroft & Company in time to see a black stretch limousine disgorge most of the principals involved with *The Ears of the Elephant* in front of the Double B. Nora waved to Tony Lyme-Regis, who stomped after Brynn Moore, Stormy, and Amber Stark into the watering hole. He didn't see her.

"I wonder what that's all about?" Nora said. "It's too early to be done shooting for the day."

"Investigation is definitely called for. Come on, Mikey, Elfie, let's boogie on over."

"Me too," Nora cried.

"Of course, you too, silly. I didn't think you needed a formal invitation."

They found Tony bellied up to the bar, slugging down what looked suspiciously like a double scotch — neat. "Another large whisky," he said, "if you would, please, Pete."

Big Mike leaped to his customary stool next to Tony. Friends shouldn't drink alone. Besides, riding around the back trails was thirsty work. He was ready for a double saucer of nonalcoholic beer.

"What's wrong, darling? Shouldn't you still be working?"

"Indeed, we should but . . ."

Pete refilled his glass from a bottle of the good stuff from beneath the bar.

"Ah, thanks, old boy."

"Chardonnay for the ladies?" Pete asked. "I know what Big Mike wants."

"Thanks, Pete."

"So, what happened, sweetie?"

"Someone stole the production's entire supply of gaffer's tape. That's what bloody happened. Do you realize a movie cannot be made without gaffer's tape? Miles and miles of the bloody stuff."

"Why didn't you just send someone to the hardware store?"

"We did, old girl," Tony said, patting Nora's rump affectionately, which had a salubrious affect on his mood, "but we lost an hour."

"That shouldn't be enough to ruin the entire day," Penelope said.

"I'm not finished."

"Oh."

Before Penelope could find out what else had happened, Stormy interrupted, putting her hand on Tony's shoulder and giving him a quick peck on the cheek. "The barbecue's at our place tomorrow night," Stormy said. "You and Andy are invited."

"Who else is coming?"

Stormy smiled. "Tony and Nora, of course, Brynn and Bobby, Amber and Pete, Laney and Wally, and some of the usual suspects."

"Can I bring Elfrida Fallowfield?"

"Sure."

Chapter Thirteen

Penelope liked her dreams to be neat and
systematic with an orderly progression of
events, preferably tending to the lurid. She
did not like the stream of consciousness
dream where everything was all jumbled
up and it would take a team of psychia-
trists, working night and day — at several
hundred dollars an hour each — to unravel
hidden meanings. This particular dream
was all right up to a point. She didn't mind
being tied to the railroad tracks with gaffer's tape, listening to the lonesome
whistle growing louder, although her nose
itched and she was irritated at being unable to scratch it. Nor did she object to the
I.A.S. spray-painted on the left breast of
her floozy gown. That all had some basis in
reality, however distorted her subconscious made it. But when Big Mike
marched across the tracks with a cigar
perched at a jaunty angle in his mouth and
an apple pie balanced on his back — at
least, it looked like apple, but it might have

been peach — well . . . that was just too damned much.

It didn't help either when Laney and Nora — her two best friends in the entire world — strolled by, each wearing one of *her* matching cat suits, by the bye, carrying perfectly good back scratchers, talking of Michelangelo, and didn't even notice her plight. One of them might have had the common decency to scratch her nose. Penelope was positive that had their positions been reversed, she would have helped them out.

Whoo-whoo.

Surely, they could hear that damned whistle. Penelope cried out to her buddies, but no sound came. Wasn't that just like a dream? Get laryngitis at the most inopportune moment. She craned her neck and saw C.D. Masterly leaning out of the cab of the locomotive. He had a fiendish grin on his face. Vixen and Buffy Anne, dressed in skimpy cowgirl outfits, were on saddles atop the engine, waving lariats, and hollering Yippie ki-yi. What in the hell was that all about?

Masterly yanked on the whistle. Whoo-whoo.

Yippie ki-yi.

It was getting time to wake up — or

else. Penelope struggled to free herself from the tape.

Whoo-whoo.

"Ow, ow."

What kind of train whistle was that?

Yippie ki-yi.

"Ow, dammit, ow!"

Whoo-whoo.

Penelope awakened abruptly to find that she had Andy in a stranglehold.

"Sorry, I thought you were a train."

"Let me go," Andy croaked.

"Oh, yeah, right." She released him.

He sat up, rubbing his throat. "I'm going to have to start wearing body armor to bed."

"Meow," Big Mike complained from the foot of the bed. Some people around here are trying to sleep.

"Don't you look at me like that, Mikey, you know I don't like peach pie, so it better have been apple."

"Good God, what a way to start the weekend."

"I said I was sorry. How would you like it if your best friends wouldn't scratch *your* nose?"

"I wouldn't."

"There you have it," Penelope humphed. At least, the damned itch was gone.

★ ★ ★

"Stealing the gaffer's tape could be a practical joke," Penelope said, "but spray-painting X's and O's and the odd swastika on all of Stormy's and Brynn's costumes is malicious. Why would someone want to delay the production?"

Andy was dancing at the stove, scrambling eggs frantically, trying to keep them from sticking to the bottom of the pan. Penelope always kept a safe distance when Andy was stirring anything. During culinary enthusiasm, he had a tendency to throw elbows about wildly. "Graffiti vandalism?" he shouted over his shoulder. He punctuated the remark with the long wooden spoon, tossing a hunk of scrambled egg in Penelope's direction. She caught it deftly and popped it in her mouth.

"Wardrobe taggers?" she said. Penelope was rather dubious on that one. Empty Creek was remarkably free of graffiti, probably because of Dutch's enlightened policy of he who spray-painted the town, however artistically, got to spend their community service cleaning the police station — twice. For a relatively small town, it was a pretty big cop shop. Who wanted to waste their time scraping bits of congealed jelly dough-

271

nuts out of Tweedledee and Tweedledum's office? "And a ring of thieves stealing gaffer's tape in quantity?" Penelope added. "That doesn't make sense. Where would you go to fence gaffer's tape? Not even electricians need that much tape at one time."

Andy plopped the eggs on plates, added strips of bacon, a piece of toast for each, and fairly leaped the short distance from counter to table. *"Voilà,"* he cried. Presentation was everything.

Penelope absentmindedly picked up a strip of crispy bacon and pointed it at Andy. "Our teenagers tend to the more humorous practical jokes," she said, "not the malicious, so it's probably someone connected with the production. But why would anyone want to interfere with their livelihood?"

"Frustrated actor," Andy offered. "Frustrated writer, assistant director, cameraman, best boy, whatever that is, baby-sitter —" He paused to bite off the end of Penelope's piece of bacon.

"Hey, that's mine."

"I thought you were giving it to me."

Penelope wiggled her nose. "Someone who wants Tony to fail?"

"Who would that be?"

"I don't know. Frustrated actor, writer, assistant director, cameraman . . ."

"And why?"

Good question, Penelope thought. Awfully good question.

After breakfast, Big Mike lazed in a pool of light cast by Mr. Sun on the kitchen tiles. Fortified by several cups of coffee, Penelope was now her usual cheerful self, humming while she finished the crossword puzzle — in ink — and turned to the comics and *Citizen Dog* to see what Cuddles the Cat was up to. That done, she jumped up and grabbed Andy from behind, carefully avoiding his neck now that she was fully awake.

"Affection attack," she announced, planting several kisses about his head and shoulders — he was doing his manly thing and sitting bare-chested at the table.

"Hug attack," he cried, pulling her down into his lap and squeezing her tightly.

"Mmm," Penelope purred.

Big Mike snored. He was experiencing a nap attack, which was probably good. His humans could get embarrassingly silly on occasion.

"What should we do for lunch?"

"We just had breakfast," Penelope said.

"It's good to have a plan."

"So long as the plan is subject to change."

"Of course."

"Double B? Afterward, I'll go up and help Stormy get ready for the party."

"Sounds good to me. Wanna fool around till then? Work up an appetite?"

After her heartbeat returned to normal and a dual shower with Andy — they washed each other's backs thoroughly — Penelope headed for her little home office and the computer. She wiggled the mouse to wake the machine up from its nap, and after some whirring and clicking around signed on to the Internet, wading through the interminable advertisements, clicking no thanks on each until the system decided to let her poke around on the information superhighway. It took a while, but she eventually found Shorty's old extra card on a casting service out of Beverly Hills. There was a grainy color photograph of the extra turned wrangler, vital details — hair color, eye color, height, weight, age. Shorty listed no language fluency or accents or dialects. He was not willing to do nudity or semi-nudity. Under wardrobe he had listed Western, formal — Penelope couldn't imagine him in a tux — and business. His special skills included riding and anything with animals, including snakes.

But I already knew that, Penelope thought. She stared at the screen, willing something to be there that wasn't.

On an impulse, she typed in Vixen's name for the same extra casting service. After a brief wait, Vixen's photograph appeared. It, too, was grainy and did no justice to the young woman's beauty. Vixen said yes to semi-nudity and nudity. Surprise, surprise. Her wardrobe included doctor, nurse, formal, and exotic. Penelope tried to imagine Vixen with a stethoscope around her neck. No go. Nurse, maybe, but even that was difficult to visualize. Under special skills, Vixen had listed screaming and go-go dancing. Her measurements were 36-24-37. If the picture didn't entice a casting director, the vital statistics certainly would.

Penelope typed in Buffy Anne's full name and waited.

THAT SITE CANNOT BE CONTACTED popped up on the screen.

Brock Hackett.

THAT SITE CANNOT BE CONTACTED.

Who killed C.D. Masterly?

The Internet was growing impatient with her. THAT SITE CANNOT BE

CONTACTED, it repeated. And then, THIS MACHINE HAS PERFORMED AN ILLEGAL OPERATION AND WILL BE SHUT DOWN!

Good-bye.

Penelope was tempted to make a rude gesture, but refrained. If the information superhighway was going to be ill mannered, there was no need to reciprocate. Penelope exited the Internet, watched her screen turn deep blue, hit the snooze button on the computer, and sat back to wonder why Big Mike was wandering through her dreams, chewing on a cigar and packing an apple pie. That made at least as much sense as everything else connected with the case.

The Arizona Diamondbacks were on television when Penelope, Andy, and Big Mike walked into the Double B — rather, Penelope and Andy walked, Big Mike scooted for his bar stool. The Diamondbacks were in San Diego playing the Padres in a weekend series. "What's the score, Pete?"

"One-one, bottom of the second."

"Owooo," Penelope said.

"Owooo," Pete replied.

It was the battle cry of the Empty Creek Coyotes.

Penelope had asked for the score automatically, even though she wasn't a big Diamondback fan. She much preferred the Coyotes, an often inept but always fun minor league team with enthusiastic young players who hadn't yet been corrupted by agents, multimillion-dollar salaries, and fame. The Coyotes still played the game for fun, although each and every one of them hoped to make it to the Big Show.

Penelope led the way to a table where Hilly Hollander was sitting, working on a crossword puzzle.

"May we join you?"

"Of course, dear lady. I would be honored." He rose and pulled a chair back for Penelope. "What's a Frome?"

"Ethan," Penelope said. "From the novel of the same name."

"I haven't read it."

"Didn't you go to high school?"

"Yes."

"I'm surprised you haven't read *Ethan Frome*, then. Most high school students are forced to read it. Or the Cliffs Notes, more likely. It's no wonder we are raising a generation of illiterates who think literature begins and ends with *Playboy* and *Playgirl*."

"Don't get her started on the state of literature today," Andy warned.

"All right," Penelope said. "I'll be good."

Debbie took their drink orders — white wine for both — and bopped off to the bar.

"What's new in the tabloid world?" Penelope asked.

"I'm afraid they're rather skittish about my expense account still. I need a good scoop. Something along the order of who killed C.D. Masterly."

"Don't bother asking the Internet," Penelope said.

"You will give me the scoop, dear lady, when you solve the crime, won't you?"

"Wait just a damned minute here," Andy said. "She's not your dear lady, she's my dear lady, and *I* get any scoops around here, preferably before my Wednesday or Friday deadlines."

"Don't fight, boys, or I'll tell Lola LaPola first."

An attractive young woman — a stranger — entered the Double B and stood just inside the doorway, looking around with interest. Penelope saw her and thought that it was probably her first time in such a unique establishment. She wore an almond-colored ribbon lace slip dress that fell only to shapely mid-thighs and a matching shirt-jacket with three-quarter-length sleeves. The bodice was low-cut, revealing pale skin. Obviously, she was not a resident of Arizona. The outfit was a perfect complement to the soft blond hair and green eyes.

When she saw Penelope watching her, she smiled and walked over to the table.

"Can we help you?" Penelope asked.

"I've come to see Hilly Hollander," she said. "The people at the motel told me I might find him here."

Hilly looked up, a puzzled expression on his face, but didn't forget his manners in the presence of a pretty young woman. He hastily pushed back his chair and rose. "I'm Hilly Hollander," he said. "Are you from *The Millennium*," he asked. "About my expense account?"

"I'm Emily Horster, from Akron, Ohio." She raised her face for the expected kiss. Her friends in the sewing club would not have recognized her.

"Good God!" Hilly cried, slumping back into his chair.

"Is this a bad time?" Emily asked.

"I'm afraid it is, dear lady," he said, glancing at his watch. "I'm leaving for Ethiopia just now."

"He is not," Penelope said. "Perhaps you'd like to join us?"

"Thank you."

It was Andy's turn to play the gentlemanly role. He jumped up, pulled a chair out for Emily, and remained standing long enough to watch her cross her legs gracefully.

I'll get you for that, Penelope thought. "What brings you to Empty Creek, Emily?" she asked politely.

"Hilly sent for me."

"I did not."

"Of course you did, I have all your e-mails, and when you sent me your column, I just knew you were too shy to come right out and say it, but I'm yours, Hilly. I've already had my things transferred to your room, but I'll sleep on the couch until we get to know each other better."

Hilly tried again. Rather desperately, Penelope thought. "Madam, I'm gay," he proclaimed.

"I'll cure that," Emily said.

"No, he's not," Penelope said helpfully. This was getting good. "He has any number of ex-wives."

"That's why I'm gay, and I don't want to be cured."

"May I see his e-mail, please?"

Emily Horster delved into her purse and handed over a sheaf of hard copies.

Penelope glanced over them quickly. "You flirted with her?"

"I was answering a fan," Hilly protested.

" 'Describe yourself,' " Penelope read, " 'I have a vision of you that must be confirmed. I see you with long black hair and soft, pale skin, stark contrasts that amplify your beauty.' That's flirting."

"Mildly flirtatious, perhaps. I try to give my fans a thrill."

"I'd say there are grounds for breach of contract," Penelope said, turning to Emily. "I can recommend an excellent lawyer."

"Thank you."

"You can't sue someone you meet over the Internet," Hilly cried. "Whose side are you on anyway?"

"Palimony, perhaps," Penelope said.

Hilly groaned and gulped his Manhattan.

"Lots of people meet over the Internet and live happily ever after," Emily said, pinching one of his cherries.

"Lots of people meet serial killers over the Internet and don't live happily ever after. They don't live period."

"Are you a serial killer?"

"Of course not. I'm Hilly Hollander of *The Millennium*."

"Well, then, we'll just have to live happily ever after, won't we?" She looked up at Debbie with a demure smile. "I'll have one of whatever he's having," she said.

"Do you want me to stir it with my little finger?" Debbie asked.

Emily looked a little uncertain. "If that's the proper procedure."

"Welcome to Empty Creek," Penelope said.

Leaving the happy couple to get better acquainted — Emily Horster was pretty cute in a wholesome, Midwestern sort of way — Andy went home to fall asleep watching a golf tournament on television while Penelope and Big Mike headed up Crying Woman Mountain, narrowly missing the pothole that had tripped up Vixen on her nocturnal run. Penelope suspected the impromptu barbecue organized by Stormy was more to cheer up Tony than a desire to entertain sundry cast, crew, friends, and suspects. Her little sister always did have a big heart that reached out to anyone or anything in distress.

A barbecue at Stormy and Dutch's place was a down-home affair, informal to the max, which meant no limousines, no valet parking, no liveried bartenders, waiters, and waitresses, no reception line. So Penelope parked the Jeep herself and entered the shrine Dutch had created to his beloved. Big Mike ran off to the kitchen to greet his favorite aunt while Penelope paused to take in the scene. The living room was decorated with posters from Stormy's own career as a scream queen and a heroine of numerous sword and sorcery exploitation flicks, where she went through hordes of villains, evil wizards, depraved kings, wicked queens, and assorted aliens and otherworld creatures.

Stormy came out with a dish towel thrown over her shoulder. "Hey, sis, what are you doing out here?"

"I was actually thinking I'm going to miss these silly little movies now that you're moving into the mainstream."

"Oh, I've got a few good years left for wasting bad guys. After *Elephant*, Myron's got me booked for the lead in *Viking Pirate Queen and the Sultan*."

"Good old Myron."

Myron Schwartzman was Stormy's agent and the guardian of her career. It was Myron who had provided Cassandra Warren with her stage name of Storm Williams, a tribute to the burlesque queens he had loved in his horny youth from the front row of the old Hollywood Burlesque House in San Diego while stationed there in the navy.

"He's flying in for the barbecue."

"Bet I can tell you what his first words to me will be."

"No bet."

"So, Penelope, when ya gonna get an answering machine? Everybody's got an answering machine." Penelope did a pretty good imitation of the agent with the permanent croak in his voice.

Stormy laughed. "That's Myron all right. Come on back. Dutch is in the kitchen too."

Dutch looked more than a trifle silly in the apron that announced to anyone who could read that he was the cook, but Penelope decided it probably wouldn't be wise to point that out to him, not while he had the big barbecue fork in his hand anyway. She settled for "Hi, Dutch."

"No business today."

"What's that supposed to mean?"

Big Mike looked up from his bowl of liver crunchies. Yeah, what's that supposed to mean? Did I miss something?

"It means no discussion of C.D. Masterly, not one word. With that said, hi, Penelope, favorite future sister-in-law-to-be of mine."

"That's redundant."

"What is?"

"Future sister-in-law-to-be. Future or to be. Take your choice."

"It's conversation, for God's sake."

"It's still redundant."

"I changed my mind. You ain't my favorite future sister-in-law-to-be."

"Put the fork down and kiss me, you fool."

"Oh, okay."

"No French kissing though."

"What fun is that?"

"Oh, right. Okay, then, but just a little."

"When you two demented juveniles are finished screwing around," Stormy said, "there's work to be done."

While slicing and dicing various veggies to go along with a healthy dip Stormy had concocted, Penelope blithely ignored Dutch's dictate and reported everything she had been doing — the great rattlesnake bite, the expert administration of anti-venom, the apparent attempts to impede shooting the film, finally including asking a belligerent Internet who had killed Masterly. "That was in the leave-no-stone-unturned department," she said.

"Stormy's right. You are unbalanced."

"Well, wouldn't you be surprised if I'd gotten an answer. Please wait while we contact that Web site. And . . . the murderer is . . ."

"The way we're going, it was worth a try," Dutch conceded.

"A whole new concept in law enforcement. Web sites for killers. It would simplify things considerably. I like it."

"I don't."

"Frankly, neither does Elfrida Fallowfield."

Dutch knew better, but he asked anyway. "Who in the hell is Elfrida Fallowfield?"

"The new P.I. in town."

"Friend of yours?"

"We're very close. Elfie wears cat suits. You'd like her."

"I doubt it."

"She adores French kissing."

"Well, maybe. Where'd she come from?"

"My fertile imagination."

"Demented," Dutch said. "Truly demented."

"Fertile. When I'm stumped, Elfie takes

over for a while. Like now. You need an alter ego for tense moments, Dutch."

"I need a beer."

"That's good too."

Chapter Fourteen

When the guests began to arrive, Penelope assumed the role of assistant hostess, leaving Stormy free to greet each new arrival. Dutch was in the backyard tending to the barbecue, an ice chest filled with beer handy at his feet. Andy took up a post behind the bar and cheerfully dispensed drinks beneath a poster of Stormy chained to a stake in *The Last Bride of Satan IV*, her ample charms about to pop out of a torn and artfully disheveled dress. Penelope kept an eye on the munchies, making sure that each bowl and platter was promptly replenished, all the while keeping track of new arrivals. Not having been consulted about the guest list, Big Mike again took a post near the electric can opener in case Stormy had inadvertently invited a kleptomaniac specializing in such devices. It also gave him a view of both the living room and the patio, enabling him to follow the action.

Amber and Pete, Tony and Nora, and Brynn and Bobby arrived simultaneously, creating a crush at the door as Stormy kissed everyone and received kisses in return.

Vixen and Buffy Anne caused a momentary lull in the conversational din and a quick rise in some male temperatures when they showed up wearing black leather miniskirts and matching halter tops which, in the interests of modesty, might have been a little bigger. But they had probably chosen the outfits in honor of C.D. Masterly. After all, they were still in mourning.

"I'm definitely getting a referral," Nora whispered to Penelope.

"It is kind of overwhelming."

Hilly no longer looked so dismayed at having acquired a new friend. Emily Horster had changed into Saturday's fabric and color du jour, a hot number consisting of a black leather bustier that laced up the front and had two thin straps over her shoulders. Between the bustier and the matching black leather miniskirt, there was an inch or two of provocative belly button and flesh showing. Emily had gone Hollywood big-time, although she had a way to go to rival Vixen and Buffy Anne in the revealing-costume department.

Penelope was mildly shocked when

Dominique Anders and Harry Duchette entered together. Dominique even smiled when she greeted Stormy. The steamy nocturnal readings must be getting to her, Penelope thought, and Andy might have found his match in Harry for the stupid grin department.

Alexander and Kelsey towed Laney and Wally in. More kisses and some hugs for the Yorkshire terriers who lapped eagerly at Stormy's face, bestowing any number of dog kisses before they were released. They bounded nimbly through the room in search of Big Mike and the chow. Mikey was never hard to find. He was always somewhere near the food — or the women.

Samantha Dale and Big Jake came directly from riding and checked their hats at the door.

Shorty showed up with a beaming babysitter on his arm, to be followed in quick order by his medical benefactor of the day before, Brock Hackett, who was paired with a third assistant director — a stunning Eurasian, originally from Singapore, named Willie.

Craig Halliday came alone and left early to keep a secret rendezvous with a dancer from the Dynamite Lounge, cheerfully admitting to Stormy that he had promised to show Suzanne his trailer.

"Be nice," Stormy said, "or I won't be shooting blanks during our big gunfight."

"Just the trailer, ma'am," her costar replied.

When the noise assumed a comfortable level, Penelope decided to be a guest herself and sashayed over to the bar. "Hey, sailor, looking for a good time?"

Andy's grin was crooked. Apparently, his customers had been plying him with strong drink. "Sure. Meet you at the train station later?"

"No more trains," Penelope said, "but I'll think of something."

"Harry, I want you to meet a good friend of mine. This is Laney. Laney, Harry. You two have lots in common. You both have the damnedest imaginations for writing sex scenes."

"Have I been in one of your scenes?" Laney asked. "I've heard about you."

"No, I have recurring characters."

Dominique looked uncomfortable.

Laney appeared disappointed. "Tell me your specialties."

Dominique looked a lot uncomfortable.

"Well, last night, my heroine, a statuesque figure of a woman —"

"Excuse me," Dominique said, a tinge of red creeping into her cheeks. "I think I'll get another glass of wine."

Harry watched her go. There was a lot of woman to watch. Finally, reluctantly, he turned to Penelope when Dominique melded into the crowd at the bar. "I've changed the title," he said.

"I think that's wise under the circumstances. What's the new one?"

"*The Perils of Dominique.*"

"Hardly original, but probably apt."

"You were telling us about your heroine," Laney prompted. "I presume that yonder beautiful Dominique provides your inspiration?"

"Yes, although I've had to use my imagination a great deal in certain respects."

"Keep writing," Penelope said. "I think she's weakening."

"You really think so?"

"She hasn't attacked you recently, has she?"

"No."

"You see."

"Can we just get on with this? I'm all atwitter."

"Anyway, last night Dominique was tied to a pier in a wild and remote ocean cove."

"How can it be wild and remote if there's a pier?" Penelope inquired.

"Don't interrupt," Laney said. "I want to hear this."

"I'm just interested in accuracy," Penelope said.

"I'm interested in the juicy bits."

Penelope ignored her friend. "Wild and remote indicates, well, wild and remote," she said. "A pier is evidence of some degree of civilization."

"The cove used to be used by smugglers."

"I'll accept that," Penelope said, "for the moment."

"Thankfully."

"Okay, so the plucky Dominique is tied to one of the pilings and the tide is coming in faster and faster, lapping at her beautiful knees, her shapely and slender thighs, her provocative hips. . . ."

"Isn't she cold?" Penelope asked. "I assume poor Dominique has been deprived of her clothing."

"She's inflamed with desire for the hero. That keeps her warm. Besides, it's summer, and el Niño has warmed the ocean waters."

"Very thoughtful of you."

"What happens next?"

293

"That's where I stopped. I always leave her in a cliffhanger. Like the old Saturday afternoon matinees. *Nyoka of the Jungle* was my favorite."

"I wish I had some ocean coves in Arizona," Laney lamented. "I'm limited in the heroine-in-peril area."

"Horsewhipping, unspeakable tortures, evil cattle barons. That isn't enough for you?"

Laney smiled. "Yes, I have made good use of my material, haven't I?"

"I must pick up your books," Harry said. "For inspiration."

"I'm sorry I didn't get back to you sooner," Amber Stark said, "but I just heard from the last writer this morning. He's been out of town."

"And?"

"Masterly initiated each script and worked closely with the writers all along, not always to the best interests of the picture. Does that help?"

Penelope shrugged. "I don't know. It's more information for the equation, I suppose."

"I kind of hope you don't find him," Pete said, "not right away, at least. It's nice having Amber around."

"Don't worry, honey bunches," Amber said, squeezing his hand. "I'll be back. I crave more dance lessons."

Penelope withdrew to a corner of the living room, where she could observe the dynamics of the group, both inside the house and out on the patio. Tony's gloom of the day before seemed to have dissipated under the tender ministrations of Nora. She was sitting on the arm of his chair, her arm draped around his shoulders. By Penelope's timing, Nora leaned over and kissed him on an average of every thirty seconds. That would certainly keep his morale up.

Vixen and Buffy Anne were also on morale duty, flirting, and teasing Andy with one thing or another while he refilled their glasses. He was stammering, an excellent indication of his spirit. Although if they got any closer, Penelope would have to throw him in the pool to cool him off — or them, although it was a good thing for him to know he was attractive to other women, within reason.

Samantha and Big Jake were in a group with Stormy, Brynn, and Bobby Danes. Brynn and Bobby were holding hands. Big Jake's paw rested familiarly on Samantha's hip. They were laughing at a tale told by Stormy. Penelope hoped Stormy wasn't talking about her peculiar style of topless gardening to encourage healthy growth in her flowers.

Hilly and Emily were huddled in a corner, opposite Penelope. He evidently had abandoned his gay ploy, for he was surreptitiously trying to peer down her bustier while expounding passionately on some topic. Emily listened intently, nodding agreement, shifting slightly to allow a better view.

Dominique reclined on a chaise longue near the pool. Her eyes were closed. Harry had pulled a chair close and was whispering to her, perhaps finishing her latest adventure in the oral tradition, or even reciting a love poem. Penelope somehow doubted that he was discussing the weather.

Perhaps inspired by her talk with the screenwriter, Laney had taken Wally into the hallway, where they were doing what Laney and Wally usually did — necking. The woman was insatiable and probably belonged in Nymphomaniacs Anonymous, Penelope thought happily, along with everybody else in town, including her and Elfrida Fallowfield.

Yes, the Empty Creek water was hard at

work. Given time, it would cast its magical spell on Dominique too. Now, if it could only assist in criminal investigations as well as it aroused libidos.

"So, Penelope," Myron Schwartzman said, "when ya gonna get an answering machine? Everybody's got an answering machine."

"Never, Myron," Penelope said, smiling and leaning over to kiss his cheek.

"You're just doing it to irritate me. It ain't nice to irritate old men."

"You're not old, Myron."

"I will be if you don't get an answering machine. What if I need to get hold of Stormy in an emergency?"

"Leave a message on *her* machine."

"I do that. She never returns my calls. What kind of actress doesn't return her agent's phone calls?"

"The kind who lives in Empty Creek."

"Yeah, that kind. Who's the bimbo?"

"Which one?" Penelope didn't take offense. Coming from Myron, bimbo was a politically correct term of affection.

"The tall drink of water with the bazooms."

"Vixen DeVaughn. She's an aspiring scream queen."

"I think I'd better say hello."

Penelope followed to eavesdrop when he went over to Vixen and looked up at her. "You wanna be in pictures?" he said.

"I am in pictures," Vixen said. "Sort of."

"Let me tell you about *Viking Pirate Queen and the Sultan.* You do nudity?"

"When it's artistic and an integral part of the story."

"Oh, it is. See, the part I got in mind for you is the Viking princess who gets abducted and put in the sultan's harem. Your sister, she's the queen, naturally, has to rescue you."

"More than ten lines?"

"Of course," Myron said. He looked insulted. "I'm gonna make you the next Storm Williams."

"Sounds good."

"Better let me see your chest. Make sure you're right for the role."

Never turn down an audition. Vixen whipped off her halter top.

The men of Empty Creek went limp — in a manner of speaking.

"Omigod," Myron said reverently. "You'll do."

Under the influence of a third glass of wine, Penelope called a meeting of the

Empty Creek Floozies to order. "Are we going to stand for this?"

"Absolutely not!" Laney said. "I'm not about to be out-ravished on my home field."

"I don't know what we can do," Nora said. "I don't think I can get a boob job in time. I haven't even made an appointment yet."

Samantha Dale sighed. "I think we've lost."

"Big Jake was absolutely mesmerized."

"I know," Samantha said sadly.

"Have another glass of wine," Penelope suggested. Sometimes, it took a little inducement for Sam to shed the conservative bank president persona to be replaced by her deliciously wicked evil twin.

"Thanks, I think I will."

Penelope and the others kept swim suits at Stormy's, and there were a number of spares for guests. Penelope led the way into the girls' locker room, one of the guest bedrooms, to choose between the modest one-piece suit in white or the skimpy bikini in black. Well, someone had to uphold the honor of Empty Creek. Penelope went for scanty. "And you, Nora," she said, "don't even think of modesty."

Blushing right on cue, Nora pulled out

the sexy little number usually reserved for solitary evenings in the Jacuzzi with Tony.

"You too, Sam."

Samantha downed her glass of wine and reached for her bikini. The gauntlet had been thrown. It was definitely evil twin time.

Laney had no such compunctions and went straight for exciting and seductive.

There was a knock at the door and Stormy peeked in. "May Brynn and I join you?"

Good old sis and Brynn.

The parade of pulchritude through the living room to poolside was pretty impressive. The men of Empty Creek had no more chance than the lemmings on their way to the cliff or the children of Hamelin following the piper. Andy gaped and emptied a full bottle of wine into an already overflowing glass. Even the diminutive agent nearly dropped his cigar. Dutch, flipping burgers on the grill, tossed one right over his shoulder to the delight of Alexander, who got there ahead of Kelsey.

The only one who wasn't impressed was Big Mike, largely because the hamburger had landed in the dirt and the cavalcade of loveliness went directly to the pool, sat, and dipped ten shapely legs into the water, depriving him of a nice lap for a quick snooze. There were any number of things that could happen to a cat near water, and none of them was good. He settled for Buffy Anne's lap, which wasn't a bad thing entirely. At least she had the good sense to keep a respectable distance between herself and the water.

Kelsey, having missed out on the hamburger, bounded over to Laney, but misjudged her leap and went into the pool with a plop and a splash and a whine. This further inflamed the male audience, because Laney nearly lost her bikini top while rescuing Kelsey, who could swim perfectly well but wanted the attention. She handed the drenched Yorkie to Penelope, who put her on the tiles.

Kelsey scampered directly to Buffy Anne and Big Mike, where she shook her fur vigorously, sending water everywhere.

Big Mike growled in disgust at the unwanted shower. What a silly twit. Some dogs just didn't know anything.

Honor restored, the women pretended to ignore the stares of their men. There was going to be one bunch of horny dudes by the time this party was over.

"This is nice," Brynn said. "It's hard to believe that this time last week we were at C.D.'s party. Has there been any progress?"

"Not much," Penelope said. "We've sifted through a lot of information, but nothing solid yet."

"I hate the thought that I might be working with a murderer. Is there any chance that it was someone outside the film?"

"Not much, I'm afraid. Someone knew Masterly and his habits too well."

"Well, they're building the gallows for my lynching next week," Brynn said. "If you find the murderer, we could have a real hanging," she added grimly. "I didn't like C.D. much, but he didn't deserve dying like that."

The Masked Madman came out wearing a black Speedo and stood at the end of the diving board, eyes closed. It was time for a little staring on the part of the females present. It was readily apparent why Brynn liked Bobby Danes. He took a deep breath, and his taut, trim body cleaved the water with scarcely a splash. The floozies applauded enthusiastically while he swam the length of the pool and back effortlessly.

Apparently, someone had forgotten to hide the cooking sherry, because Tony Lyme-Regis mounted the board clad in a pair of gaudy boxer shorts and belly-flopped into the pool, dog-paddling mightily to the far end. The ladies gave him a five point five for effort and a nice round of applause. By the time he huffed his way over to Nora, Tony had entered the stupid grin contest with Harry Duchette and Andy, both of whom wisely refrained from the swimming competition.

If it was good enough for a mad Englishman, it was apparently okay for an Empty Creek native.

"My God," Penelope whispered when Big Jake jumped up and down on the diving board, "I hope you didn't buy those for him."

"I like them," Samantha protested.

Big Jake was certainly leading in the colorful underwear contest and, having found the resiliency of the diving board satisfactory, took a mighty bounce, curled into a ball, and did a credible backward somersault, right up to the point where he forgot to complete the dive, hitting the water still tightly wrapped in a ball. That splash nearly emptied the pool.

Feeling a little left out at his lonely post

behind the barbecue, Dutch did something uncharacteristic. He went over to his wife-to-be and nuzzled her neck. That wasn't so out of character, but his next action was. He pushed her into the pool.

Stormy, warmed up for some good nuzzling, shrieked before she disappeared beneath the surface. She came up flailing and spitting water.

Always quick to defend her little sister, Penelope gave Dutch a little nudge, enough to cause him to lose his balance. He teetered on the edge of the pool, arms windmilling frantically before he went facefirst into the water.

Tony, garish shorts billowing, played crocodile-on-the-Nile, swimming underwater to Nora's dainty ankles. The next thing that particular floozy knew, she was being carried off to his lair for a little underwater kissing.

"Bobby, no!" Brynn cried. "My hair."

Too late.

Star of stage and screen got a good dunking.

Samantha was held at arm's length — he could just as easily have been called Big *Strong* Jake — and slowly lowered into the water, kicking and laughing.

Penelope watched the water lap at

Samantha's beautiful knees, her shapely and slender thighs, her provocative hips, and wondered if Big Jake had been talking with Harry Duchette.

"Penelope doesn't like your shorts," Samantha said just before going under.

Laney scrambled to get out of harm's way, but Wally caught her at the Jacuzzi, carried her back to the pool over his shoulder, and unceremoniously tossed her in.

Kimberly was next. She put up the obligatory struggle, but she was no match for Shorty. He removed his cowboy boots and hat before jumping in after her.

Brock Hackett looked like he might remain standoffish, but the temptation to see Willie's black mane wet — and a few other things — was too great. Willie giggled and backed away, but not too quickly. She very much wanted to be a second assistant director.

Hilly and Pete looked wistfully at their dates but both refrained — each for different reasons — from dragging them poolside and throwing them in. Always fashion conscious, Hilly did not want to ruin Emily's outfit, although he wondered if the leather would shrink when wet. For his part, Pete didn't want to introduce

Amber to the wild mores of Empty Creek too quickly, for fear of scaring her away.

He needn't have bothered. Amber pushed him in and jumped in right after him.

Emily sighed. Sometimes a girl had to do everything. She threw a devastating cross body block at a shocked Hilly and they tumbled into the pool. That took care of that.

Penelope observed the splashing and dunking from the side of the pool. It was important to release energy, especially when you were not the one being dunked.

Dutch, however, a trained observer, saw Penelope getting off the hook entirely. "Get her, Wally," he ordered. It was probably all Penelope's fault anyway. It usually was.

Penelope, equally trained, immediately knew Dutch's command was not intended for the mail person. She dashed for the kitchen and safety.

Andy blocked the door. He was now clad in some geeky Bermuda shorts.

"You wouldn't."

He grinned fiendishly and caught her wrists.

"Traitor."

Wally took her ankles from behind,

pulling her feet out from under her. They carried her to the deep end of the pool and swung her back.

"One," the pool inhabitants chanted.

"I'll get you for this, Andy," Penelope cried. "You too, Wally."

"Two."

"Don't you dare!"

"Three!"

After the great water fight, everyone changed and lined up for the real meal of the event. Everything up to then had been prelude, little snacks to keep the stomach growls at bay. Big Mike and the Yorkies scarfed down in the kitchen, while everyone else sat at folding tabies scattered about the patio.

Penelope went into I.A.S. mode, but the only information she acquired, looking around the little gathering, was that the horseplay in the water seemed to have whetted any number of appetites. Good old Empty Creek water.

Penelope put her hand on Andy's shoulder. "Hurry up and eat," she said.

Buffy Anne stared at Emily Horster over a paper plate filled with a hamburger and coleslaw. "Don't I know you from somewhere?" she asked.

I.A.S. ears perked up.

"I don't think so. I just arrived yesterday. From Akron, Ohio. Have you ever been there?"

"No, but I'm sure I've seen you somewhere. Have you ever been in Los Angeles?"

"I was born there, but my mother moved to Akron when I was two. I've never been back."

"This is very weird," Buffy Anne said.

Despite an eagerness to be hitting the bedroom highway, Penelope took charge of cleaning up. Others joined in. Penelope washed. Brynn dried. "I don't know what it is about Empty Creek," the movie star said, "but I can't remember a time when I've felt better. There must be something in the water."

Penelope handed her a bowl and smiled. "Hormones raging?" she asked.

"As a matter of fact . . . I hope Bobby didn't forget his vitamins."

"I know!" Buffy Anne cried. "You were in C.D.'s scrapbook."

Penelope dropped the sponge in the sink and rushed to the door.

"A Constant Companion?" Hilly said. He was aghast.

"Not that one," Buffy Anne said. "The family scrapbook."

"What family?" Penelope asked, her heart leaping to somewhere in the vicinity of the moon.

"His long-lost family. He hired a private detective to find them."

Everyone stared at Emily Horster of Akron, Ohio.

"Why, I thought you knew," Emily stammered.

"Knew what?"

"C.D. Masterly was my half brother."

Chapter Fifteen

A beautiful sunrise filled the eastern horizon with streaks of pink that quickly brightened to red. To the west, the full moon that had been overhead when everyone finally got to bed lingered.

Penelope, Andy, and Big Mike missed it all.

Soon, the cloudless sky turned a deep and icy blue, promising a brilliant day.

Penelope and Big Mike missed it, although Andy sat on the back patio, drinking coffee, reading the Sunday paper, and marveling, as always, at the natural splendor all around him and the beautiful woman he loved.

When the sun bathed the surrounding hillsides in a golden light, Penelope missed it, but Big Mike joined Andy to sit in reverence watching over his domain — after a quick stop at the liver crunchy bowl. Sleeping was hard work, and the body needed sustenance.

When the woman of the house made her

appearance, tightly wrapped in a white Frette terry-cloth robe monogrammed with her initials in gold and the Peninsula Beverly Hills beneath the P.W., the slight morning chill had disappeared and Andy had brewed fresh coffee, timing her arrival to within five minutes.

"Thank you," she mumbled. He was further rewarded with the first kiss of the day.

"You're welcome."

On the other side of Empty Creek, half a dozen riders wound their way into the hills — something Penelope would be doing in the normal course of an Empty Creek Sunday morning. Usually, Laney and Wally would ride by with the dogs and Penelope would have Chardonnay saddled and ready, Big Mike in the saddlebag and they would ride off to the Double B for brunch. Andy, who preferred his horses on the other side of the corral, always went ahead to save their favorite table.

Oh, well, Penelope thought, tasting her coffee. After several sips she might be ready to try for a complete sentence. "Did you have any great revelations during the night?" she asked.

"The 4:52 didn't show, thank God."

"That's it?"

"It's not nice to wake up being choked

by the woman of your dreams. Dampens the relationship."

"I can see how it might." Penelope giggled. "I'll have to remember that choke hold in case I ever really need it."

"I hope you'll practice on someone else. How about you?"

"In the revelation department, nothing. Everything gets curiouser and curiouser."

"Well, we're not in Kansas anymore."

"You're mixing references."

"Sorry. I was a journalism major."

"All the more reason to be precise."

"Does that mean I can't be a network journalist?"

"Afraid so, sweetie." Penelope sighed. It was so much more convenient when a murder victim had a family or close friends. Often, the case could be tidily wrapped up almost immediately with the cops playing pin the rap on a fed-up wife or husband, angry sister or brother, irate son or daughter, enraged boyfriend or girlfriend, or a drunken friend. C.D. Masterly, however, had few friends, and no visible family in the beginning, and when one turned up, it consisted of a half sister with two-thirds of a continent for an alibi and a brother who was nowhere to be found.

Emily Horster had produced copies of two birth certificates — one testified to the birth of Clarence Davis Masterly and the second introduced Robert James Masterly to the world. Emily had been born one husband and three years later. "I didn't know any of this until my mother was dying. She was practically on her deathbed when she told me. She felt guilty all those years about leaving her sons with their father, but he beat her and she had to run away. She didn't have much luck with men. My father was abusive too. That's why she ran away to Akron with me."

"Did she ever try to contact them?"

Emily dabbed at tears trickling from her eyes. "No."

"Not even when C.D. became famous?"

"Especially not then. She didn't want to appear a gold digger. She was pleased that he had turned out so well."

"What happened to Robert?" Penelope asked.

"I don't know. Clarence became famous. Robert didn't."

"And you." Dutch pointed an accusing finger at Buffy Anne. "Why didn't you say anything about his family earlier?"

"They were lost," Buffy Anne said petulantly. "And C.D. wanted them to stay lost.

313

I think you should respect the wishes of the departed."

"Not when they might have assisted in the departed's departure. I ought to throw your butt in jail again for withholding evidence."

"Ms. Horster was in Akron," Hilly said, "and can prove it."

"What about the long-lost brother?" Dutch demanded. "I ought to throw all your butts in jail."

"It's not big enough," Penelope said.

"I'll build an extension and you can help."

The accusatory finger shifted to Vixen. "What's your sad tale?"

"I didn't know any of this," Vixen said.

"She didn't," Buffy Anne said. "C.D. told me only because he was feeling maudlin one night when Vixen was at her acting class. It was the only time I ever saw him cry."

And that was that.

"Oh, balderdash," Penelope said, sighing again. She was also annoyed at the sleep she had missed since the film company had moved into town. It was one thing to stay up half the night listening to Emily Horster relate a convoluted tale of a dysfunctional family that made soap operas seem role models for the American family structure, but it was quite another to have to get up before noon and report to the police station for another go-round. Damn that Dutch anyway. There were civilized hours for conducting police business. And she was down for another early call on Monday morning. Damn Cecil B. De Mille too, or whoever it was that started the precedent of making movies in the middle of the night.

"I just love the way you say *balderdash*. It's so sexy."

"I picked it up from Elfrida Fallowfield."

Chardonnay whinnied disappointment after breakfast. The mare knew it was Sunday morning and time for the ride down to the Double B. Penelope reassured her that nothing was wrong in the equine world, a statement that she couldn't make for the rest of Empty Creek.

Driving through town, normal people were going about ordinary activities — heading for church, breakfast, or brunch, the stables for a morning's ride through the desert, a pick-up softball game — or sleeping in. Damn them too.

Grumpy old police chief was about to meet a grumpy blonde and an even grumpier cat.

"Want a jelly doughnut?" Tweedledee said.

"Bleeh. Don't you keep anything good around here? A nice English muffin, for instance? Or a bagel?"

"Bagel or muffin?" Tweedledum asked. "I got some for you."

"You did?"

"Know how you get."

"I'm touched. Thank you."

"Which is it? Bagel or muffin?"

"Bagel."

"Coming right up."

"No," Penelope said. "A muffin."

"Jeez, make up your mind."

"Muffin. Definitely muffin. And coffee. Lots of coffee."

"Andy?"

"Coffee, please, and a muffin."

"You're sure?"

"I was a journalism major. I'm very precise."

"So, what do you make of it all?" Dutch asked. He had his feet crossed on the desk and stared at Stormy's movie poster for *Amazon Princess and the Sword of Doom*. He had reluctantly left the warmth of her body against his and her comforting arm thrown possessively over his chest for this

— a conference where people couldn't even make up their minds whether to have bagels or muffins. He could think of any number of ways to spend a day off, most of them involving chasing Stormy around the house.

"I was hoping, for once, you could tell me," Penelope replied.

"Stumped, huh?"

"Yep."

"Anyone want to hear my theory?" Tweedledee asked, coming through the door with coffee cups and toasted muffins artfully arranged on a tray.

We might domesticate him yet, Penelope thought. "Not really," she said.

"Come on, be nice."

"Sorry. We'd love to hear your theory so long as it doesn't involve Vixen DeVaughn."

"Oh, never mind."

"Law offices," Miss Matilda Grimes answered.

Good, Dutch thought, hoping she had left a nice warm cuddle behind, but he doubted it. "Stanley Barkingham, please," he said.

"Who shall I say is calling?"

"The person who arranged this call. Police Chief John Fowler of Empty Creek, Arizona."

"One moment, please, I'll see if Mr. Barkingham is available."

"He'd damned well better be!" Dutch shouted, but Miss Grimes didn't hear. She had already cut him off.

Dutch drummed his fingers impatiently while he waited for the attorney to pick up. After an interminable wait, Barkingham's speaker phone squeaked.

"This is Stanley M. Barkingham."

"What's the M stand for?"

"Montgomery. Is this germane?"

"Just curious. I like to know who I'm dealing with."

"Who's calling, please?"

Dutch rolled his eyes. "Police Chief John Fowler. Doesn't your secretary tell you anything?"

"Oh, yes," Barkingham said. "I've been expecting your call. Are you alone?"

"Is that germane?"

"I like to know who I'm dealing with."

"Stop playing mine is bigger than yours," Penelope said crankily.

"Who's that?" Barkingham demanded.

"Penelope Warren. She's assisting in our investigation. Detectives Larry Burke and Willie Stoner are also here, along with Harris Anderson, editor of the *Empty Creek News-Journal*."

"Is that wise?" Barkingham asked. "To have a reporter present?"

"Not if there's nothing to hide."

"Yes, well, I suppose you know your business."

"Yes, I do."

"I should be at the Peninsula hotel right now," Barkingham complained. "The Belvedere restaurant serves an excellent champagne brunch. Dom Pérignon."

"I know," Dutch said. "I've been there."

"You have?" The attorney sounded dubious about a backwoods sheriff ever having been . . . well, out of the backwoods.

"I always stay at the Peninsula when I'm in town."

"So do I," Penelope said. "Doesn't everyone?" The Peninsula Beverly Hills was the best hotel she had ever stayed in — witness her Frette robe — although the old Norfolk in Nairobi was more exotic with its mosquito nets and the long bar where Lord Delemere and his cronies drank and fought around the turn of the century, but if the Beverly Hills city council allowed mosquitoes within the city limits, the Peninsula would have state-of-the-art mosquito nets. Penelope was sure of it.

"Can we just get on with it?" Dutch said.

"There's no need to be curt."

"There is a need to find out what the damned will says. Today, if at all possible."

"I'm looking, I'm looking. Poor C.D. kept changing the will."

"You'd think you could remember your client's latest wishes. What about a brother, for God's sake. Can you remember that?"

"C.D. had no brother. He had no family. He kept changing things for his latest slattern. Ah, here it is . . . hmm . . . in this case, three slatterns."

"Do they have names?" Dutch was about to reach into the speaker phone and grab the shyster by the throat.

"Dominique Anders, Vixen DeVaughn, and Buffy Anne Mulholland."

"Yes!" Tweedledee cried, snapping his fingers. "The missing motive."

"And opportunity," Tweedledum said. He cracked his knuckles.

"Along with accomplices," Tweedledee added gleefully. "I like it. What do you think now, Penelope?"

"Meow," Big Mike said. Are you finished with that bagel?

"Get 'em in here," Dutch said. "Now."

"Can I go to brunch now?" Stanley M. Barkingham, Esquire, whined.

"In a minute."

320

★ ★ ★

For one hundred sixty-eight hours — a full seven days — Penelope, Big Mike, and the authorities had floundered with a plethora of suspects and a paucity of meaningful leads. Now, in the space of less than twelve hours, their victim had suddenly acquired an estranged family and three of the suspects had abruptly been provided with sufficient motive to hasten the demise of the late C.D. Masterly.

Unfortunately, the latest developments, while interesting, didn't clarify the situation one damned little bit for Penelope. Tweedledee and Tweedledum were ready to clap the three beautiful beneficiaries in irons to await trial, conviction, and execution by lethal injection. There were still the nagging details like a missing hypodermic needle and some incriminating fingerprints, which they would probably never find, a rattlesnake, which they would probably never find, and even if they did, so what? "All right, talk, or we're going to make rattlesnake chili out of you and your loved ones." Penelope was ready to take up a new hobby, something quiet and sedate, like climbing Mt. Everest in her bikini.

Tweedledee thought it was too bad that

they couldn't take one or another of the women up to the roof and dangle her over the edge by her heels until she confessed like the cops in *LA. Confidential.* It was Tweedledee's favorite movie — he had seen it twenty-two times, even before it came out on video — and thought it should be a required training film for police officers. He'd have to start with Buffy Anne because she weighed the least. He wasn't sure he could hold Dominique or Vixen very long. Of course, since the Empty Creek P.D. was only two stories high, it might not have had the same impact as in the film. And, unlike James Ellroy's creations, they were hampered somewhat by the unenlightened attitude of the Supreme Court toward confessions garnered in such a manner. Too bad. Tweedledee sighed. Sometimes he longed for the good old days.

"Nope," Penelope said. "They didn't do it."

"Why not, Miss Smarty Pants?"

"Too complicated," Miss Smarty Pants answered. "All they had to do was give Masterly the hotshot and go to bed. They wake up, find the body, and dial 911. Coroner rules accidental death by an overdose of cocaine. They're home free. Why screw everything up with rattlesnakes and running around naked?"

"We're not talking IQ here. Everybody knows Masterly was a jerk. They hated him and wanted him to suffer before they made him dead."

"Penelope's probably right," Dutch said, "but this is what were going to do when they get here. . . ."

"Aw, man."

"Don't whine. You sound just like Stanley M. Barkingham, Esquire."

The three women were shown into Dutch's office and offered coffee and their choice of jelly doughnuts, English muffins, or bagels. They accepted coffee and declined food in a figure maintenance gesture.

When everyone was settled, Dutch said, "We've just gotten some information, which you should know about."

"What's that, Chief Fowler?" Dominique asked pleasantly. As the personal assistant to Mr. Lyme-Regis, she outranked the stand-ins and naturally took charge.

"C.D. Masterly's will leaves everything to the three of you to be shared equally."

Dominique Anders listened to Dutch's terse announcement impassively. Vixen

DeVaughn was stunned and nearly dropped her coffee cup. Buffy Anne Mulholland's fist flew to her mouth. "I can't believe it," she said.

"Me neither," Vixen said.

"Shouldn't you be reading us our rights?" Dominique suggested coldly. "I assume we've just moved to the top of the suspect list."

"You got that right," Tweedledee whispered.

"Oops," Vixen said. "George is going to be mad at us."

"All I said was I can't believe it."

"He said not to say anything."

"I know, but . . ."

"Ladies, please," Dutch said. He recited the Miranda warning for them and then allowed Vixen to use his telephone to call George Eden's beeper. He called back almost immediately, and fifteen minutes later was in Dutch's office.

"Circumstantial," he said immediately. "How much did they inherit?"

"A lot," Dutch said.

Buffy Anne could save a substantial portion of the rain forest with her share and still have enough left over to make Rodeo Drive look like a ghost town, Penelope thought.

"It's still circumstantial."

"We just want to ask a few questions. One, actually, but three answers."

"I'd like to confer with my clients."

"Fair enough."

They were gone for ten minutes. When they returned, George Eden nodded. "Go ahead and ask your question."

Dutch looked at Dominique. "Did you know that you were named in the will?"

Again, the defense attorney nodded, giving permission for her to answer.

"No," Dominque replied firmly.

Dutch asked the same question of Vixen and Buffy Anne. Each immediately replied in the negative.

"I still think they did it," Tweedledee said. "They're all actresses, for God's sake, and they had time to rehearse when they were with Eden."

Penelope didn't bother to point out that Vixen was the only one with acting ambitions.

"I didn't say it was a great plan," Dutch said. "But at least we know what you have to do."

"What's that, boss?"

"Get me some damned evidence."

Penelope thought that was a very good

plan, indeed, and resolved to put Elfrida Fallowfield on the trail immediately. She'd had enough vexing developments for the moment and had other plans for the afternoon.

Despite her resolve to ignore the case for a few hours, Penelope dragged Andy and Big Mike out to Frontier Town. She craved a frozen yogurt and that was as good a place as any to get it. And there was always the chance that she might run across a saboteur with a motive to slow production *and* kill a famous director.

Frontier Town was busy with tourists attracted by *The Ears of the Elephant*, although there wasn't much evidence of the film on Sunday afternoon except for the half-finished gallows on the street in front of the jail. Base Camp Elephant was cordoned off and now patrolled by rent-a-cops in an attempt to prevent further sabotage. AUTHORIZED PERSONNEL ONLY, a new sign proclaimed. So much for a happenstance encounter with a killer, saboteur, or practical joker.

The gallows, even incomplete, was a grim edifice and sent shudders racing up and down Penelope's spine, and she squeezed Andy's hand tightly. The thought of someone dying in such a manner horrified her, even if it was make-believe.

Big Mike bounded up the steps that Brynn Moore would slowly climb a few days hence. The script called for Brynn to be rescued at the last moment, of course, during a diversion caused by Stormy, who would set the weekly stagecoach on fire and send it racing headlong down the street. While everyone rushed to stop the stampeding horses and extinguish the blazing coach, Stormy would face down the vigilantes, blasting two or three of them in the process, throw Brynn on the saddle of a waiting horse, and gallop out of town in a wild shootout.

The trapdoor on the gallows clanged open.

"Meoargh!" Big Mike exclaimed as he dropped into the darkness.

"Now what, Mikey?"

Penelope and Andy hurried around the base of the gallows and found the entranceway.

Always casual and nonchalant when he screwed up, Big Mike looked up and seemed pleased at having ensured the trapdoor on the gallows worked. It was one less thing for Tony to worry about. Penelope knew it was a cover-up. He hated to be embarrassed, like falling off the windowsill in the kitchen while napping in the warm sunlight. He kept doing it despite the logic that said he was too big for the narrow space provided, but each time he pretended he had done it on purpose. Now Big Mike batted at a tattered cover from a script of *The Ears of the Elephant.* There were always scripts and parts of scripts lying around, carelessly left behind by one or another of the company. Penelope picked the cover up. There was a block B written on the top corner. Probably Brynn's copy had gotten loose from the fasteners — two fasteners, although it had been three-hole-punched, that was a movie rule — that held it together while she studied her lines. There were some other pages lying about as well. Penelope shook her head. Film people weren't supposed to litter the local countryside. That was one of the rules too. She picked everything up and tossed it in a handy trash receptacle.

"Come on, Mikey, Andy's going to buy us a frozen yogurt."

Cool.

"I am?"

"Did I forget to tell you?"

"I thought you were on to some hot lead."

"I hope they have pistachio nut today."
Penelope had to settle for nonfat cherry.
That figured, she thought. Just like every-
thing else around here lately.

Chapter Sixteen

Penelope once heard that if you ate a frog promptly upon rising, it was the worst thing that could happen to you all day. She didn't believe it. A toad, probably. Swallowing a goldfish, maybe? And whoever said it didn't live in Empty by God Creek, Arizona, and never had to get up for an early morning trek to Base Camp Elephant without a limousine. Her eyes were open, but she was on automatic pilot driving through the deserted streets, shifting smoothly, sipping coffee, observing speed limits, traffic lights, and navigating precisely to her intended destination rather than someplace like Tucson or Santa Fe, which was a distinct possibility for one of the living dead — and this was accomplished without the assistance of Big Mike, who had jumped into the Jeep and fallen asleep again before he hit the seat cushion. All in all, it wasn't a bad feat for a woman whose soul was still in bed back at the old ranchette.

No longer a virgin, Penelope sleep-walked past the baby-sitters, ignoring Milan Penwarden's and Kimberly Ferrell's attempts to flag her down to check in, wiggling her fingers limply at them on her way to the coffee urn to join other former virgins on call for the day. She was greeted with a chorus of good mornings. Penelope nodded and poured coffee. There would be time for the niceties when additional caffeine propped her eyelids open.

The scenes to be shot that day called for the floozies, Penelope and Nora first, and then Laney and Samantha, to visit the local mortician's office, where two of Craig Halliday's cutthroat gang had been laid out for viewing. It was appropriate for the floozies to pay their last respects to their former customers, killed when they attempted to ambush Stormy, who was having no part of *that.* The ladies in the Temperanee Union would make their appearance at the mortician's to tut-tut their disapproval of such wild goings-on in their town.

"Quite some revelation at Stormy's," Nora said. "And then to find out Masterly left everything to his girlfriends . . . well . . . they must feel like they won the lottery."

"Unless," Laney said, "their particular lottery was rigged."

"I really can't believe one or all of them killed him. They seem so nice. Even Dominique is warming up. What do you think, Penelope?"

"I think . . . I think . . . I hear a blueberry muffin calling my name."

"No blueberry muffins," Nora said. "In fact, no muffins. Just Danish."

"What kind of movie set doesn't have blueberry muffins? I'll bet the assistant directors have muffins."

"You're not going to start a muffin fight, are you?"

Penelope glared at the Danish. Who wanted Danish when the tummy was all set for a blueberry muffin? She measured the distance to Milan Penwarden before realizing it was too early and her arm wasn't properly warmed up. "No," she relented, "but can't you use your influence with Tony to better our morning fare?"

"He hardly slept at all last night. He's getting paranoid about what might happen today. He doesn't want to fall behind and go overbudget on his first feature film."

The eastern skies had lightened somewhat, when a hideous shriek, sounding much like Big Mike the time Grandmother Warren had inadvertently introduced him to the perils rocking chairs held for creatures with handsome tails, rang over and through Frontier Town. It was immediately followed by a second screech and a third.

Penelope jerked awake — finally — and ran to the sound of trouble.

She was followed by a gaggle of floozies and temperance ladies.

Another day of adventurous filming was under way.

A floozy gown flew from the doorway of wardrobe and landed on the head of a seamstress. She screamed and danced, attempting to dislodge the offending garment from her body. That accomplished, she brushed frantically at her clothing, dancing all the while as though someone had filled her shoes with hot coals.

Mrs. Finney leaped from her wardrobe domain with an alacrity that belied her stoutness. She, too, was frenzied and joined her assistant's dance, brushing wildly at her ample bosom. What they lacked in choreography, they made up for in energy, rather like two women in the throes of delirium tremens. "Get them off me!" Mrs. Finney screamed. "Get them off me!"

Big Mike, who had taken the lead,

skidded to a halt. He had no intention of joining *that* chorus line.

Penelope nearly stumbled over Big Mike, but managed, with some delicate footwork of her own, to avoid him. The gaggle thundered to a halt.

The trailer rocked. Inside the wardrobe department, someone was tap dancing on a table and shouting, "Help! Help! Save me!"

Penelope and her band of rescuers were more than willing to save the wardrobe department, but from what? "What's wrong?" Penelope shouted.

"Bugs!" Mrs. Finney cried. She was now ripping her clothes off and flinging them away. Her blouse landed on top of the trailer. Her skirt went underneath. The striptease went on until she and her assistant were hopping around in their underwear.

It was too bad Myron Schwartzman wasn't present for the burlesque retrospective, Penelope thought, although Mrs. Finney couldn't match the likes of Tempest Storm and Irma the Body.

"Bugs!"

Penelope advanced rather tentatively. While she wasn't particularly afraid of bugs, deranged women were quite another matter. Drawing closer, she leaned over and saw a tiny black shape scurry for safety beneath the trailer, its little pointed tail curved aloft. She straightened up and announced, "Those aren't bugs, they're scorpions."

Identification of the order Scorpionida did not have a fortifying impact on Mrs. Finney. "Scorpions!" she screamed, taking off in bizarre emulation of Vixen De-Vaughn's midnight run, followed closely by her assistant. Legs pumping, arms flailing, they thundered through Frontier Town, much to the amazement of cast and crew.

"Now what?" Anthony Lyme-Regis said, watching his wardrobe department, clad only in foundation garments and support hose, disappear around the corner of the jail.

"Don't leave me!" the unseen tap dancer cried.

The wardrobe call — and subsequent filming — was delayed while about a million little black scorpions were shaken out of the costumes that Mrs. Finney and her assistants had worked frantically all weekend to clean and restore from the damage inflicted by the mysterious spray can wielder. So much for the security provided by rent-a-cops. Mrs. Finney, fully clothed again but no less hysterical, was near to a complete nervous breakdown. Still, she shook floozy gowns energetically, shrieking whenever another scorpion flew out. The floozies — hardy souls all and used to the vagaries of desert life — pitched in. Penelope, armed with a broom, swept scorpions out the door gently. After all, it wasn't their fault. They didn't particularly want to be in the wardrobe department when they could be out doing whatever it was that scorpions did to while away their lifespan — probably foraging for food and procreating, just like humans. Penelope did wish, however, that Mrs. Finney would stop all that hollering. It was getting on *her* nerves. They were just little scorpions, for God's sake.

Things were back to normal on the set of *The Ears of the Elephant*, which was to say the atmosphere was remarkably peculiar. Not only had someone brutally murdered the film's original director, but someone was certainly trying to undermine the production. It had to be one and the same person — but why? The heiresses stood to benefit by Masterly's death, but what reason could they have for trying to delay or shut down production of *Ele-*

phant? Others among the film's company or hangers-on had revenge motives for wishing to see Masterly dead, but even the killer should want to get paid. It was the American way.

Wasn't it?

Penelope was putting on her bonnet — the head floozy was concerned about her delicate skin complexion being exposed to the desert sun — when Lora Lou Longstreet cried out, "I've been bitten." She then let loose a string of words that would hardly be uttered by a lady of the Temperance Union.

Penelope dropped her hat — an ugly white number with feathers — and leaped to Lora Lou's assistance.

"Ow, damn, it got me again." She pulled the shoulder of her dress away. Penelope reached in and held up a straight pin.

"Oh," Lora Lou said sheepishly. "It felt like a scorpion."

Milan Penwarden clapped his hands briskly. "It's time, ladies."

Penelope had lost all track of where they were in the script. This business of skipping around from scene to scene was irritating. How was a floozy supposed to get into character when one day Tony was filming interiors in the middle of the script and shortly thereafter moved to exteriors some forty or fifty pages away and out of context? She complained about this all through rehearsal and while waiting for the dearly departed to arrange and compose themselves in their respective coffins.

"You're just being obstinate," Nora said.

"Is it too much to ask for a little continuity?"

"Yes."

"Oh, all right, then," Penelope said cheerfully. "Who are the deceased? What are their names?"

"I don't know," Nora said. "Corpse Number One and Corpse Number Two in the script."

"How am I supposed to mourn people named Corpse Number One and Corpse Number Two?"

"Think of them as Tom and John."

"Real cowboys aren't named Tom and John."

"Ellsworth and Hector, then."

"For lack of time, I suppose Ellsworth will have to do." Penelope closed her eyes and took a deep breath. Exhaling slowly, Penelope opened her eyes. "Poor Ellsworth," she said, "he was a good boy really. Respected his mama. And he was a big

tipper. I'm sure going to miss them tips."
Solitary tears trickled from each of
Penelope's eyes.

"My God," Nora said. "That's good.
How'd you do it?"

Penelope sniffed, still caught in the emotion of Ellsworth's passing. "I," she announced imperiously, "am an actress,
dahling."

"You are a fraud."

"That too," Penelope agreed promptly,
"but I'm damned good at it."

"All right," Tony shouted. "This is a take."

Everyone who had shouting in their job
description shouted something.

"Action!"

A fly lit on Corpse Number One's nose
and rubbed its little paws together. Old
Ellsworth was a trouper. He didn't even
twitch. Now, that was acting, Penelope
thought. If she hadn't watched him climb
into the coffin and repose himself, she
might have thought he really was dead or
that Tony had obtained a real body somewhere for added verisimilitude. Penelope
moved on to Corpse Number Two, restraining an urge to applaud Corpse
Number One's performance.

An equal opportunity pest, the fly
buzzed over to Corpse Number Two's

cheek and walked boldly up to his eyelid. Probably Corpse Number Two did not have the same experience as Corpse Number One. Indeed, that was doubtless the reason he was relegated to the secondary role in the first place. His lips curled. He opened his eyes.

"Cut!" Tony said. "Lose the damned fly, please."

A third assistant director leaped forth with a fly whisk. Penelope hadn't seen a real fly whisk since Africa. She had to give credit to the moviemakers. It would never have occurred to her to have a third assistant director in charge of losing flies with an authentic fly whisk. Now, that was logistical planning at its best.

"This is so exciting," Emily Horster said at lunch.

"Yes, it is," Penelope said politely. She really wanted to point out that's because Emily hadn't been standing around in the hot sun all morning, wearing a stupid bonnet, in front of two make-believe corpses, while the cameraman polished his lens.

"Tony graciously offered Emily a small role in the crowd scene at the lynching," Hilly Hollander said.

"I can hardly wait. They'll never believe it back in Akron. Me. In a real movie."

"You'll be a triumph, dearest."

"Canceled your reservations for Africa?"

"Oh, yes," Hilly replied smoothly with a wink.

Well, at least someone was happy, Penelope thought. She speared a stalk of steamed broccoli and admired its delicate contours. "Just by the bye, Emily, you haven't seen your missing brother around the set anywhere, have you?"

"Oh, I wouldn't begin to know what he looks like. I have no memory of him at all."

The afternoon was devoted to watching a confrontation between Stormy and Craig Halliday before the gallows. The floozies were in the background behind Stormy, while the Temperance Union looked on approvingly from behind Halliday and his gang.

"I'm going to kill you one of these days," Stormy said pleasantly.

Halliday flipped his duster back and was ready to draw. "No time like the present," he drawled.

Penelope cringed. It sure wasn't "make my day" dialogue.

"Another time." Stormy smiled. "When

the odds are better. Like six to one instead of ten to one." She turned deliberately and walked away.

Halliday's hand twitched at the butt of his revolver, but even he couldn't bush-whack the second lead in the back on the main street of town.

"Cut," Tony said. "Very nice. Very nice, indeed, but I'd like to do one more, please."

Between takes, Penelope ducked beneath the gallows to check on Big Mike. He had taken a liking to that particular hidey-hole. It was cool and inviting in comparison to the dusty main street of Frontier Town. Winter was definitely over and the temperature was climbing daily. They would soon be in a string of days when the temperature would be above a hundred for weeks on end, but it was a dry heat as the skeleton on a popular T-shirt proclaimed.

Big Mike stretched and yawned, arching his back, beneath Penelope's touch. His claws uncovered a computer disk. Penelope picked it up. There was no identification on the little sticky thing.

"Places, everybody." Several dozen voices repeated the command.

"See you later, Mikey." Penelope hurried out and grabbed a bullhorn from an assistant director. "Anybody lose a computer disk?" Her voice echoed through Frontier Town.

When no one claimed it, Penelope shrugged, returned the bullhorn, and slipped the disk into her purse, which was just as ugly as her bonnet.

"The set is up!"

By the time shooting wrapped for the day, most of a full moon had climbed above distant mountains surrounded by the bright pinpricks of stars. The moon looked like a pale hole in the black sky, the opening to a tunnel where answers might be found.

Penelope opened the door of the Jeep and Big Mike leaped in, bounding across to his seat. Penelope climbed in wearily. Shooting two pages of script a day was damned hard work, and she was glad they weren't doing a television show where ten or twelve pages each day was the norm. Slipping the key in the ignition, she saw a rectangular piece of paper taped to the horn. She switched on the interior light and read a piece of dialogue from the *Elephant* script.

It came from the scene when Craig Halliday warned Brynn Moore to leave the valley. Penelope had watched when the scene was filmed. Halliday made a fine villain, and he delivered his lines vehemently, dripping with menace.

"Sell out," he said, "and get out, or else."

"We'll see about that," Brynn retorted bravely.

"Yes, we will," Halliday said. He smiled, but there was no warmth or humor in his expression. It was the smile of evil.

"We'll see about that," Penelope repeated, ripping the dialogue from the horn and sticking it to the dashboard, but she didn't feel any more effective than Brynn during the filming. The words from the movie were mere bravado. Brynn knew it then. Penelope knew it now.

There was a bad moon rising.

Despite the warning, Penelope was not particularly frightened — yet. The parking lot was crowded, and she took the time to plug the portable CD player into the Jeep's cigarette lighter, opened the console, and riffled through the discs. Big Mike said, "Meowrr." Penelope knew what that meant. He wanted to hear Jimmy Buffett's "Let's Get Drunk and Screw," while she was ready for a little Credence Clearwater and "Bad Moon Rising." It was appropriate for the moment, but she was nothing if not always fair to the extreme. She took a quarter from the change compartment — she kept loose change handy in case somebody suddenly erected a toll bridge without her knowledge — and said, "I'll flip you for it. You call."

"Meow."

Penelope took that to mean tails. Big Mike always had been a little vain about his tail. She tossed the coin expertly. "Heads," she said. "You lose."

She slipped the disc in and soon the Creedence guys were into "Bad Moon Rising," what had become the theme song for *An American Werewolf in London*, where the hapless heroes had ignored the warnings of the locals —"Whatever you do, don't go on the moors."

Penelope listened to the lyrics that promised calamity and disaster, seeking elusive clues. Someone was sending her a message to get the hell off Empty Creek's metaphorical moors, the sole domain of a killer, and he — or she — wanted to keep it that way. Well, to hell with him — or her. Penelope had a silver bullet on her key chain and that would take care of any werewolf that happened to trot down the pike — or was the silver bullet for vampires? Damn, it was hard to keep things straight in Transylvania. Better stop off and get a clove of garlic or two. The way things were going, it wouldn't hurt to be prepared for any eventuality, although she had yet to see either a werewolf or a vampire in Empty Creek. Still, in this community, one could never tell. . . .

Penelope switched discs. When Jimmy Buffett blasted away, Big Mike meowed his appreciation and settled in for a bawdy ballad or two. Penelope sang along. Under the circumstances, it wasn't a bad idea at all. Andy would go along with the plan. He always did. Never once in their relationship had he pleaded headache — good thing too.

There was just one little thing to take care of first.

Penelope went to the top shelf of the master closet and took down Tweedledee's snub-nosed thirty-eight. She took the revolver from its ankle holster and flipped the cylinder open, emptying the shells into her hand. She checked the barrel. It was lightly oiled and free of obstructions. She knew it would he, but she never took anything for granted where firearms were concerned. She reloaded, closed the cylinder, and replaced it in the holster before putting it on the nightstand.

"It's me." Andy identified himself from the doorway. When Penelope was locked and loaded, he knew from previous experience that things were about to get a little dicey, and he wanted to ensure that he wasn't part of the excitement. "What happened?" he asked.

"Our killer told me to butt out today," she answered grimly.

"I don't suppose I could convince you to follow that advice."

"Nope."

"I didn't think so. Well, while you're not butting out, would you, at least, please watch out for your pretty little butt?"

"That I can do." She went back to the closet.

"Now what?"

"My weapon of choice." She emerged with her AR-15. Penelope knew that if the killer were standing about two feet away from her, she might, *might,* be able to scare him to death, if not actually hit him with the thirty-eight. She preferred confrontations with killers at about two hundred yards. She could pop him good at that distance with the AR-15. She inserted a magazine into the rifle but didn't chamber a round. "We still have to feed the critters."

"You feed, I'll be your gun bearer."

"Deal."

Despite his concern and excellent intentions, the sight of Andy on sentry duty with the AR-15 slung over his shoulder, guarding her while she went about the mundane tasks of feeding a slew of rabbits and an Arabian mare, almost gave Penelope a fit of the giggles. Still, someone had warned her off the case, which meant she was getting too close to the killer — at least in his mind.

The problem was, Penelope had no idea what she had done or discovered to warrant such an admonition.

Chapter Seventeen

If she hadn't introduced Andy to Elfrida
Fallowfield, Penelope might have remembered the computer disk before three a.m.,
when she awakened and found herself
alone in bed — without Andy's comforting
hand on her breast and the reassuring
weight of Big Mike on her legs. Where'd everybody go? She struggled out of bed —
somehow she'd managed to entangle herself in the sheets. That didn't seem right.
After Elfrida made Andy cry uncle — for
the second time — Penelope had straightened the bed while Andy recovered from
the prolonged encounter with her alter ego.
Penelope rather liked being Elfrida. Whatever inhibitions remained from Catholic
school, and there weren't many, had disappeared with Elfrida's cat suit.

She flipped on the lamp and blinked
against the harsh glare. Everything seemed
the same as when she'd turned the light
out and told Andy and Mikey to "Sleepy
tight." She did wonder how Elfrida's bra

had managed to get on the ceiling fan. Elfrida hadn't disrobed with that much gusto. But the fact remained that two people, two rather important people, were missing from her bed in the middle of the night.

She made it down the hallway without stubbing any toes and entered the kitchen, where Andy was sitting with Big Mike — and the AR-15 — at the kitchen table.

"I thought I heard a noise," he explained.

"Don't scare me like that," Penelope said. "I thought Elfrida had given you a heart attack."

Andy grinned. "She very nearly did. If she hangs around, I'm going to have to double my vitamins."

"What kind of noise?"

"You know. A noise noise."

"No, I don't. Was it a thump-in-the-night noise or a more subtle rasping of a tree-against-the-roof noise?"

"You don't have a tree."

"I know that. I'm trying to determine what kind of noise you heard."

"A noise-in-the-night noise. How do I know? I was asleep, and when it woke me up, it was gone."

"Oh, that kind of noise. The mysterious noise in the night that you didn't really hear because you were asleep."

"Exactly. Haven't you ever heard anything like that?"

Penelope shook her head and touched his forehead with her wrist. No temperature. That was reassuring. "Did you see anything or anyone?"

"I didn't imagine it."

"Of course you didn't, sweetie. Where did I leave my purse?"

"In the living room, I think." It was a part of Andy's job to remember where Penelope put things — her keys, her brush, her purse, her shoes, her head.

"I'll be right back."

She returned, rummaging through the bag. "That's strange. Where did I put the disk?"

"What disk?"

"The computer disk I found under the gallows. Actually, Mikey found it. I just picked it up."

"How did we get from my noise in the night to a computer disk?"

"It's perfectly logical. I woke up and you and Mikey were gone, but I found you, and you had heard a noise in the night and I remembered it was dark and

351

cool under the gallows, ergo the computer disk. You see?"

"No."

"Well, where is it, dammit?"

"When did you last see it?"

"I stuck it in my purse just before the last take. Oh, hell. That was the prop purse. I forgot to put it in *my* purse after I turned everything back to wardrobe. Damn. I wanted to see what was on it."

"Just go to wardrobe in the morning and get it back."

"An excellent idea."

Elfrida Fallowfield seemed to have a propensity for getting Penelope into trouble of one sort or another. Not only did the beautiful, if ethereal, blonde in the leather cat suit distract Penelope from following up on the computer disk in a timely manner, she also diverted Penelope's attention away from the warning she had received, an omission that Dutch was not pleased with.

"Dammit, Penelope!" he roared. "Why didn't you tell me last night?"

Penelope pondered her answer. She didn't think explaining Elfrida's healthy interest in sex was going to placate him.

"Well?"

"I'm thinking."

"There's nothing to think about. You receive a dire warning on your life, you report it." He pounded the desk. Bam! "To me." Bam. "Immediately." Bam!

Big Mike jumped at each bang on the desk.

"It wasn't dire, and it wasn't a threat on my life. It simply said get out of town."

"What do you think 'or else' means? Read between the lines."

"Are you just going to sit there and yell all day? You're upsetting Mikey."

"Yes, dammit! That's exactly what I'm going to do. Sorry, Mikey."

"I don't see how that's helpful."

"It makes me feel better."

"Good. I'm glad to contribute to your mental health."

"Want some coffee?"

"Sure."

"And then you're going to tell me everything that happened yesterday."

Dutch followed Penelope and Big Mike out to Base Camp Elephant. Walking toward wardrobe, Dutch said, "It still doesn't make sense. The only slightly unusual thing you did was find a computer disk and offer to return it. If there's something incriminating on it, just say it's mine and no one thinks anything of it."

Penelope shrugged. "If I've stumbled across something, I sure don't know what it is."

Mrs. Finney was sitting outside reading the latest issue of *W* when they approached the wardrobe trailer. Although she wasn't working at the moment, the head of wardrobe still had a mouthful of pins. It was cheaper than smoking and not nearly as dangerous — unless she swallowed them all at once.

"Hello, dear, how are you today?"

"Just fine, thanks. Could I see the purse I used yesterday on the set? I left something in it."

Mrs. Finney looked over her shoulder. Her right eye twitched. "Would you mind getting it, dear? You know where I keep them. I haven't recovered from that mean little episode yesterday. I had nightmares about scorpions. I didn't sleep a wink."

"Not at all."

Penelope entered the trailer. Big Mike trailed along just in case Uncle Dutch pitched another temper tantrum. All that banging could get on a well-bred cat's nerves.

Penelope picked out her purse and

opened it. Empty. She opened a dozen other bags with the same result. An entire shelf of props and not a computer disk to be seen.

Outside, Mrs. Finney was telling Dutch how awful it was to come to work and find your place of employment infested by such terrible little creatures.

"Mrs. Finney, did you by any chance find a computer disk in the purse I used yesterday?"

"Why, no, dear. We just locked up and got out of here. I'd had quite enough for one day."

"Could anyone else have taken it?"

"Absolutely not. I insisted that a guard be posted all night if they didn't want to see me on the next plane back to civilization."

Penelope looked at Dutch and shrugged an apology.

"I hope it wasn't important, dear. I know how writers get when they lose something."

"If it turns up, you'll let me know?"

"Of course, dear. It's a locked room mystery, isn't it?"

"It does appear that way." Penelope hated locked room mysteries. They were so annoying. Even bumbling vicars, always serving tea and crumpets, were vastly more interesting to Penelope's mind.

"Hey, Sheriff, Penelope."
They turned to see Shorty running up.
"I'm a police chief, not a sheriff."
"Sorry, it's all this Western stuff. I just keep thinking sheriff, but I'm glad you're here."
"What can I do for you?"
"The rattlesnakes are gone."
"All of them?"
"Every damned one of 'em. Those things are valuable. Somebody's gonna have a piece of my butt for this. Can you get 'em back?"
"Just what you need, Dutch. An all-points bulletin on a bunch of diamond-backs. 'Be on the lookout, rattlesnakes, last seen slithering down Empty Creek Highway.'"
"That would be the good news."

The three heiresses hovered behind Tony, who was seated in his director's chair wearing an *Ears of the Elephant* baseball cap.
They were filming the first steps of Brynn Moore's journey to the gallows. The

vigilantes guarded the door of the jail, rifles and shotguns at the ready. Shorty was in the background, slouched against the wall of the general store, close to several horses tethered to a hitching rail.

"All right," Craig Halliday said, "bring her out." His eyes darted up and down the street, ready to shoot if Stormy made the move to rescue her screen mother.

Brynn Moore appeared in the jail's door, two vigilantes clutching her arms. She wore a dress that was her Sunday-morning-going-to-church finest. If she was going to hang, she wouldn't do it in some dowdy outfit. Brynn's wrists were bound behind her back, and another length of rope encircled her chest, binding her arms tight against her body. Her hair was tied back in a bun to facilitate slipping the noose around her neck.

She exchanged cold stares with her nemesis. The look in her eyes told it all. No dialogue was needed with an actress like that. Halliday nearly matched her talent.

"Fine day for a hanging, boss," a vigilante said.

Brynn cowed him with a glance. "Let's do it," Brynn said. She shook off the hands and stepped proudly into the street.

"Cut!" Tony said. "Beautiful, Brynn,

simply beautiful. Well done, everybody, but I'd like to do one more just to be sure."

"Tony, could we take a short break first?" Brynn asked. "I've been tied up forever."

"Of course, Brynn. Fifteen minutes, everybody."

Bobby Danes stepped into the scene and quickly loosened the ropes from his beloved and led the star to her director's chair. He gently massaged her wrists. "You're such a dear," Brynn said.

"How's it going, Tony?" Penelope asked.

"Smoothly for a change," he said. "We haven't had a repeat of the scorpion incident." He glanced nervously at Dutch. "Yet."

"You haven't heard about the rattlesnakes, then?"

Tony groaned. "What about the bloody rattlesnakes?"

"They're missing."

"Who in the bloody hell wants my rattlesnakes?"

"Good question."

"Quite. Mumsie always told me I should enter the Foreign Office. I'm beginning to think she was right."

"What did Dadsie think?" Penelope asked.

"He didn't, really. He was always off murdering the poor little grouse during the season when he wasn't with his regiment. He was quite disappointed with me, really. He blamed it on my public school and their fixation on the arts."

Dominique massaged Tony's shoulders.

"Ah," he murmured. "Ahh!"

Vixen and Buffy Anne slipped Tony's sneakers off and rubbed his feet. "Does that feel better?" Vixen cooed.

"Much. This is why I entered the arts. Old Dadsie doesn't know what he's missing."

"It's a good thing Nora isn't here."

"Quite," Tony repeated. He closed his eyes and smiled.

Hilly Hollander and Emily Horster came down Main Street holding hands. With their arrival, all the likely suspects with the exception of Claude and Harry Duchette were again gathered. It's too bad, Penelope thought, that I can't believe any of them did it.

"Hello, Tony, do you mind if we watch for a bit? Give Emily a sense of what's going on?"

"Always room for one more frontier trollop," Tony said.

"When will you need her?"

"Day after tomorrow, most likely. *If* nothing else happens and we can keep to the bloody schedule."

"This is *so* exciting," Emily said.

"Yes, it is, rather," Tony said.

"I'm ready whenever you are, Tony," Brynn said.

"Well, let's get you tied up, shall we?"

Brynn stood and crossed her wrists behind her back. "I'm beginning to like this," she said.

"I know where you can get a bondage starter kit," Penelope said.

Brynn smiled. "Better check it out, Bobby."

The crew laughed politely. Brynn Moore was a kick to work with.

Brock Hackett grabbed the length of rope and quickly, expertly, tied Brynn's wrists.

"Ow," Brynn cried, "not so tight. I don't like it that much."

"Sorry, Brynn. Is that better?"

"Much, thank you."

"Places, everybody."

They went through the entire rigmarole, shouting all the various commands.

"Background."

Shorty slouched against his wall.

"Action!"

"All right," Halliday said, "bring her out."

Brynn and Big Mike, the ham, appeared in the doorway.

"Cut!" Tony said calmly. "Lose the cat, please."

"Sorry, Tony." Penelope picked a squirming Mycroft up and carried him out of the scene.

"Let's try it again."

Brynn retreated.

"Background."

"Action!"

"All right, bring her out."

Penelope turned away from the scene and stroked Big Mike's fur in an effort to soothe his disappointment at being banished from his big scene. Glancing up, she saw a flash of light reflecting off what appeared to be the barrel of a rifle. "Sniper!" she cried, dropping Big Mike rather unceremoniously.

So much for that take.

"Cut!" Brock Hackett cried.

Give it a rest, Penelope thought.

"Where?" Dutch hollered, pulling his service weapon from the shoulder holster.

"On the roof of the saloon." Penelope pulled up her pant leg and drew the snubbie from the ankle holster.

"Clear the street!" Dutch shouted. "Now!"

Cast and crew did not need a second invitation. Assistant directors convened a meeting beneath a handy buckboard. Craig Halliday gallantly shielded Brynn until Bobby Danes arrived, picked her up, and carried her around the corner of the jail. Halliday stayed in character, backing away slowly, steely eyes glinting, pointing his rifle at the roof, belatedly realizing an unloaded carbine from the prop department wasn't of much use against a hidden sniper. To hell with character. He bolted around the corner and down the alley.

Tony stood in the middle of the street, shouting, "Go ahead and shoot, you bloody bastard."

"I'm going up there," Penelope said.

"The hell you are. Stay here. I'm going."

Even as he took off for the back of the saloon, Dutch knew he wasn't going to win that argument. All he could do was beat her to the staircase that led to the second floor and the roof. He hit the landing first — barely — and pounded up the stairs, slowing only at the top. Penelope bumped into him. Big Mike was right there. "Meow," he complained. No fair, you had a head start.

"See anything?"

"I haven't looked yet, dammit. I just got here."

"Well, look."

"On three," Dutch said. "One . . . two . . . three!"

They popped over the ledge and drew down on a thoroughly perplexed paparazzo holding a camera with an enormous telephoto lens.

"Don't shoot," Brendon Mack, National Talent Search, Inc., cried. "Don't shoot."

"Some sniper," Dutch said.

"How was I to know?"

Bobby Danes held his hand out.

Disconsolately, Mack opened his camera and gave him the roll of film.

"All of it," Bobby said.

Two more rolls appeared from a pocket in Mack's official photographer's bush jacket straight out of Safari Land.

"You're banished from my set," Tony said. "Again."

Mack glared at Penelope before trudging away down the street, scuffing his feet angrily. How was a paparazzo supposed to make a living with people beating him up and pointing guns at him all the time?

With order restored, Brynn and Craig

did another brilliant scene together, the malevolence between them showing without a spoken word.

"Cut," Tony said. "Check the gate."

"We're fine."

"Print it."

Penelope joined the crew in applauding the performance.

"Wow!" Emily Horster said.

"Moving on."

Penelope and Dutch watched them set up for the next shot — the vigilantes escorting Brynn down the street to the steps of the gallows. Although Vixen and Buffy Anne were prepared to stand in for their female stars, Brynn remained on the set and Stormy appeared from her trailer well ahead of the time she would be needed.

"Hi, sweetie," Stormy said. "I didn't expect to see you here."

"Thank your sister."

"What'd she do now?"

"Oh, just conveniently forgot to tell me she got a threatening note and then saw a telephoto lens and thought it was a sniper on the roof. Other than losing a computer disk that might have been a piece of evidence, she's been pretty normal. For her."

"What threatening note, sis?"

"Don't worry about it, Cassie. I can take care of myself."

"I know you can, but I still don't like it. Who's going to be my maid of honor if something happens to you."

"Big Mike can fill in."

"He's the best cat."

"I'll be careful, sis."

"Can't you put her in protective custody or something, Dutch?"

"She'd just figure a way to break out of the jail. Probably blow out a wall or two in the process."

"I suppose you're right."

Penelope watched Big Mike amble around to the back of the gallows and disappear. She stared after him for a moment. Big Mike always did have a knack for finding things, but what was a computer disk doing under the gallows in the first place? What was anyone doing down there anyway? Mikey, at least, had a reason. He needed a hidey-hole to get away for a bit. "Hidey-hole!" Penelope exclaimed, snapping her fingers. "Got a shovel, Dutch?"

"Not handy. Why?"

"I should have thought of this earlier," Penelope said. "I want to dig under the gallows. See what else might be there."

"What are you talking about?" Stormy asked.

"That's where I found the computer disk. *If* the killer dropped it there, he might have been hiding something else. What else would he have been doing under there?"

"Maybe taking a nap," Dutch said. "Like Mycroft. Or," he added with a lecherous grin, "a little hanky-panky between takes. Haven't you ever made love under a gallows?"

"Actually, no."

"How long do you have, Stormy?"

"Oh, no, Dutch. Don't even go there."

"Damn, and I thought it was a pretty good idea too."

"Mine is better," Penelope said. "Are you going to get a shovel or not?"

"If it will shut you up."

"I'll be damned," Dutch said. "The earth is loose." He threw the dirt aside and started digging energetically.

Two minutes later, the shovel clanged, striking something hard.

Bingo!

Finally.

Dutch scraped the dirt off metal, tossing it aside.

"Hey, not on me."

"Sorry."

"What is it?" Penelope asked. "Let me see."

"In a minute. Calm down."

"I am calm, dammit."

Dutch pulled a small rectangular toolbox from the hole and brushed it off.

"Hurry up," Penelope cried.

"I'm preserving evidence here, dammit."

"Preserve it after it's open."

Dutch carefully flipped the latch and raised the cover with the tip of a ballpoint pen.

There were several items in the metal box — an old-style Western revolver that looked very much like a missing forty-four, a plastic bag containing a white substance that *might* be flour, a hypodermic needle, and a reprint of the old WPA Federal Writers' Project guide to Arizona. Dutch used the pen to flip the book's cover back.

Penelope peered over his shoulder and saw that Shorty had printed his name on the flyleaf.

Chapter Eighteen

The discovery of the toolbox halted filming for the day just as Brynn was ready to take her first dramatic steps up the scaffold. The crew crowded around, clamoring to see the discovery.

"What is it?"

"What'd they find?"

"What's in it?"

"Stand back," Dutch commanded, waving people back as though someone had fainted and needed air. "Don't touch it." He looked around for the wrangler and found him standing with Kimberly, trying to see what was in the toolbox like everyone else. Dutch motioned him forward. "Take a look, Shorty," he said, "but don't touch anything."

"Well, damn," Shorty drawled. "I wondered what happened to it."

"You better come with me," Dutch said. "We need to talk."

"I reckon we do."

"Dammit!" Tony protested. "You can't

arrest my wrangler. I need him for the big rescue scene."

"I'm not arresting him. I'm taking him in for questioning."

"I've been set up," Shorty said.

"We'll talk about it in my office," Dutch said.

"We'll ride with you," Penelope said, tossing her keys to Stormy. "Will you bring the Jeep in, sis?"

"Sure."

"Let us know if we can help, Shorty."

"Thanks, Brynn, but I'll be okay, I reckon."

"Shorty . . ."

The big wrangler leaned over and kissed Kimberly. "Don't you worry, darlin', I'll see you tonight."

Penelope approved of the plastic covering Shorty used to protect the dust jacket of the Arizona guidebook. Shorty was obviously a man who cared about his books. She didn't, however, appreciate the dog-eared page that marked the account of the Pleasant Valley War. Real men don't dog-ear pages. They treat their books with respect and use bookmarks, just like real women. But real murderers might use bookmarks too, and Penelope had seen Shorty's temper erupt at the Dynamite

Lounge. By all rights, Dutch should have cuffed Shorty even if the guidebook was circumstantial evidence at best. But macho Dutch hadn't embarrassed the wrangler in front of his friends, and Penelope had no intention of letting her future brother-in-law get jumped by someone who might be a murderer, not when she and Big Mike could cover his six from the backseat as a precautionary measure. Besides, she didn't want to miss anything.

She didn't have to worry about that. The drive to the police station was made in silence. The first words spoken were by Dutch when he told the crime lab guys to go over the toolbox and its contents. He bypassed the interrogation rooms as well for the warmer atmosphere of the conference room adjoining his office, calling for Tweedledee and Tweedledum on the way.

"What's up, boss?"

After Dutch explained, the Tweedles looked at Shorty with interest. Shorty shrugged. "You want to hear my story?"

"That's what we're here for."

"I don't know how my guidebook got in there."

"When did you see it last?"

"Couple of days ago. I thought it was with my gear."

"Why was the book dog-eared at the Pleasant Valley War?" Penelope asked.

"Probably because whoever took it knew I grew up in Pleasant Valley. Throw a little more suspicion my way. I wouldn't dog-ear a book anyway."

Good, Penelope thought, he might be a murderer, which I doubt, but he has the proper reverence for the printed word. "How many people knew where you were from?"

"Most of the crew. It was no secret. I told them the *true* story of the feud one night at the Dynamite."

Penelope shook her head. Everybody knew except us. Damn secretive film crews anyway. "Who was there?" she asked.

"Oh, hell, I can't remember. A whole bunch of us. Claude, Brock Hackett, Brynn and her guy, Kimberly and her boss, Penwarden, Harry Duchette, the columnist from *The Millennium.* Some others maybe."

"Have you ever thought about writing?" she asked.

"Only when I saw what a dog Masterly was making out of a good story."

" 'The imitation of an action that is serious and also, as having magnitude, complete in itself.' "

"Yeah."

"Did you ever talk to Masterly about the Pleasant Valley feud? Perhaps give him a treatment?"

"I just thought about writing. I didn't do it. Besides, Masterly didn't talk much to people like me."

Penelope sat back, frowning. Filmmaking began and ended with words. Despite all of the complex illusions now possible in movies, it still began with words. No one ever filmed one hundred and twenty blank pages. Movies started with FADE IN and ended with FADE OUT, no matter in what sequence the scenes were actually shot. Penelope couldn't get rid of the idea that Masterly's murder began and ended with the power of words.

"Where you going with this?" Tweedledee asked.

"I don't know," Penelope replied. Words and screenwriting and plots nagged at her. Masterly had been sued — and settled out of court — for allegedly stealing story ideas.

Harvey Curtis interrupted with the preliminary report from the crime lab. "No prints, boss, except on the book. All from the same person. And it was coke. Very high quality apparently."

"I'll stipulate that the fingerprints are probably mine," Shorty said, "but not the rest of that stuff."

Penelope smiled. He had read a courtroom drama or two, in addition to Aristotle.

"We got enough to hold him on suspicion," Tweedledee said.

"There is the matter of my alibi this time," Shorty said.

"Let's hear it," Dutch said. "It's about time someone in this case had an alibi."

"All this stuff had to have been done during the night. Too much activity and too many people around to do anything during the day. Right?"

"I'll stipulate to that," Penelope said. Shorty wasn't the only person around who enjoyed a good courtroom drama.

"So I've been with Kimberly Ferrell the last few nights, or she's been with me, actually, to be precise. My room's bigger."

"Check it out," Dutch said to Tweedledee and Tweedledum, "and while you're at it, talk to the rent-a-cops again."

"Jeez, we've talked to them. They don't know anything. That's why they're rent-a-cops."

"Talk to them again."

"Oh, man."

After warning Shorty not to leave town — he'd been watching too many cop shows on television — Dutch offered him a ride, but Shorty said he'd walk back to the Lazy Traveler.

With the wrangler gone, Dutch turned to Penelope and demanded, "Well?"

"Too easy."

"Yeah, someone's writing a really bad script for us here. Every time we're stuck, someone or something shows up. Emily Horster pops in from Akron, Ohio announcing that she's Masterly's half sister and there's a brother out there somewhere who, incidentally, we can't find."

"Still no luck in L.A.?"

"*If* this long-lost brother exists, he's still lost. He disappeared into the child welfare system. There's probably a record of him somewhere, but it hasn't shown up. You know what bureaucracies are like. 'Tsk, tsk, whatever did we do with little Johnny? He was here just last week.' And then the shyster tells us Masterly's three most recent girlfriends stand to benefit from his death . . . now this."

"The killer might have planted the book,

but he couldn't have known about Emily or the will necessarily."

"Unless they're in it together, hoping the half sister might inherit."

"Who's in it together?"

"The whole damned crowd — girlfriends, Emily, missing brother, Shorty, Claude Gilbert and his stupid snakes, the right-wing conspiracy, the left-wing conspiracy, the Evil Empire, Darth Vader, the Playmate of the Year."

"What year?"

"Any year. I don't know. Somebody's playing big time games with us." Dutch stood and kicked his chair. "I'm going home to soak my head."

"Good idea."

Penelope sat at her computer and typed.

Harry Duchette, Hilly Hollander, both writers who disliked C.D. Masterly intensely.

Three women, heiresses all, great motivation.

Shorty and Claude, both adept at losing things that might or might not have a bearing on the case.

Arizona guidebook — a classic.

Revolver found. Needle found. Cocaine found. Buried beneath the gallows. Why?

Rattlesnakes gone. Why?

Brock Hackett, skilled with hypodermic needles.

Penelope thought about adding the rest of the cast and crew as possible suspects. For all the real information they had, anyone could have done it. But that was too much typing. In her mind, she had not eliminated anyone except the obvious. Big Mike, for example, had a solid alibi.

Penelope stared at the screen and her short list of suspects and long list of unanswerable questions. Too many strange things had occurred of late — a spray painter attempting to ruin costumes, Emily Horster's revelation of the family connection and a missing brother, the reading of the will — such as it was — naming Dominique, Vixen, and Buffy Anne as beneficiaries, a scorpion invasion, and buried instruments of Masterly's death. Why? What was the connection?

Nancy Drew wouldn't be able to decipher this mess. It might even drive Sherlock Holmes to a seven percent solution.

FADE IN: Penelope typed.

To a shadowy figure skulking outside the master bedroom at Paradise Regained. The CAMERA zooms in on his face, revealing . . .

Dammit, who are you?

Now is the time for all good women to track down a murderer.

What would Elfrida Fallowfield do?

Penelope exited the document without bothering to save her frustrated ramblings and put the computer down for its nap.

She reached for the telephone and dialed a familiar number.

"Adult Bookshop and Marital Aids for the Discriminating Individual."

"I'd like to order a black leather cat suit, please."

Penelope dreamed of a rattlesnake wearing her cat suit. That was worse than a bunch of scorpions nesting in her floozy gown, and she fought her way up from the murky depths of nightmare to lie awake, listening to Mikey snore and Andy's deep, regular breathing until he rolled over on his back and went, "Sniff, gargle, sniff." She hated it when he did that. His breathing became so irregular. It took her ten minutes before she was able to coax him on his side again and get his breathing back to normal. Then she wiggled her legs. That shut Mikey up — he was sleeping on her legs, as usual — for a minute before the wheezing started again. Andy took that opportunity to try for his back again. "Gargle, sniff, gurgle," he said. "Oh, no, you don't," Penelope whispered, pushing back. She won that round. Waiting for sleep and the next nightmare, Penelope wondered if her friends had to put up with such shenanigans during the night.

In point of fact, Samantha Dale and Big Jake slept peacefully, their limbs intertwined comfortably, after she had beaten him for the four hundred fifty-first time at strip poker. But he was a good loser and never held it against her because the aftermath was always so much fun.

Nora Pryor was giving Tony a full body fingertip massage, which drove him crazy and made him forget completely about the various pitfalls that might befall his set on the morrow. When she had reduced him to a whimpering little Englishman, Nora broached an important subject. "Tony dearest, would you like it if I was . . . you know . . . bigger?"

"I like you just the way you are, precious," he said, and commenced to prove it, which reduced Nora to a little happy whimpering of her own.

Laney suggested that a trapeze installed above their bed might be interesting. Wally agreed.

Stormy prepared a nice hot chocolate for Dutch, which he sipped in the Jacuzzi while the water bubbled all around them, easing the tension in his neck and shoulder muscles.

Brynn and Bobby borrowed some ropes from the prop department and spent the evening trying to figure out how to tie a square knot. "I wasn't a very good Boy Scout," the Masked Madman explained.

When Penelope finally fell asleep again, the rattlesnake was waiting for her.

After filming the shot of the gallows being tested, and a weighted bag dropped ominously when the lever sprung the trapdoor open, Tony ordered the trapdoor nailed shut, inspecting it carefully himself once the job was done. The way things had been going lately, he sure as hell didn't want to hang his leading lady by mistake.

With that accomplished, it took all damned day to get Brynn Moore down the dusty street, up the steps of the scaffold, and the noose around her neck, despite the fact that Tony only once had to say, "Lose the cat."

All the while, the background became increasingly complicated. A makeshift band played "There'll Be a Hot Time in the Old Town Tonight." Penelope suggested "The Marine Hymn" as an alternative — she never tired of hearing it — but Tony rejected it as inappropriate for the scene.

Ranchers brought their families into town for the festive occasion. Even the sheepherders trickled in to see one of their own hung. It was better than listening to the wind blow across their hard-scrabble land, which was the other chief form of entertainment near the turn of the century. Snake-oil salesmen took advantage of the occasion to hawk their wares. Boardwalk vendors offered lemonade and sarsaparilla for the thirsty. A photographer ducked under a black hood and aimed his old box camera at families posed before the gallows (he had already taken a number of shots of Brynn, recording her every last step and stoic wait with the noose around her neck for the newspapers back east).

Penelope twirled her yellow parasol endlessly through take after take, finally estimating enough revolutions to approximate the distance from the earth to the moon. The floozies, gathered to the right of the gallows steps beside the chairs set out for local dignitaries, were barely tolerated by the temperance ladies on the opposite side, who sniffed and tossed their heads haughtily while waiting for the great moment that would rid the town of the cigar-smoking, profane creature with the noose around her pale, slender neck. Their only regret was that it wasn't a double hanging. It wouldn't hurt to get rid of the gun-slinging daughter at the same time, but, alas, that wasn't in the script.

A nervous and trembling Emily Horster — all tarted up — made her film debut while Hilly watched with Amber Stark from behind the cameras. "She's quite good, don't you think?" Hilly asked.

"Hilly, she's just standing there," Amber said.

"But she does it so well."

It was Reggie Pryor's big moment. She was the leader of a gang of town kids who were forbidden by their parents to watch the lynching. She got around that by marshaling her troops in an alley, the shortest ones in front, the taller kids in the back, so everyone would have an excellent view of the lynching of Brynn Moore.

Between takes — there were several interchanges between the condemned and the sheriff, the preacher, the hangman, and each had to be perfect — hair and makeup clambered up the steps of the gallows to touch up Brynn's hair and face.

"Hanging in there, Brynn?" Tony asked.

"In a manner of speaking." The actress smiled. "This must be the longest death scene in movie history."

"It just seems that way."

"It's not your nose that itches. It always happens when I'm tied up."

"Scratch Ms. Moore's nose, please."

Half a dozen assistant directors and production assistants leaped for the honor.

"Thank you, all, but one will be sufficient."

"Anything else itch, Brynn?"

"Not that *you're* going to scratch."

Everyone laughed. That Brynn. She was a trouper.

There was a brief discussion between director and writer over whether or not to have the mayor lead the assemblage in the Pledge of Allegiance before singing the national anthem.

"It's a nice touch," Harry Duchette said.

"I agree," Tony said, "with one minor exception."

"What's that, Tony?"

"Arizona didn't become a state until 1912. Why would they pledge allegiance and sing the national anthem?" He had studied his

American history when he decided to join the upstart Colonials, if rather belatedly.

Harry, born into the society, had cut any number of American history classes during high school and college. "Planning ahead?" he said hopefully. "They already know they're going to become the fiftieth state?"

"That was Hawaii."

"Whatever."

"Sorry, Harry. We must be historically accurate whenever possible."

"Well, how about we have them sing 'Nearer My God to Thee' instead?"

"Now, that I like, old boy!"

Penelope did too. Anything to stop that infernal rendition of "There'll Be a Hot Time in the Old Town Tonight," especially since the hanging was to take place at noon, with a barbecue immediately after to be hosted by the church ladies. "There'll Be a Hot Time in the Old Town This Afternoon" lacked accuracy.

After the lunch break, Vixen stood in for Brynn while continuity was ensured among the extras.

"Shouldn't I be tied?" Vixen asked. "For realism purposes?"

"Someone tie Ms. DeVaughn," Tony said absentmindedly.

Volunteers leaped to carry out his command and hang around the gallows in case *her* nose needed scratching.

Satisfied that everything conformed to the morning's shoot, Tony called for the first team to take their places.

"Someone can untie me now."

"In a moment, dear," Tony said, and promptly forgot about her.

Without a command from God, no one dared untie the stand-in, so she spent most of the afternoon rehearsing stoic acceptance of fate until three takes later.

"Good God," Tony said. "Who tied you up?"

"You did."

"I did? Well, someone untie her."

Penelope rolled her eyes.

And so, the afternoon slowly became evening.

The entire day's filming went without one appearance of a plague of locusts, an outbreak of plague, or any other calamity. Penelope supposed the killer lacked certain resources. After Tony said, "That's a wrap," and a weary cast and crew began to disperse, Penelope watched them, waiting for a killer to give himself away, and wondering what the morrow would bring.

Chapter Nineteen

Cue the stampede.

Although a great deal of *The Ears of the Elephant* had yet to be filmed, this would be the climax of the finished piece of work. Forget the chariot race in *Ben Hur* and the cattle stampedes of the "move 'em out" Westerns. Retire the cavalry charges in *Rio Grande* and *Fort Apache.* Stuff the great car chases of movie history — *The French Connection, Bullitt,* the *Terminator* flicks, *Lethal Weapon I* to *IV.*

This was going to be, without doubt, the mother of all rescue scenes, with a runaway stagecoach, stampeding horses, a gunfight to make the O.K. Corral look like a schoolyard scuffle, floozies and temperance ladies fleeing for their lives, stunt men and women tumbling from roofs, and a really good explosion — all filmed right here in Empty by God Creek, Arizona.

All they had to do was keep a killer at bay and prevent any unforeseen disasters befalling the set.

Excitement permeated the players although preparations were still going on. Even Penelope was caught up in the moment, feeling just a little of what it was like to make movie magic. As for Big Mike, well, he was a bundle of little cat nerves, galumping here and there, ready for his big part, although no one had as yet explained his role in the major scene of the movie. Born to greatness and ready to take his place in the pantheon of famous cat actors, Morris and that darned cat could just move right on over and make room for Big Mike. Little did he know.

The set was chaotic with crew members dashing hither, running yon, shouting commands through bullhorns, responding to orders issued through headsets. Horses whinnied nervously. Tony checked all the cameras.

The bell ringer at the town church rehearsed his role. The bell tolled mournfully twelve times. When the last lingering sound of the twelfth ring died, the executioner would pull the handle and spring the trapdoor. The church bell was another late addition by Harry Duchette. It was much easier working with Tony Lyme-Regis than the former wunderkind. Tony listened to all ideas, accepting the good and rejecting the bad — without rancor or humiliating anyone.

The band tuned its instruments raucously, ready to swing when the vigilantes sprang the trap on Brynn Moore.

The town kids killed time playing spin the empty beer can in the alley. A regal seventeen-year-old Reggie Pryor ignored them, although she might have joined in if that hunk of a bad guy with the droopy mustache had noticed her wistful glances.

The baby-sitters escorted their charges to the appointed place. Penelope lifted her skirts and led the floozies down the dusty street, not caring who might see the thirty-eight in its ankle holster. She was making a fashion statement.

Vixen and Buffy Anne came around opposite corners of a storage building that was normally used by the shops of Frontier Town but which now served to house the overflow of materials necessary to support the filming of a Western epic on the scale of *Elephant*.

"What are you doing here?" Vixen asked.

"I got a message from Dominique," Buffy Anne replied. "She said we needed to talk."

"I had the same message. I wonder where she is?"

"Inside?"

"Probably." Vixen pushed the door open. "Come on."

The cavernous building was crammed with saddles, tack, trunks, lighting equipment, boxes, and row after row of shelving filled with boxes of one size or another.

"Hello," Vixen called. Her voice echoed.

"This is spooky," Buffy Anne said.

"Dominique? Are you here?"

"Let's get out of here."

"Hands up, my pretties."

Buffy Anne whirled and looked into the muzzle of the biggest damned gun she'd ever seen. All of Rodeo Drive flashed before her eyes. Vixen was so startled that for once in her life she forgot to scream, a mistake that might prove costly — and life-threatening.

Dutch showed up with Tweedledee and Tweedledum, along with Sam Connors, Peggy Norton, and Sheila Tyler in uniform. They scattered to strategic points around the set, out of the way of the day's shooting.

To the consternation of Milan Penwarden, Penelope immediately left her

388

mark and went over to Dutch. "What's going on?" she asked.

"Nothing."

"You show up with half the cops in Empty Creek and nothing's up?"

"Nothing's up. Simple precautions. I read the script for today. If something's going to happen, this would be a good day for it."

"I had the same thought," Penelope said. "I'm glad you're here."

"Gotta protect the bride-to-be and the maid of honor." Dutch grinned.

"That'll be the day."

"To say nothing of the guest list," he added, looking around. "Most of them are here today."

"Let's hope for Tony's sake, the killer takes a day off and leaves his scorpions and spray paint at home — wherever that is."

"That's the point of the reinforcements. If we can't catch him, we can maybe scare him off."

"Ms. Warren, please," Penwarden pleaded. "We need you."

"How nice of you to say so."

When Tony called for a rehearsal, Vixen DeVaughn didn't ask to be tied for realism's sake. In fact, she didn't ask for anything. She was nowhere to be found, nor was Buffy Anne Mulholland, Stormy's stand-in. "Bloody hell," Tony said. "Where are they?"

The word went out over headsets that the stand-ins were needed, but no one had seen them. They weren't at craft services, wardrobe, holding, props.

Tony turned to Dominique. "See if you can find them, would you, please?"

"Of course, Tony."

The rehearsal continued with Kimberly standing in for Brynn on the gallows and Amber Stark pressed into service to lurk in Stormy's place in the alley.

Tony conferred with the first and second assistant directors and the cameramen. Production assistants hovered, ready to carry out the slightest order. "Something's wrong," Tony said, appraising the background critically. "An extra's missing. Where's Emily?"

"She was here a minute ago," Penelope said. "Maybe she went to the loo."

They turned to Hilly for confirmation.

"She's a little nervous still," Hilly said. "She'll be back in a minute."

"We can't wait," Tony said. "We'll put her in the next scene."

"Break a leg, hon," Nora said, drawing

applause from the crew when she kissed Tony.

"I probably will," Tony said glumly. "I wonder if Cecil B. De Mille ever had to direct from a hospital bed?"

Kimberly shrieked and disappeared through the trapdoor.

"Good God!"

Penelope beat Dutch up the steps. "It was nailed shut yesterday," she said. "I watched them do it."

"Dammit, who is this guy?"

"I don't know," Penelope said, echoing her second favorite line in *Butch Cassidy and the Sundance Kid*, "but he's very good." She looked down through the trapdoor. "Are you all right, Kimberly?"

The young woman, assistance already at hand, looked up and nodded. Kimberly, only a little shaken, brushed her knees off.

"Are you all right?" Tony repeated.

"I'm fine," Kimberly said. "I think."

Penelope and Dutch exchanged glances. "I'm calling for backup," Dutch said. "Our boy is just too weird."

After Kimberly limped off for first aid and the trapdoor was securely nailed shut again, the first team was called.

If Stormy was nervous, she didn't show it, striding confidently through the set, winking at Penelope, kissing Dutch, and taking her place in the alley. Brynn Moore traded quips with cast and crew. Craig Halliday scowled, already in character, at his villainous-cattle-baron best.

Brynn ascended the gallows regally, replaying the scenes already shot. By the time she took her mark beneath the noose, she had assumed the persona of the courageous heroine — calm, beautiful, stoic. Do your worst, her expression said. She acted with consummate skill while being bound, using the opportunity to truly become someone else.

Penelope thought Brynn might be sending a message to the murderer who had removed the nails from the platform. You can't frighten me, Brynn's face said when she scanned the crowd below, all eagerly awaiting her demise.

When Brynn had been tied, the ropes were once again compared with still photographs taken the previous day for continuity. Her hair was also scrutinized by her stylist, ensuring the bun was the same.

"Perfect," Tony finally announced.

The now-familiar singsong shouts necessary to get the cameras rolling and the actors acting counted down to "Action!"

The preacher read verses from the Bible.

Brynn Moore disdainfully refused the black hood offered by the hangman. Craig Halliday smirked. His victory was at hand. Penelope twirled her parasol. The bad guys passed a whiskey bottle back and forth, taking big swigs.

The first take was okay in Penelope's opinion. The second take was better. The third was perfect. So were the fourth, fifth, and sixth.

After the seventh, Tony said, "Check the gate and let's move on."

It was time for the big scene.

"Over here, Dominique. I think they're in the storage building."

"I certainly hope so. I'm tired of looking for them, and Tony needs me."

"Oh, he'll be able to get along without you for a few more minutes."

While the vigilantes made their preparations to hang Brynn Moore, Stormy and her henchwomen were busy as well. When the scene was ultimately shot — after all the town scenes were completed — it would show Stormy and her gang ambushing the weekly stagecoach. Leaving the driver and the cowpoke riding shotgun afoot in the desert, two of Stormy's gunslinging molls donned dusters and slouch hats for disguises for the ride into town. It would all be done quickly, expertly — after all, time was running out on Brynn — with Stormy dousing the rear luggage compartment and a case of dynamite with a flammable liquid that would be lit just before the coach raced into town. A burning stagecoach, horses running wild, would provide a suitable diversion for the rescue of Brynn Moore. The stunt women on the coach would dive off and come up shooting, while the rest of the gang rode into town from opposite ends of Main Street, blasting away. Stormy would emerge from the alley, guns blazing, and rescue her mother from the rope, while the extras scattered, screaming, running for their lives.

"It took you long enough," Brynn would say when Stormy removed the noose from her neck.

"I was busy, Mother," Stormy would reply just before shooting Craig Halliday dead and tossing Brynn her shotgun.

Piece of chocolate cake with jalapeño topping. At least, that's the way the script went.

"Where's Dominique?" Tony asked. "I need her."

"Haven't seen her, Tony."

"Damn."

"I'll see if I can find her," Nora said.

"Would you, please, luv," Tony said, "and see if you can find those other infernal women as well. We've got work to do today."

Penelope counted heads, about the most useful thing she could think of doing. The heiresses and the half sister were off doing something mysterious. Harry Duchette had hung around, staring wistfully at Dominique until she went off to look for stand-ins. Claude Gilbert passed out blanks to everyone who would be involved in the gunplay. She knew Shorty was getting the stagecoach ready. Brock Hackett had been in and out all morning. Hilly Hollander was off looking for Emily. After that, Penelope lost track. There were still just too many damned possibilities.

Away from Main Street, everything was quiet, ominously so, and Nora's imagination kicked into overdrive. She was the last human being left in Frontier Town. The inhabitants of the little Western community had all been abducted by aliens, well before aliens became fashionable with flying saucers, Roswell, New Mexico, and Area 51. The Porta Potties were unoccupied. Still, Nora called out, "Vixen, Dominique, Buffy Anne?"

A little dust devil swirled at her feet by way of answer.

"Emily? Emily?" Hilly Hollander emerged from the alley beside the general store. "Have you seen Emily?" he asked.

Nora shook her head. At least, he wasn't an alien, despite his newspaper's propensity for conjuring them up. "Have you seen Dominique, Vixen, or Buffy?"

"No," Hilly replied, wrinkling his brow. "I'm worried. She should have been back long ago."

"She's probably just lost in this maze back here."

"Let's split up. You go this way and I'll go down here."

"Okay."

Nora moved on to the storage building. She knocked politely on the door, and when there was no answer entered tentatively.

Nora found the missing gaffer's tape, but it looked like the thief had used most of it to make mummies out of the beneficiaries named in C.D. Masterly's will, with a half sister thrown in for good measure. Vixen

DeVaughn, Buffy Anne Mulholland, Dominique Anders, and Emily Horster were swaddled in the damned stuff, from their ankles to their shoulders. For good measure, additional strips had been criss-crossed over their mouths. Vixen and Buffy Anne mumphed a greeting. Dominique was doing her stoic Amazon routine for real this time. Emily's eyes pleaded with Nora for release. This wasn't the sort of thing that happened to nice girls from Akron, Ohio. The four women had been crammed into trunks, circa 1870 or so. Wooden trays were stacked next to the trunks. A fifth trunk was empty. Four women, five trunks, Nora thought. That didn't make sense.

Dominique's eyes widened. "Uummp!" she said.

That's when the lights went on in Nora's brain — and went out in the room.

Too late.

In the sudden darkness, someone grabbed her from behind, stuffed a silk scarf into her mouth, and slapped a piece of that same tape over her lips. "Mumph," Nora cried, struggling to break free of the enfolding clinch that lifted her off the floor. She kicked at her assailant's legs before he threw her to the floor, straddled her, and twisted her wrists behind her back for binding with more of what Nora was coming to think of as that damnable tape, wishing now that the tape had remained missing. Another strip was plastered over her eyes. "Mumph," she repeated. That was going to hurt when it came off, she thought, and I don't want my eyebrows plucked.

Although Nora flailed her legs, her captor easily wrapped the tape around her ankles. This was no time to be five foot three and one hundred ten pounds, she thought while more tape was wrapped around her thighs just above her knees. That done, the weight left her body.

Even if deprived of sight, voice, and easy mobility, Nora, if anything, was not lacking in mettle. She kicked out with bound legs, but found no target, and decided to make her escape by rolling away through the door. In theory, this was a good plan. In actuality, disoriented during the struggle, she went the wrong way and banged into a trunk. She rolled the other way but was stopped by a foot planted on her backside. In addition to kidnapping and assault, Nora planned to add sexual harassment charges when she got this bozo under control, which wasn't going to be easy, since he now picked her up effortlessly and slung her over his shoulder.

Hanging upside down, she felt the blood rush to her head. Still, Nora kicked at his chest, but it was hard to get any leverage. He whacked her across the butt, then stuffed her into that fifth vintage traveling trunk. A fitted wooden tray was inserted and pushed her farther down, pressing against her. Nora didn't like what came next. She heard the distinctive buzz of what appeared to be a very big and very pissed off diamondback rattlesnake being dropped on the tray before the lid was slammed shut.

Tightly bound and crammed awkwardly in the trunk, Nora was not pleased. She had read the script and knew what was going to happen to certain trunks when they were loaded on the top of a stage-coach. The script didn't call for women — or rattlesnakes — to be inside when it happened either. Someone was improvising. This was not good. An escape plan was definitely called for — and soon.

Nora hunched her shoulders against one end of her prison and set her feet against the other end, ready to break out of the little slammer. She paused. What was going to happen if she freed herself — and the rattlesnake? Well, it was better than the alternative. Besides, the snake had been milked of its venom. She might be bitten, but she wouldn't be poisoned. Here goes. She strained mightily until her muscles ached, but she didn't feel the slightest movement. Damn that old time workmanship. A modern trunk made of plastic and cardboard would have been no problem. She gathered her strength and tried again. The damned thing just wouldn't budge. Nora wondered if Dominique was attempting the same thing. The Amazon might be able to pull it off. Nora strained to hear, but the outside world was silent, blissfully unaware of the plight of five women. At least, the snake had settled down.

Nora tried to relax in the confines of her temporary home, but this was definitely not good.

If all went according to schedule, Tony would direct her fiery and explosive demise in just about an hour.

"Has Emily returned yet?" Hilly asked.

"Haven't seen her. Did you see any of the others?"

"I passed Nora. We took different directions."

"Well, we better shut down and find them," Tony said. "I'm getting worried."

"No," Dutch said. "That's what he wants. You keep going. We'll find them."

"If you think that's what we should do . . ."

"Spread out," Dutch ordered the posse he'd assembled. "I want them found. Now!"

"You got it, boss," Tweedledee said. "Where do you want us to look?"

"Everywhere, dammit."

"And keep an eye out for Mycroft too," Penelope said. "I haven't seen him for an hour."

"Jeez," Tweedledum said, "the big fur ball too? Where's everybody going?"

"Keep everybody out of our way, Tony. We'll find them."

"Beware of the Hun in the sun," Tony said. He turned to Brock Hackett. "Is the stagecoach ready?"

"I loaded it myself, Tony."

"We have grips for that sort of thing."

"I didn't do the actual loading. I just supervised. I wanted to make sure it was done right."

Tony nodded. "That's a good show, then. Jolly good show."

There had been a good deal of bumping around and muffled shouts when Nora's

401

trunk was pitched to the top of the stage-coach. She mumphed as loud as she could through the gaffer's tape, but her entreaties went unheeded. She faintly heard a man complain about the weight of the trunk and took it personally. Not one of her one hundred ten pounds was excess or out of place. And the damned snake seemed to have gone into hibernation. The least it could have done was rattle loudly, alerting the crew to its presence. Stupid snake. Never rattled when you wanted it to.

It was getting pretty damned uncomfortable in the trunk, and Nora wondered how the others were holding up. As tall as they were, Dominique and Vixen must be getting pretty cramped. Like Nora, the slighter Buffy Anne and Emily would fare somewhat better in their confined quarters.

Shorty had a faint buzzing in his ears that sounded just like a rattlesnake. From a safe distance he stooped and looked under the stagecoach just in case. He didn't have to force a yawn to clear his ears. Kimberly was keeping him awake well past his customary bedtime. If she kept up the pace, he would have to plead a headache or check into a prescription for Viagra. At least, the damned buzzing had gone away.

After a final check of the stagecoach and a brief, soothing conversation with each of the six spirited horses, Shorty climbed up to the box and collected the lines. He released the brake and urged the horses on. "Okay, kids."

The stagecoach swung into motion.

Uh-uh. Think fast, Nora, think fast.

Chapter Twenty

Penelope might have joined the search party under different circumstances, but with the additional officers Dutch had called in, they'd be running into themselves everywhere. After all, Frontier Town wasn't that big. Nor was she concerned about Big Mike and Nora. They might have gone off together somewhere. Nora was a big girl and Mikey a big cat. They could take care of themselves. Still, Penelope hoped Big Mike didn't catch a mouse to present to Nora. She could be squeamish about the silliest things.

She wasn't so sure about the others. Dominique was probably fine, but Vixen and Buffy Anne, while not complete airheads, could experience a blond moment or two on occasion. As for Emily, Empty Creek was not Akron, Ohio. . . . Well, ten cops ought to be able to find a few missing women and a cat in the rather small confines of Frontier Town.

In point of fact, Big Mike wasn't missing

at all. He knew exactly where he was. He could have taken the steps to the roof of the saloon, but where was the fun in that? Instead, he jumped to the top of a trash can, measured his distance to the arm of a saguaro cactus, and used it as a springboard to the edge of the roof, which he grabbed with his front paws and pulled himself over easily. He stared at Brendon Mack, the persistent paparazzo, for a moment before deciding there was room for two on *his* roof and settled down to bask in the sun.

Shorty passed the waiting stunt women, going into the desert at an easy trot along a dusty trail, reluctant to give up the lines to others. Some women had all the fun. But after a quarter mile or so, he swung the team around and headed back slowly, prolonging the moment as long as possible. Driving a well-schooled team in open country was almost as much fun as driving in front of the cameras. It was going to be one hell of a scene, and he wasn't part of it.

"You kids, do good, now, you hear!"

Vixen regretted not screaming when she'd had the opportunity. Now, with gaffer's tape plastered across her mouth, all she managed to do was make her throat raw and her ears pop with what were pretty feeble attempts to make herself heard. Tears welled in her eyes and her heart beat faster with the growing panic. You'll never break me, she told the evil warden just before the iron lid on the hole clanged shut. Do your worst. She drew a deep breath through her nostrils and exhaled slowly. You'll *never* break me. That was very good. I'll have to speak to Myron about a women-in-prison flick. I could even write it. The camera closes on Vixen's beautiful face. She is strong and determined, her spirit indomitable. Do your worst. Do your *worst!*

Vixen continued her nervous rehearsal, knowing that someone *was* about to do his worst. And she was so perfect for the Viking princess too.

Penelope furled the yellow parasol, sat down next to Harry Duchette, and watched him save the computer file he'd been working on. "What's poor Dominique up to in the latest chapter?" she asked.

"I'm running out of imagination," Harry said. "I may have to dig up *The Joy of Sex* for inspiration."

"I find that hard to believe."

"Really. I've been reduced to the missionary position. It's the only one I haven't used."

"Actually, she might like that. Just for a change, you understand."

"She did seem to enjoy it when I read it to her last night. She didn't hang up on me anyway."

"I told you all along. Perseverance wins the fair lady's heart."

Harry closed the laptop computer and sighed. "It was just doodling anyway."

"It's the longest love letter I ever read," Penelope said, "and one of the strangest; but then, we can't all be William Shakespeare or Elizabeth Barrett Browning."

"Ah, Dominique, how many ways can I love thee. . . ."

"Close, Harry, close."

"I wonder where she is anyway?"

"Probably off writing a love letter to you."

"Do you really think so?"

No, Penelope thought, but she didn't want to disappoint Harry, even though he was still a suspect.

In fact, although unable to physically compose a billet-doux, Dominique was thinking of Harry and willing him to rescue her, just as he did at the end of each cliff-hanging episode. It was better than thinking of the alternative end to this particular chapter. She maintained courage by humming "Guenevere" from *Camelot*. The beautiful queen stood at the stake, waiting for her Lancelot to champion her cause, wondering if he would arrive before they lit her pyre.

The stagecoach swayed in a big turn.

They were about to burn the queen.

Write fast, Sir Harry, write fast.

"Another gun's missing," Claude Gilbert reported disconsolately, "and there's never a cop around when you need one."

"What was it?" Penelope asked, shaking her head.

"A forty-four. At least, he's got good taste."

"Dutch'll be back soon. We'll report it then."

"Dammit, why me? I had everything locked up. Next time, I'm taking the damned things to bed with me."

The stagecoach rocked to a halt. Shorty set the brake and turned the lines over to the female desperadoes. "You all set?" he asked, looking down the trail toward Frontier Town. There was a good long run for the horses to gain speed for their spectacular entrance.

"Yep."

Shorty whacked Buffy Anne's trunk with the flat of his hand and jumped down. "Break a leg, ladies."

Buffy Anne whimpered desperately to no avail. Dammit, if all you people would stop shouting out there, you'd know there were some women in trouble in here. What is the rain forest going to do without me? Buffy was seriously beginning to regret not following her mother's advice to learn to type. "A girl who can type can always get a job." The maternal words thundered in her mind, loud enough to reach poor C.D. You'd think a few crew members could listen up for a change. There was never anyone around to yell "cut" when you really needed it.

The girls and the cat were still on the missing-creature list, but on the set everything was dangerously close to filming. Penelope was still amazed at the amount of patience it took to make a movie, and told Tony so.

"It's fun, really," he replied, turning

away from the bank of monitors. "The writer has a vision and gives it to the director to translate into his own vision. What do you see when you look from the various camera angles?"

Penelope stepped closer and looked at each monitor. "I see Mrs. Finney with a knitting bag, a mouthful of pins, a computer on her lap, a syringe in her hand, and Brock Hackett handing her something. On this one, Harry Duchette is mooning over his lady love, and over here there are a bunch of my friends dressed for a cowboy Halloween party, gobbling up all the doughnuts."

"Not in the safe area, old girl."

"What is she doing?" Penelope said, looking back at Mrs. Finney.

"She's diabetic," Tony said, "and she uses the computer to design costumes. They have programs for everything nowadays. Now look again and tell me what you see."

"I still see a bunch of sloppily dressed people standing around waiting for the shouting to start."

"And I see a carefully choreographed action scene with every actor and actress performing beautifully in their assigned roles. I see it on the big screen. God, I loved cowboy movies when I was a kid."

"Even in England?"

"Especially in England. Obviously, you never attended public school. It was a frightful bore."

"I did attend public school, and I agree. I was ready to graduate from high school in about the sixth grade, but they made me go anyway."

"My public school was a private school."

"I know that. It's what I love about England. Public is private. Only mad dogs and Englishmen."

"Quite."

Not having read the script, Emily Horster was more angry than afraid. She couldn't imagine why that odious person had pointed a gun at her and then wrapped her in tape before stuffing her in the trunk. Well, she had a very clear vision of the perpetrator, and when Hilly released her, someone was going to get a black eye or two. They had laws against this sort of thing back in Akron, and if Arizona couldn't protect its citizens, she would just have to do it herself. Surely, Los Angeles and Hollywood would be more civilized than this place.

"The set is up!"

Penelope anticipated her cue and twirled

411

the parasol, wondering too late to ask Tony if parasol twirling wasn't a little too festive for a hanging, especially when the head floozy was secretly sympathetic to the beleaguered sheepherders.

"Rolling!"

Penelope exercised a little creativity of her own and stopped the parasol in mid-twirl. She drifted away. That's it, her right brain said.

"Sound speed!"

What's it? Her left brain asked.

Brynn Moore stared impassively over the crowd.

"Sound!"

Oh, my God, I must have had a blond moment of my own.

Clappers clacked their slates to mark camera A, camera B, camera C, and camera X.

"Background."

"No, wait," Penelope cried. "I know who the killer is."

Too late. With all the shouting going on, no one of importance on the set heard her.

"Action!"

Reggie, I'll never ground you again, Nora thought. She rocked against her prison frantically in a futile effort to dislodge the trunk, but someone had loaded the stagecoach all too well. Maybe, just maybe, it was time for the teeniest little bit of panic.

Hysterical City, here I come.

The stagecoach careened around the corner and down Main Street, heading directly for the gallows, smoke and flames from the boot trailing behind. The horses were running hard, ears flattened, having a great old time. Extras shrieked and fled. Craig Halliday drew his revolver. Bad guys dropped their whiskey and leveled their rifles.

The horses, all pros, hit their mark and the coach skidded to a halt in front of the saloon. Bit players hollered for a bucket brigade. The stunt women leaped from the stagecoach and started shooting. The bad guys returned fire with their blanks. Stormy raced from her hiding place and ran for the gallows, firing along the way, dropping two bad guys in front of the mortician's office and shooting another from the roof. He tumbled into a handy water trough.

Penelope searched desperately for her quarry, but there was too much organized confusion. Idly, she hoped it transferred well to the big screen. At least, no one was bored anymore.

Big Mike ignored the melee below. He had his eye on a plump pigeon perched on the eave of the saloon. The bird sat there, cooing arrogantly, taunting Big Mike. Neener, neener, neener. I can fly and you can't.

Patiently, Big Mike put his target acquisition system into operation, creeping forward an inch at a time, ears flattened, tail swishing — slowly, ominously, until . . .

It was dead-meat time.

Big Mike leaped.

The pigeon fluttered into the air, just out of reach, although Big Mike swiped at him as he went by.

As it turned out, the pigeon was wrong. Big Mike could fly — after a fashion, although not with the ability of his winged and feathered prey. Fur and flailing paws just didn't cut it. Still, he was a pretty graceful sight soaring over the edge of the roof, realizing it was now time for the old always-land-on-four-feet trick.

Tony ignored the cat sailing into the shot and kept the cameras rolling. Some things could be dealt with in the editing room.

Big Mike crashed into a trunk on top of the stagecoach, but he landed on four feet.

Take that, you stupid pigeon. He was looking around to make sure everyone knew he had done this on purpose, when he was distracted by strange sounds from within the trunk. *Buzz whir mumph thump.*

He arched his back and scratched energetically at the lid of the trunk.

Buzz mumph whir thump scratch scratch.

Penelope watched Big Mike, knowing immediately that he had found something interesting. Ignoring her role — she was supposed to drop the parasol and take cover in the bawdy house — she ran for the stagecoach, now smoking from the fire, and climbed up, not without difficulty in the damned dress, but made it.

Tony groaned. The editing room would be working overtime on this one.

"I've got it, Mikey!"

Big Mike jumped to the next trunk and scratched away. Penelope was sure his claws didn't need sharpening that much.

She reached for the clasp and found it locked. Undaunted, she pulled the thirty-eight. "Look out below," she cried even though she knew the coach had no passengers according to the script. Her gunshot was hardly heard in the furious firefight going on all around her. Besides, she'd always wanted to shoot a lock off. There might be something to making movies after all.

There was one small hitch in that, however. Having blasted the lock free and opened the trunk, she had never wanted to find a coiled rattlesnake waiting to strike, but strike it did. Its aim was bad though, probably something to do with the sudden blast of bright sunlight in its eyes, and it sailed off the side of the stagecoach.

"Snake in the hole!" Penelope hollered.

An errant pail of water from the bucket brigade doused the snake, and it wiggled rapidly out of Dodge, taking shelter beneath the steps of the saloon.

This was moviemaking at its finest — Empty Creek style.

Penelope lifted the tray inside the trunk and tossed it after the rattlesnake.

"Mumph!" Nora said.

"What are you doing in there?"

"Murgle."

"Oh. Well, I'm busy just now. We'll have you out in a minute."

Penelope looked around. Bad guys were dropping like trailer parks in a tornado.

Stormy had freed her mother now, and Brynn's shotgun added a distinctive boom to the proceedings.

Big Mike scratched at another trunk. Penelope had a pretty good idea where the other women were, but there was no time for that now.

Penelope finally spotted him just as Tweedledee and Tweedledum ran around the corner of the blacksmith's shop.

"Stop him!" Penelope shouted.

"Who?"

Penelope pointed. "Him! Brock Hackett!"

Hackett, seeing the accusatory finger, looked for an escape route. Tweedledee and Tweedledum were running for him now. Hackett untied a horse at the hitching rail and leaped into the saddle, looking pretty good for a second assistant director. The horse reared, but Hackett controlled it easily, reaching into his shirt to pull out what looked suspiciously like a big stick of dynamite. He managed to light it before jerking the horse around violently and heading out of town, throwing the sizzling stick of dynamite to clear his way. He nearly ran down Dutch, who appeared in the middle of the street from somewhere. Hackett then pulled a revolver from beneath his shirt, where he had tucked it into the belt in the small of his back. One shot whizzed past Stormy's ear. No faint heart she, Stormy blasted away, although her blanks were not nearly as effective as Hackett's real bullets.

Fortunately, his path veered right past the stagecoach. Unfortunately, Elfrida Fallowfield was nowhere in sight, nor were any stunt women or loaded rifles — she really would have to learn to shoot a handgun — leaving Penelope a nanosecond to make up her mind. What the hell, she had seen any number of cowboys do it in the movies. How hard could it be? If a man could do it . . . She hastily reholstered the revolver and waited, timing her jump perfectly, leaping off the stagecoach, hitting Brock Hackett in a chest-high tackle, throwing him out of the saddle. She didn't land as gracefully as Big Mike, but when they hit the ground, Penelope fared the better simply because she landed on top. The air left Hackett's lungs with a big oof, but Penelope was taking no chances. Sitting astride his stomach, she bounced up and down, all the while pummeling him severely about the head and shoulders.

Craig Halliday could ad-lib with the best, so he scooped up the stick of dynamite and threw it on the roof of the saloon.

"Coo," said the pigeon, who saw it coming and took wing.

"Great stuff," Brendon Mack said, who

didn't see it, and took wing rather unexpectedly.

"Cut!" Tony finally cried. "Cut! I hope you got all that."

"Ready when you are, C.B.," the head cinematographer shouted back. "That was a good rehearsal."

"I hope that was a joke."

"Just kidding, Tony."

"Leave me alone!" Hackett screamed.

Mrs. Finney charged, knitting needles poised for a killing blow. "Get off my son," she screamed. "Leave him alone. He's a good boy."

Enough! Penelope pulled her skirts up and drew down on Mrs. Finney with the thirty-eight. That stopped the head of wardrobe. She dropped her knitting needles.

"I didn't do anything," Hackett pleaded.

"Oh, stuff and nonsense," Penelope said. "Cuff him and read him his rights."

"You sure you know what you're doing?" Dutch asked.

"I've got a pretty fair idea. Dutch, let me introduce you to C.D. Masterly's long-lost brother."

"That thieving son of a bitch was no brother," Brock Hackett cried.

"Mrs. Finney has a laptop computer.

Get it. I also think you'll find a computer disk in her knitting bag."

"Sheila, go get it."

"Okay, boss."

"Mumphery-mumph!"

"Damn," Penelope said. "I forgot about the girls. Nora and the others are in the trunks on the stagecoach. Better get them out."

Tweedledee and Tweedledum hopped to it.

"And, just as an afterthought," Penelope said, "someone might want to put the fire out."

"See to it," Tony instructed the bucket brigade.

"Hey, boss, we found them."

"Mycroft found them," Penelope said indignantly. "And you better watch out for rattlesnakes."

Too late.

Two big diamondbacks flew off the stagecoach in one direction and two cops in the other.

"Oh, hell," Tweedledee cried when he hit the ground awkwardly. "I sprained my ankle."

Tweedledum groaned and clutched his knee. "Medic!" he hollered. "Medic!"

If a big Abyssinian alley cat from Abyssinia could be said to snicker, Big Mike did. Several times. Tweedledee and Tweedledum were no cats.

Shorty was called in to release Buffy Anne and Emily and to handle the snakes. He was a lot better at it than Tweedledee and Tweedledum, both of whom managed to scurry quickly away on hands and knees despite their injuries.

When the gag was removed from Vixen, she screamed lustily. "That felt good," she said. "I was afraid I'd never scream again."

Harry Duchette released Dominique and was rewarded with a kiss. "I'll never complain about being rescued again," she said.

"They'll never believe it back in Akron," Emily said after receiving several kisses of her own from Hilly.

Buffy Anne, having no one to exult over her rescue, administered first aid to Tweedledee and Tweedledum, making them forget all pain in the process.

"I wasn't worried," Nora said after checking her eyebrows and getting a good hug from Tony along with a shot of medicinal brandy from his flask. "The snake had been milked."

"Nope," Shorty said cheerfully, "not this time." He held up his sleeve where the snake had struck. It was stained with venom.

Too bad the cameras weren't rolling then. They might have caught the greatest swoon in movie history when Nora's eyes rolled back and she fainted dead away in Tony's arms.

When Sheila returned with the computer, Hackett clammed up and refused to help. Mrs. Finney glared and said, "We're going to sue."

It took several minutes for Penelope to figure out the system, but she eventually found the directory and opened a file designated "Ears. Act I."

A title page appeared on the screen.

```
The Ears of the Elephant
  An Original Screenplay
           by
  Brock Masterly Hackett
```

"That's a wrap," Penelope announced.

"How did you know?"

"I always thought that a writer had to be connected somehow," Penelope said. "Writers and directors are natural enemies in the greater scheme of Hollywood.

There were lawsuits accusing Masterly of stealing ideas, but there was never anything I could point to and say, 'Ah-ha!' Just this nagging feeling and the fact that there were enough writers around with a grudge against him. Harry and Hilly disliked him intensely. The guidebook cast suspicion on Shorty for a while. Every time something showed up, it indicated a writer might be involved. I just didn't connect sibling rivalry with a writer until it was almost too late.

"And then I saw Mrs. Finney with a hypodermic needle in the safe area. Hackett said his mother was diabetic and he had learned to give shots in case of an emergency. That's when I started putting things together. Remember the needle we found in Masterly's bedroom?"

"Yeah."

"I just figured at the time, Mrs. Finney dropped it when she was working on the buckskin dresses for Vixen and Buffy Anne, but once I made the connection between Hackett and Mrs. Finney, it seemed plausible that she might have been at the murder scene. It was just a regular old needle, not the kind you'd use for buckskin."

"That's a bit of a stretch," Dutch said.

"You leave my sister alone," Stormy said. "She's had a tough day."

"That's the trouble with you, Dutch. You're too logical."

"How did you know she was his mother?"

"I didn't, but I figured it was time to make something happen. If he hadn't jumped on the horse, he probably could have brazened it out. At least, for a while longer."

"Stop the presses," Andy shouted.

"The presses aren't running yet," Penelope pointed out.

"They will be. I've finally got a scoop. Sorry, Tony, I've got a story to write."

Penelope smiled, watching her lover boy lope down the street. She wasn't going to alert Lola LaPola, not this time. She could always make it up to the TV reporter later.

"What I don't understand is why he kidnapped Nora?" Tony said. "I can understand the beneficiaries of C.D.'s will and his half sister, but not Nora."

"Nora blundered in by accident," Penelope said. "I'm afraid the fifth trunk was meant for me. Everyone was used to me wandering around, and he thought it would be easy to kidnap me but, for once, I stuck close to the set. When he warned me off earlier, he didn't realize I was no closer to solving the case than anyone else."

"I can't imagine hating a brother enough to do what Hackett did to his."

"He stole his idea, relegated him to the second unit, and browbeat him the whole time. Hate and revenge can be a powerful, even overwhelming, emotion. Enough to kill in the most brutal manner, especially after stealing *The Ears of the Elephant.* And then, when the word got around that Masterly left everything to his girlfriends, Hackett couldn't take anymore and snapped."

"Still . . ."

"I know," Penelope said. "It wasn't the best of families."

"It wasn't a family," Hackett cried. "He stole everything I ever did for him. He was a no good hack. I had more talent in my big toe than he had in his entire body. He kept promising that things would be different, but he always stuck me with the second unit. Whatever happened to good old-fashioned nepotism? And then it was too late. He had the reputation and I had nothing. He thought he was some sort of king. Well, I'm the king now. He's dead and I'm glad we killed him. The king is dead. Long live the king." Hackett giggled. "Whoopee-do, whoopee-do. Hallelujah, baby."

"Now, Brock sweetie," Mrs. Finney said, "don't work yourself up. You know how you get."

"Where's my scepter, Mummy? I want my scepter."

"Dutch, you might want to consider a straitjacket," Penelope said.

"Nice work," Elfrida Fallowfield commented.

"Thanks, but where the hell were you in my hour of need?"

"Being fitted for a new cat suit. You have no idea how difficult it is to remain stylish."

"Moving on," Tony cried. "Let's make some movie magic."

"Coo, coo," said the pigeon from what remained of the saloon's roof.

That was a bit of unfinished business. Big Mike took off for the back of the saloon and a handy trash can. After all, Mother's Day was coming up, and he didn't have a present for Penelope yet.

The Cutting Room Floor

No cats, rattlesnakes, pigeons, cops, or paparazzi were harmed during the making of *The Ears of the Elephant* (sprained ankles, wrenched knees, and black eyes don't count).

Brock Masterly Hackett and Mrs. Finney — who turned out to be Hackett's foster mother — showed absolutely no remorse for their brutal deed and were both sentenced to life in prison without the possibility of parole.

In due course, *The Ears of the Elephant* completed principal photography in Empty Creek.

The location wrap party was held at the Double B. Vixen and Buffy Anne offered Paradise Regained, but no one really wanted to revisit the site where all the trouble began. The Double B outdid itself on this occasion. The party began with a huge buffet and ended with a wet T-shirt contest won by Amber Stark, which was only right since she provided all the

T-shirts for the contestants. As usual with such events at the Double B, there were cries of foul and jury tampering that subsided only after Pete the bartender threatened to close his bar if the standings were not ruled final — and damned quick too. In order to prevent such a catastrophe, Andy, the jury foreman, convened a presentation ceremony — and damned quick too — awarding the trophy to Amber. Second- and third-place trophies were given to Debbie Locke, who took time out from her waitressing duties to participate, and to Lora Lou Longstreet, thereby upholding the honor of Empty Creek. Lola LaPola's honorable mention helped her forget that she had been scooped by a print reporter — on a biweekly paper at that.

Upon hearing a reliable report at the party that hell had frozen over, Dominique Anders later slipped down two doors at the Lazy Traveler, knocked softly on Harry Duchette's door, and jumped his bones when he answered.

There was a lot of that going around in Empty Creek that night. Penelope, of course, was pleased that the local water supply still worked better than Viagra — and a prescription was unnecessary.

After things returned to the Empty

Creek version of normal, Dutch came home early one afternoon to find his beloved bouncing higher and higher on a trampoline. Since Stormy happened to be wearing only her birthday suit, it was a rather inspiring sight for a weary police chief.

Nora Pryor remained au naturel, although she did consider a butterfly tattoo on her shapely derriere. That plan went awry, however, when Regina announced her intention to get a tattoo, and Nora, instinctively, grounded her for a month. Mother and daughter are currently in a tattoo stalemate.

Penelope's cat suit arrived, delivered personally by Ralph and Russell, twin brothers the size of small redwood trees, who, along with their mother and girlfriends, owned and operated Empty Creek's adult bookstore and marital aids shop of choice, even though it was located in downtown Phoenix. Ralph and Russell are currently considering an expansion into Empty Creek proper in order to accommodate their many local customers.

Brynn Moore and the Masked Madman finally mastered the square knot.

Vixen DeVaughn did such a superb job in *Scream for Your Life 6* that she was immediately signed to reprise her role in *Scream for Your Life 7*. Vixen was also a smash in *Viking Pirate Queen and the Sultan*, demonstrating a talent for sword fighting as well as screaming, almost upstaging the Viking Queen herself. Almost.

Myron Schwartzman left Empty Creek with a goodly supply of water — at Penelope's recommendation — and is frequently seen at Spago with the statuesque Vixen on his arm. He does find her nocturnal rehearsals somewhat unnerving, however.

Buffy Anne Mulholland opened charge accounts at every boutique on Rodeo Drive and currently serves on a subcommittee of a presidential commission on ecology and is dating an Ivy League attorney who is counsel to the commission. He is trying to convince her that the nation's capital has shops every bit as good as those on Rodeo Drive, but Buffy isn't buying into that.

Emily Horster moved into Hilly's Hollywood Hills bungalow and immediately cleared his bachelor's clutter away. He can now find the floor of his home office and, in gratitude, helped Emily procure employment at *The Millennium*, where she quickly worked her way up, demonstrating quite a flair for writing headlines regarding alien abductions and other matters supernatural.

Shorty and Kimberly remain an item, and she is a willing pupil in a crash course on Aristotle.

Milan Penwarden never again looked at steamed broccoli without cringing.

Elfrida Fallowfield visits on occasion and always makes things interesting for a certain mild-mannered reporter of no relation to Clark Kent.

Tony Lyme-Regis created a souvenir videotape for Penelope and Big Mike that captured their dramatic leaps in the pursuit of justice. Penelope gave herself a nine point seven for style in knocking Hackett off the horse. Big Mike judged himself rather more harshly for missing the pigeon, although he nailed the landing. He never did manage to corral the stupid bird and had to settle for a lizard for Penelope's Mother's Day present.

About the Author

Garrison Allen has been a Peace Corps volunteer in Malawi, an English instructor in Ethiopia, creative director for a public affairs and advertising agency, and a tank commander in the Marine Corp Reserve. He now lives quietly in Long Beach, California with his placid black cat, Oliver.